Schrödinger's City

MATTHEW BUSCEMI

Schrödinger's City

FUZZY HEDGEHOG PRESS

SEATTLE
www.fuzzyhedgehogpress.com

Published by Fuzzy Hedgehog Press
Seattle, Washington USA
www.fuzzyhedgehogpress.com

ISBN 978-1-62802-126-4
Library of Congress Control Number: 2015930126

First Paperback Edition: August 2015

Printed and bound by Gorham Printing
Centralia, Washington USA
www.gorhamprinting.com

Typeset by Matthew Buscemi at Fuzzy Hedgehog Press
in Adobe Garamond Pro and Adobe Fangsong with Gibson display.

To Serdar

for the gentle nudge
in the direction of my voice

Th' Table of Th' Contents

"The world is given to me only once, not one existing and one perceived. Subject and object are only one. The barrier between them cannot be said to have broken down as a result of recent experience in the physical sciences, for this barrier does not exist."

Erwin Schrödinger
Mind and Matter, 1958

Skyward

((now))

"Everything's different," Naim said.

Gwei glanced about, her skirt twirling as she turned from side to side. "I don't—?" she stuttered, bewilderment overtaking speech.

Naim clasped his hands behind his back, craned his neck back, and slowly shut his eyelids. "Don't worry, Gwei. You'll be fine. I've shown you everything. This has been due a long time."

Gwei frowned deeply, gulped, fidgeted with her hands, but failed to find words to express her dismay. "Naim," she mumbled absently.

Naim held his eyes shut. He tensed his muscles, relaxed, tensed again. "You can feel it too, can't you?"

Gwei wanted to argue with him, but she found no words with which to do so. All around her, City was… it had changed. Bizarre, unfamiliar facades lined their street—except, Gwei realized with a start, they weren't quite unfamiliar. She recognized many of the structures, just not their configuration. And then there was the street itself. Gravel, chipped pavement, worn stone, broken sidewalk. It wasn't right.

Where had Alabaster Way gone? They were supposed to be standing at the place where it met Emerald Square, with the entrance to Lavender Alley across the plaza. The plaza had vanished, and they stood now in this new place. And yet this was certainly still City.

A dingy green sign hung precariously from one bolt off a nearby rusted post, hugely thick and ponderous and dented. It announced the intersection of Negative Seventh Street and Twenty-Fourth Avenue. Gwei had never seen such an intersection before, but recalled that Naim had spoken of this.

She scanned the buildings to ground herself in something familiar. Zen's apothecary stood at the corner with its dirty windows, and beside it the store of the gone-away greengrocer, and beside that the entrance to Ochre Arcade. She'd been to all those places before, but never this intersection. In fact, those places weren't supposed to be anywhere near one another.

Where was Alabaster Way from here?

Gwei looked down Negative Seventh Street and gulped. The road went on straight and disappeared over the horizon five blocks away. The tall buildings arced and fell away into the curve, their tops peaking up at ludicrous angles over City's edge.

She had never seen the horizon before.

"You shouldn't be here, Gwei," Naim muttered. A warm breeze whistled past him and tossed his stringy black hair to one side. "I won't tell you to… It has to be your choice. But you shouldn't be here now."

She swallowed her fear. "You're scaring me, Naim."

"We should all be scared."

"Why? Why can't we just go back to the way things were?"

"Because nothing stays the same, Gwei. That's what I've been trying to teach you about City. I wanted things to keep going on forever just as they were. But I couldn't have it and neither can you. People change. We grow. We learn things. And you can't be the same after that. Once you know something for sure, like that, you can't keep going on like before. Everything's… it becomes different."

"How did the roads get this way, Naim?" She bunched up her fists. "Did you do this?"

Irritation welled up in Naim, but he forced it down, refocused his attention on his breathing, on being in the moment. Gwei's hand on his shoulder jerked him back realityward.

"Naim," Gwei whispered into his ear. "For me?"

Naim opened his eyes just a crack, turned his head ever so slightly toward Gwei's fierce brown eyes, and whispered back. "It's okay. Don't worry. You'll be fine. And I'll be fine, too."

His shoulder slunk out from under her grasp, and he sidestepped gracefully to the right. He stood up on his tiptoes and reclosed his eyes.

"Naim…" Gwei gulped. "Goodbye."

"I'm not going anywhere," he said.

Another blast of wind. The ambient light dimmed, and the gusts increased intensity and frequency. Naim's t-shirt rippled and his hair whipped about, yet he stood, still on his tiptoes, poised against the elements.

Gwei closed her own eyes, turned, and walked away down Negative Seventh Street. The storm whipped at her back. Rain poured down in sudden torrents, spattering her face and clothes. Thunder roared from directly above her head. And yet she held her eyes tightly closed.

She counted each step. One. Left foot. Two. Right foot.

Onward. Drenched, frightened, and alone, she endured the wind and futile rain pelting her from all sides.

Fifty-seven. Left foot. Fifty-eight—

She contacted a person, stumbled, and fell.

"Oh!" a man's voice.

Gwei opened her eyes. A hand lay outstretched before her.

"So sorry." The man stood over her. The storm was gone. The ambient light had returned to its usual piercing brightness, which sank into the gray facades.

Gwei grabbed his hand, and he pulled her to a stance.

"What happened to you?" He stood there, completely dry, unafflicted by any storm, while Gwei dripped on the pavement. "You alright?" he asked, when she didn't answer him.

Gwei looked him over. Blue overalls, white sleeveless shirt, a plastic orange hat; brown skin and well-muscled. He carried a metal box in his other hand. His skin and clothes were covered in patches of dried dirt from head to toe.

"I'm fine." Gwei turned and glanced the empty thoroughfare behind her. "Did you see Naim?"

"Sorry? Was someone with you?"

"He was right behind me." Gwei looked at the ground, dripping dejection and despair. He'd found a way out. He'd actually found a way out. And the selfish jerk had taken it. Had it been naïve to think that he cared…?

"No one here but you, miss. Say…" He bit his lip. "The funniest thing just now. I went to tell you my name, and I can't remember what it is."

"Wander long enough and you'll find it," Gwei sighed and looked at the ground as she wicked raindrops from her arms. Anger seethed within her, anger with herself for her sadness.

The man was staring at her blankly, she knew it. She'd done the same when she'd first arrived.

"What does that—?" The contents of his box rattled.

"Welcome to City," Gwei said.

City is Transition

(( ))

Philosophers and scientists have both come to City. Neither have discovered what it is. How can they? They do not know themselves.

To witness City is to witness change, the inexorable contortion of reality, form and substance shifting, skewing into a new configuration, forever altered; its original state, an unknowable certainty, forever lost in a super-cosmic haze of twirling blue.

The philosophers said that City was an outward manifestation of humankind. It changed because its inhabitants changed. But some changes could not be attributed to its inhabitants. They simply were.

The scientists said that City obeyed an internal logic all its own, that one could pick apart its workings by prying into its guts, pulling apart rafter after rafter, tearing up foundation after foundation. Digging and digging, only to discover—more City.

City is change. People arrive in City. People leave from City.

Those who leave are remembered. Their mark remains. Those who stay continue the change. City's change is part of them, just as it works independently of them.

Naim has just made his own escape. He is no longer part of City, and City is no longer part of him.

To say that City is awakening would be imprecise, for City is constantly falling to slumber and reawakening, though one can never say at any given moment which state it occupies. The ebb and flow is ceaseless. But Naim's transcendental scientific philosophy has infected City with something new.

And City, rumbles onward.

Relentless

((before))

Orange flower petals hung like draperies from the vines, forming a wall around the grove. Light breezes wafted onto the small hill at its center, joined Kaia, mingled and dozed with her, then left, off to explore other parts of Evermore. The park had dozens of groves, after all.

Naim lay, naked, his head propped up on one arm, and he watched her. Kaia lay naked, too, her chest rising and falling gently.

He found himself tracing his eyes across all of her. He'd never done that with any of his previous lovers. He'd seen the breasts, the face, the hips, sure. With Kaia, his gaze could fixate on the minutest of details—a parting of her hair, her gentle smirk, her curly eyelashes, even just the shape of her bellybutton—all of her was beautiful.

Unable to resist, he rolled closer, wrapped his arm around her. She mumbled a bit, her eyelids fluttered, and she smiled.

"I fell asleep again."

"Yeah."

"I shouldn't fall asleep."

"I've been awake the whole time. Kept an eye out."

A wry smirk traced its way over her features. She took hold of his shoulders and rolled him onto his back. They laughed.

She sat atop him, tossed her hair back, then leaned down. Naim propped himself up on his elbows, the grass soft and dewy beneath him.

"You know what I mean, Naim."

Naim retorted with a grin. "Asleep or awake, I won't let City take you away from me."

"I still don't trust it here."

A small pang of fear struck him. "You still get the feeling it will be soon for you?"

She stretched out her legs, lay atop him, her head on his chest as though it were a pillow. "I don't want it to be."

"Hey!" Naim wrapped his arms around her. "I'm not going to let City take you anywhere."

"Can you remember their names, any of the ones who left?"

Everyone knew the answer to that question—no. One moment they were here, and then they were gone. But their stores remained, their houses, their lives. Everything they were, still there. Memories became fractured, incongruent. You knew that someone had been there, that you'd had a conversation, or you'd done something with them, felt something together, but the memory of the person was wobbly and blurred at the edges. The names never stuck for those City took away.

"I won't blame you if you want to stop." Kaia looked away.

Naim sat up fully, pulled her up into his arms. "That's no way to talk. I won't leave you, Kaia."

"What if you don't have a choice?"

"I love you so much. I can't imagine anything could make me leave you. Not even City."

"It doesn't work like that." She shook her head against his chest. Tears slid down his torso. He held her closer.

"I'm not going anywhere. Not while you're still here. Let City be a dream or a figment or whatever it wants to be. City doesn't matter. You do. We do."

Kaia steadied her breathing. "We do."

Naim felt his eyes water and clenched them shut. He held Kaia tighter. The intensity of his emotions scared him, and he retracted from them as though they were a viper, ready to strike.

"Kaia?"

"Yeah?"

"How about we go for a walk?"

Kaia nodded.

Naim reached out, grabbed up their pile of clothes, and they dressed. He watched as Kaia slipped effortlessly into a sleeveless blouse. His precarious emotions already forgotten, he felt himself harden as she pulled on her underwear. She shot him a wry grin, eyeing him enticingly, and he was glad that she too had escaped from the brink of distress.

Fully dressed, he took her hand warmly, and they pushed through the wall of vines and orange flowers, through leaves and branches and brambles, crunching, stomping, finally emerging onto a dirt path, which took them to the wooden sign, standing stalwart at the entrance to Evermore Public Park.

City lay before them.

Kaia gaped.

Fear struck Naim, and he tightened his grip on her hand.

"Wha—what happened, Naim?" she asked meekly.

Naim shook his head. "I don't know."

The couple walked slowly out into the street, a blank, boring concrete street, one lane traveling each direction and one lane of parking on each side. The center was delimited with a yellow, broken line, and white boxes outlined the parking spaces along the curbs.

The mossy, curving, slightly dilapidated brickwork of Myrtle Parkway, where Evermore Public Park was supposed to lie, had vanished. A sign at a nearby intersection, sternly fixed atop a drab metal pole, announced their location to be the confluence of Negative Forty-Fifth Street and Negative Fourth Avenue.

Naim watched with morbid curiosity as Kaia mouthed the names of the streets silently.

They pulled closer to one another.

"Have you ever heard of these streets?" Kaia asked.

"No," Naim said.

"Is it still City?"

The street was deserted, though that was nothing new. Most of City lay empty and unused.

A scuttling sounded in the distance, a dull rumbling, growing louder by the moment.

"There!" Kaia pointed.

A two-story home before them, with siding a shade of gray-blue like the scales of dead fish, grew a patch of shimmering, seething translucence. Part of its door and a chunk of adjacent wall morphed and twisted.

Naim pulled at Kaia. "Back into the park!"

She shot him a look more inquisitive than fearful. "Wait. There's a voice. Hear it?"

"Kaia!"

She held her ground as he tugged at her arm.

The rippling wall congealed and formed all at once into a twenty-something man atop a skateboard. A red bandana capped a hairless head. His shirt flew out behind him like a tail, tucked into the waist of baggy jeans. His chest bare, hairless, he hurtled out of the building, landed on the pavement with a clap of plastic wheels on concrete.

All at once, confidence and pride, eyes of mirth and arrogance morphed into shock, then utter horror.

Naim pulled Kaia's arm as the skateboarder hurtled toward them, off-balance and flailing, and this time Kaia lent her own strength to the effort.

The couple fell to the grass at the edge of the park, and the skateboarder hurtled into the curb, flew into the dirt path, and rolled to halt a few meters away.

Kaia picked herself up and helped Naim to his feet.

"You alright?" he asked.

"Fine. You?"

He nodded.

The skateboarder groaned loudly.

The couple crept toward the forest path.

"Eh… Uh…" The skateboarder clasped his head with his hand as he pulled himself up out of the dirt. "The *fuck* was that?" he roared.

Naim ambled toward the skateboard, which lay propped up against the curb, its back wheels still spinning. He picked the contraption up. Heavier than he expected. He ran his fingers across the red and gold paint, a design that looked like urban graffiti. He'd never learned to read those bulbously flourished letters.

"You alright?" Kaia had strode down the path. She stood now, just in front of the skateboarder.

Naim shuffled the skateboard to his other side so as to carry it properly and moved to join them.

"I'm fine," the man said. His face was boyish with bright, big eyes. He had a slender jaw and narrow shoulders. His naked torso revealed a sinewy musculature. For all that, his voice was deep.

"Do you have your name?" Naim asked.

His gaze turned from affable to wary as it meandered to Naim. "Yeah."

"I'm Naim."

"And I'm Kaia."

The skateboarder held out a hand and raised his eyebrows. Naim cautiously handed over the skateboard.

"Grey," the skateboarder said.

"I've seen some strange things in City," Kaia said. "But I've never seen anyone shoot out of a building's wall before."

Grey tilted his head, took a step back. "What're you sayin'?"

Naim crossed his arms. "You and your skateboard kind of… formed out of that house—" Naim pointed behind them. "—and hurtled toward us."

Grey's face turned up into an exasperated sneer. "Fuckin' City."

"How did it look to you?" Kaia tried.

Grey leaned into his skateboard, eyeing Kaia much too fondly for Naim's liking.

"Dunno." He stared at the couple for some time, then sighed. "All I know is I was grindin' down Tangelo Relief, and I took the curve at the end like always, but all of a sudden there was no more road, just all these trees and shit."

Naim couldn't help but notice how Grey directed all of his speech toward Kaia. And he was smirking. Naim knew he had nothing to be jealous of, but still. He couldn't help but level a sinister expression at the younger man.

Grey seemed to register this, scoffed, grabbed up his skateboard in a swift, controlled jolt, and crunched away past the couple toward the street. "Fuckin' City can't even make up its mind where to put its fuckin' roads." He tossed his skateboard onto the sidewalk of Negative Fourth Avenue and glided away without a second glance.

Good riddance, Naim thought. He took Kaia's hand once more, and they returned to Negative Fourth Avenue. Kaia's eyes scanned the buildings.

"It's weird," Naim said. "I'm sure I've never been to this particular intersection before, but all the buildings are familiar."

Kaia nodded. "Like down there." She pointed. "That's the roller rink, right?"

Naim smiled. One of their first dates. "Yeah. And there's the restaurant that has the spaghetti you like."

Kaia turned. "Huh. The roads… Negative Fourth Avenue and Negative Forty-Fifth Street. Maybe… we should go looking for the parkway?"

Naim shrugged. "Sure."

There was no way of knowing if it would be safer to stay put or explore, so they might as well explore.

They walked down empty Negative Forty-Fifth Street, gray buildings looming over them, some towering above, others only a few stories tall. City's architecture had always been random. Naim and Kaia both recognized styles of construction from their homes' modern day and its history, from big cities and small towns, and even some styles that defied both, seeming to be no part of their respective worlds' civilizations at any point in time. Exotic skyscrapers reached up toward a sky that twisted and morphed like blue oil on water. Beside such towering monstrosities might sit a modest, single-story brick domicile.

Strangest of all was the way that City drained its building's facades of hue. All the structural components' paint and lacquer seemed to sink toward grayscale tones, while streets and signs and people remained vibrant.

Naim remembered his arrival in City. Terror and loneliness had ruled his world. He'd avoided and run from all others he'd encountered. He'd learned his City name by listening to faint echoes from within a conch shell in a beachside supply store with a tattered sign atop its entrance labeling it 'The Basics.' Huddled in the corner for a day or more, he'd survived on junk food while listening to the shell's dull, repeated whisper of 'Naim.'

Three new arrivals, a merry band apparently happy to be free of their previous lives, had raided the shop one day and sent Naim flying out its emergency exit. He'd wandered Emerald Square, then Terracotta Lane, which twisted up and over, spun back around itself to Myrtle Parkway, which had led him to Evermore Public Park.

He'd hidden there, amongst the many groves, and it was there, four weeks ago, that Kaia had arrived, terrified out of her mind, screaming and howling. And immediately, without even thinking, he'd wrapped her in his arms and promised he'd protect her. Instantaneously. Reflexively. And just like that, they were inseparable.

The stark division stood out in Naim's mind. He'd always been a loner, always solitary, always in his office thinking and analyzing. Meeting Kaia was not a line drawn through his City existence, it was a line drawn through his entire life. All City had done was added some extenuating circumstances. Kaia had changed everything. And for the better.

So much better.

He squeezed her hand tighter.

She stopped.

"You hear that?" Kaia asked.

Naim perked up his ears. He did, indeed, hear something.

The couple turned. A woman walked down the street's opposite sidewalk from behind them. She wore a long red dress, high heels, a fanciful blouse with a white flower pattern, and carried two large, paper grocery bags. Even from a distance, Naim could tell she was wearing too much makeup. Blazing red lips stood out against a face painted ghostly white. Her words, at first a gentle murmur, developed into audible speech as she grew nearer.

"—can't believe that they've done this. Can you? How on earth will we get home in time now? My husband and children will be so upset if they don't get dinner in time. … Yes, I know. City *will* do as it pleases. I wish it would consult us though. You know, when I was younger, I thought I would make a point of writing a letter once a week. That's how democracy is supposed to work, you know. Our representatives are supposed to hear what we think. They're supposed to know that they'll be kicked out of their jobs if their actions stray too far from the will of their electorate. … Of course. City is clearly anarchy. Or a despotism. But listen! One minute I'm on Filemot Way and I know exactly where I am, and the next I'm on a street with a negative number for its name. It's just not right, I tell you. This is not a healthy way for a society to run. My husband runs a strict household, but it's an ordered household. Everything in its place, as he says. I know you think he's too strict—"

Naim and Kaia watched her pass by from their side of the street. She looked over her shoulder occasionally, as though an invisible interlocutor strode beside her, but never did she look across the street to the very visible Naim and Kaia.

"That could have been me," Kaia said.

Or me, Naim thought. He squeezed Kaia's hand tighter.

"We'll be okay," Naim replied.

Kaia touched her hand to Naim's cheek. "The only way I want to leave City is with you."

He looked directly into her eyes. "I don't want to leave City as long as you're here. Let it bring and take others. So long as the tribals don't cause us any trouble and we can keep each other safe." But he knew that

City was no place for them. They needed somewhere better. Somewhere without the constant fear. But how?

"I suppose that's up to City," Kaia said.

Naim pulled her close. "I'd fight the world to keep you in my life." They shared a kiss.

Kaia looked at him and smiled. Her fingers brushed over his features, twirled his hair. Naim couldn't restrain himself and kissed her again.

"We'll go back to the park later," Kaia suggested.

Naim nodded vigorously, and Kaia shot him a wry smile.

Her face turned serious. She pointed to the next intersection. Negative Forty-Fifth Street had come to intersect a street called Zero. Not Zero Avenue or Avenue Zero. Just Zero, a circle with a diagonal line terminating its existence. Or qualifying its negation.

Momentarily, Naim realized it was not the intersection she pondered, but a building at its far corner. Spires of metal jutted up out of a silver glass dome. A dull hum sounded, accompanied by clicks and whirs. A tube erupted from the top of one spire and spat out a belch of steam, then retracted.

"Have you ever seen it before?" Kaia asked.

Naim shook his head. A vague disgust worked its way into his belly like a parasite. "The streets are all wrong, Kaia. We should stay away from places we've never been to."

"I don't see any purple," Kaia retorted, referring to the tribal miasma that permeated their district. "Do you?"

Naim could not help but answer in the negative. He looked around for anything that might suggest Amaranthine architecture, but found nothing. A couple of houses, a five-story office building and the entrance to an abandoned amusement park dotted the right-angled intersection, all gray and lifeless.

The building that had caught Kaia's attention felt admittedly more alive than most parts of City.

Kaia pulled him by the arm. "Let's check it out."

"Fine, but then let's find the supermarket, okay? I'm getting kind of thirsty."

Kaia smiled and poked a finger into his chest. "Deal." She pulled him onward with the other.

The dull hum grew into a roar as they approached. A metal door lined with bolts and without a visible handle was their only greeting. A panel of buttons lay beside it.

Kaia began tapping.

"Kaia!" Naim squeezed her hand.

"One of these ought to—" The door opened with a hiss.

A hall stretched out before them, a single row of lights dotting its ceiling, each casting a circle of light onto the floor below it, creating a staccato of dark, light, dark, light down the hall.

"Real bad vibe, Kaia," Naim pulled her away from the door. "Please, let's just—"

"Hello?" a voice burst from the empty hall, deep and masculine, a bit hoarse. "Who are you? Why are you trespassing?"

"Trespassing?" Kaia shouted into the hall. "We were just curious."

"We didn't mean any harm," Naim said. "We'll just be leaving."

"How long have you been in City?" the voice asked.

Naim and Kaia looked at each other.

"A month," Kaia said.

Naim shifted his weight. "More for me."

"I will grant you access to a secure storage area at the rear of this building in exchange for your answers to various questions. It will take roughly fifty minutes."

"How big a storage area?" Kaia asked.

Naim shot her a look.

"One cubic meter."

Kaia looked at Naim pleadingly. When the supermarket ran out, they'd have to search for a new source of food and water. City's inhabitants tended to converge on a new food supply when it appeared, though one had to be careful if it appeared near the Amaranthine District. The tribals tended to grab up food stores in their own way, and it wasn't pretty. Naim and Kaia had been lucky to find the supermarket early, but its location had become common knowledge, as its stockpiles had steadily declined in previous weeks. No place in City constituted a safehouse, since no law enforcement existed to ensure public order. A cubic meter of secure storage space between them? They could haul off a couple months worth of food from the supermarket and be done with scavenging for months.

Naim nodded his consent.

"What do we do?" Kaia called out.

"Enter. Walk down the hallway. My office is the third door on the right."

"What's your name?" Naim asked.

"Taum," the voice said.

Naim and Kaia walked inside together, and the door hissed shut behind them. Both looked over their shoulders. Kaia looked up at Naim with the first signs of hesitation and warning visible on her face, and Naim gazed back as if to say he'd told her so.

They walked down the hallway hand in hand.

Below the blazing lights it was too bright to see anything, and neither in the dark interstices could any details be discerned, but in between, Naim spotted glass pipes running in and out of the walls and ceiling, each churning with liquids of various viscosities and colors, all chugging along to who knew where and for what purpose.

Naim spotted a door on the right wall, just barely visible as its frame peaked out of a dark zone.

"Is that the second?" Naim asked.

"Yeah," Kaia said. "I saw one already."

The third door also stood half in total darkness, half beneath the dim edge of a zone of blazing lamplight. It opened automatically as they approached. The couple peered inside and gazed around the brightly lit room. Computer pads lay stacked atop one another in piles. Against the back wall atop a table stood row after row of glass cubes, all suspended in a metal lattice and each holding a different substance. Some minerals, some metals, some decayed plants, and on and on.

A man, slight and mustached, with wiry black hair, stood amongst it all. Not elderly, but older than Naim and Kaia, perhaps in his forties. He held himself guardedly, his shoulders slouched, but his eyes were alight with passion and energy.

Kaia squeezed Naim's hand. Apparently Taum was giving her the same vibe Naim felt.

"Welcome," Taum said.

"Hi," Naim and Kaia said together.

Taum smiled at them warmly. "Please don't be alarmed."

"What do you do here?" Kaia asked, her eyes still scanning the computer pads and rows of glass cubes.

"I study City," Taum said solemnly.

Naim remained nonplussed. "I'd like to see this questionnaire."

"Certainly," Taum said. He walked with a bit of a hobble—was his left knee bad?—to a nearby desk. He pulled up one tablet computer, looked at it, threw it down, grabbed another, then another. He eventually found one that suited him, though his face remained stern, and he continued scavenging. After acquiring a second device, he hobbled toward Naim and Kaia.

"Are you all right?" Kaia asked.

"Yes," Taum stated more than a bit defensively. "I'm fine."

He handed them each a computer. Naim scrolled through the list displayed upon its screen. Questions prompted him for information about his life before City, what he'd done since arriving here, his diet, exercise, people he'd interacted with.

Naim dropped the computer to his side and locked eyes with Taum. "What do you want all this for?"

Taum bunched up his brow, as though the answer were obvious. "To get us each back to our homes."

Naim and Kaia instinctively grabbed one another's hands.

"Ah." Taum looked away in disappointment. "The tribals don't want to leave either, you know. I've had so much trouble with them. I've had to move my facility twice now. If you tell them my location, I'm afraid I'll have no choice—"

Naim took a confident step toward Taum. "We're not with the tribals. And you can do whatever you want. Just please leave us out of it."

Taum held up his hands. It was not in his nature to trap defenseless creatures. They needed his benevolent guidance, not a cane to the head. Unless they interfered with his work, which these two decidedly would not. If they wanted to live in ignorance, then so be it. Their loss. It was too bad. Partly his fault. He shouldn't have been candid about his intentions until they'd at least filled out the initial survey. He'd gotten so used to people wanting out that he'd just assumed everyone did. Not a mistake he'd make again. Ah, well. Live and learn.

Taum motioned to the open doorway behind the couple. "You're free to go."

"Thank you," Kaia said.

Taum nodded solemnly, walked to his sample wall, and gazed over it, listening to the couple pathetically scamper away behind him. They wanted to stay here? How ridiculous. City. What a horrible place, a waste of his talents. The sooner he got back home, the better.

The great worry welled up in him. After three years gone, his only hope for continuing his life's work, the most important research project of his age, was if City time were divergent from real time. If the two were co-continuous, it grew more likely with every passing day that his life's work had been usurped in his absence. Taum found the presence of mind and the clarity of purpose to research City in the hope that his eventual return home would leave him right where he'd left off.

Perhaps, he thought, the couple would be open to collecting samples for him. Those were only indirectly related to his work on pan-City decoherence. The chemical analyses merely supplemented his primary research. He could let his offer of the storage space stand. He had, after all, lost two errand boys in the past two months. Perhaps he could gain two new assistants.

He pulled up his computer and activated the intercom.

"Please wait," he spoke into the microphone.

He hobbled out the door, then down the hallway in fits. Dark. Light. Dark. Light. He spotted their silhouettes just outside the door. He'd caught them just in time.

He approached the portal, a coruscating rectangle of blinding luminescence. City's ambient illumination strained his poor eyes. Sweat beaded on his brow, and he held up his hand to shield himself.

"I have a project…" He gulped, took a few deep breaths. "It's only tangentially related to my work on leaving City. I wondered if you'd be willing to help me collect—"

Taum's heart fell. His eyes fully adjusted, he gazed about the intersection. The buildings… were wrong. Everything was wrong. His laboratory stood at a right-angled intersection. A right angle? Of streets in City? Dark, gray pavement and sidewalks lay strewn beneath his feet. Where was the refurb plastic of Cesious Boulevard? What had happened to the nanite-lumen sensor posts he'd installed in order to illuminate the streets if City's ambient light were to fade?

His eyes strayed back to an impatient Naim, who stood tapping his foot, his lip turned up in a half-sneer.

"Help you collect…?" Naim repeated.

"Just a moment," Taum looked around.

"We should go." Kaia tugged on Naim's shoulder.

Urgency shot through Taum like a hypodermic needle. "Please wait! What has… What has happened to the streets? And the buildings? What is… Negative Forty-Fifth Street?"

Kaia rolled her eyes.

Naim shrugged. "It's the place we promised we wouldn't tell anyone about."

Kaia looked at Taum unkindly, as though he were sad and pathetic. It made his heart race, and his head twitched uncontrollably. Anger threatened to overwhelm him.

"See you around, Taum," Kaia said.

The couple departed.

Taum watched them go, their rejection causing his anger to boil over. He took deep breaths to calm himself, and he found his eyes wandering up to the sign above his laboratory's new intersection. Negative Forty-Fifth Street. So, City could change that much. All of his analyses, everything he had done so far, wasted. He had to go back to the beginning. Of everything.

"…and Zero." He read the sign aloud. The dull green thing hung limply, and swung and squeaked in a passing breeze.

Torturous

((before))

Fuck City.

And you know what, fuck its stupid name, too. Why just City, huh? Not 'the City' or 'a City' or 'shithole where damned losers end up until some divine fuckin' hand swoops out of the gnarly-blue-ass sky and snatches 'em away City.'

Nope. Just City.

Fuck, I hate this place.

My board takes me down Alabaster Way, which really is the best place in all of City for boarding. Downhill for a good half kilo, halfpipe at the end, some handrails scattered along the way. Just perfect.

But not today. City's got other plans.

I turn right from Alabaster Way onto Tangelo Relief, and then blam! Street turns into air, right in front of me. For a few moments, I don't even know it's happened, then all of a sudden, I realize I'm about five meters higher off the ground than I thought and I'm falling hella fast, and I can't brake or anything. There's just a curb hurtling toward me and I kinda flail around so as to aim myself toward the dirt instead of the pavement. It's all I can do.

My board slams into the curb, and I go flying into a bunch of dirt and gravel and green shit.

Did I mention I hate green shit? No? Well, I hate green shit. I hate eating it, and I certainly hate getting thrown into it 'cause some asshole of an invisible despot wanted to do some impromptu urban renewal.

I cough and groan. Patches of skin on my legs and arms are on fire.

I've probably scuffed the fuck out of myself. I pick myself up, wipe the dirt off and I am *pissed* beyond belief. "The *fuck* was that?" I shout 'cause it makes me feel better.

But then I start looking for my board, hoping she's alright, and some dude's standin' there pickin' 'er up. Fuck, man. Talk about a guy who doesn't know how to handle a board. He's holding her like she's a piece of fuckin' lumber. Idiot.

Now there's this chick walkin' toward me and she's hella hot. But she and the dude are clearly involved, so I keep it cool. I'm not gonna mac on another guy's girl. Even trapped in a fucked up metropolis, I'm not that desperate. I got food and water waiting for me back at the house. I got my board. I don't have fuckin' rent to pay. Not gonna screw that up.

But I don't really feel like that's up to me. The hand of god could swoop down and whip me away anytime. That's up to him and City. Don't know why Yessel thinks he can dictate otherwise. Religious people are so funny. God's never helped me fix shit.

"You alright?" the chick asks.

"I'm fine." I say. Do I look like I'm in trouble? I ain't a broken fuckin' doll.

Her boy toy walks up, stands next to her like I'm some tribal shithead about to jump her. Pisses me off at him even more.

"Do you have your name?" he asks.

"Yeah." I bite my lip and narrow my eyes.

"I'm Naim," he says.

"And I'm Kaia."

Fuck, I couldn't care less about these two. I just want my skateboard back, and I motion as much to Naim. He hands her over, and I inspect her for damage. Thankfully, she's alright.

"Grey." I mutter my name, hoping that if I give it, they'll go away.

"I've seen some strange things in City," Kaia says. "But I've never seen anyone shoot out of a building's wall before."

That freaks me to the core. Then I think maybe they're high or somethin'. Now, I know boarders who've gotten themselves fucked up, but that ain't me. Junkies are flat out whack. You won't get me anywhere near that shit. Not in a million years.

I take a step back, wary. "What're you sayin'?"

Now Naim gets defensive 'cause I've insulted his girlfriend. "You and your skateboard kind of… formed out of that house and hurtled toward us."

Now I think it's probably not drugs, but just City being fucked up as usual. "Fuckin' City."

"How did it look to you?" Kaia asks.

Naim's eyes are spewing daggers, but I tell her what I saw, how Tangelo just turned into their fuckin' love nest and City hurtled me into it. I'm not stupid enough that I can't guess what those two were doin' here. All of sudden, I realize I'm talking directly to Kaia, and Naim looks like he's about to burst a gasket.

Fuck me.

"Fuckin' City can't even make up its mind where to put its fuckin' roads." I grab up my board, jog out to the street, slap the board down onto the pavement and cruise away.

I don't say goodbye. At first I'm happy to be rid of them, but then I think back to some of the assholes I've met since I got here. Businessmen, celebrities, hippies, people who think the world revolves around them. Can't fuckin' stand the lot of 'em.

Those two were alright, I guess.

I cruise on down the new streets, hoping to figure out where the hell City spat me out, but nothing is familiar and everything is flat. I ride through an intersection and find out that this gravelly, pothole-infested strip of shit is called Negative Forty-Fifth Street. Annoyed, I push forward. The avenue numbers decrease—I pass Negative Seventh, Eighth, Ninth...

Now the buildings themselves I recognize, but everything's all mixed up. Nothing's in the right place. I spend most of my time dodging potholes, but I spot the laundromat where I slept a few times after I first arrived and the abandoned convenience store that finally ran out of supplies just a few days ago.

Funny. The laundromat was kilometers away from the convenience store, but now they're just a block apart.

I shake my head.

Fuckin' City.

Sick of the flat monotony, I take a left on Negative Twenty-Fourth Avenue, since it looks a little less potholed than the street I'm on.

I dodge grime pits and watch the street numbers increase. I go through the negative thirties, then twenties, then teens, and fuck, what I wouldn't give for some Alabaster Way right now. This new configuration of City is just flat, flat, flat, and every fuckin' road is shit.

I lose all remaining patience and start turning at random, but the monotonous grid follows me wherever I go. An hour passes, maybe more. Sweat streaks my body, and my bandana feels itchy. Fed up, I park, prop my board against a street pole, kick the pole, throw off my bandana, sit on the curb next to it and run my hands over my stubbly scalp.

"Fuck."

I look up.

Another dingy, right-fuckin'-angled intersection, Negative Seventh Street and Twenty-Fourth Avenue.

I wick sweat off my brow, and that's when I notice it across the street: Ochre Arcade.

I smile a bit. Been forever since I've been here. Yessel told me to quit with "childish things," his way of saying 'kiddie crap' (boarding's part of that), and Taum keeps hounding me to collect samples, so it's been a while since I played a video game.

I pick up my board and head into the arcade.

The dark blue lighting is still functional. No one's at the register, but there's electricity to all the games. The token machine's been torn apart. Its guts lay open and exposed, a big pile of tokens bursts from torn metal and frayed wires. They litter the floor.

The familiar sounds of my childhood fill the arcade, the electronic bleeps and screeches of early synth. I take up my post at a Teenage Mutant Ninja Turtles game machine, prop my board up against it, and proceed to kick the crap out of Foot Clan soldiers courtesy of my best friend Donatello.

I try to forget the streets, forget City, but it's still there, just behind me. Ochre Arcade, man. I guess I've always been using these places to hide. These games have never been anything but—

"Mister?"

I jolt around and slam my back into the machine. My heart races a mile a minute.

A kid stands before me, maybe eight or nine years old. He's wearing jeans and a yellow t-shirt. He looks up at me with big, scared, hazel eyes. I exhale my fear. Fuckin' a.

He sniffles. "What's going on, mister? Where am I?"

He erupts into tears.

"Kid… C'mon kid." I kneel down. "It's okay."

"Why-why can't I remember my name?!" He crouches on the ground, bawling his fucking head off. Jeezuz, City. Talk about heartless. It's one thing to take a guy like me or Taum or Yessel, but a fuckin' kid? You're one sick motherfucker.

"Kid, it's okay. You'll remember your name soon, I promise."

He just keeps bawling. I want to do something to calm him, make him feel better. Like, maybe I should put a hand on his shoulder or something. But I get an image in my head of my old man belting me across the face and I cringe.

Fuck, I can't handle a kid.

"Mooooom!" the kid yells long and loud. He alternates between screaming for his mom and dad.

"They're not here!" I shout three times. He keeps bawling. Shit. I just wanted to play my game for a bit. You know, unwind. I look out at the streets, and the right-angled intersection is still there. Damn. I need to get him to Yessel.

"Kid!" I shout at the top of my lungs.

He stops crying, but still sniffling, looks at me with swollen eyes.

"I can take you somewhere safe. A church." Never thought I'd fuckin' utter those words, but Yessel's the only one I trust with shit this heavy. "You want to go for a skateboard ride?"

The kid nods.

"Now I can't just keep calling you kid. So you're gonna be…" I look around. "Mario." The kid does look kinda like he might be the same ethnicity as the famous video game plumber. "You wanna be Mario 'til you remember your real name?"

He nods.

"Good." I grab my board. I take a deep breath, and extend my hand. Memories of my drunken asshat of a father assault me once more, but somehow I make the offer stick. Mario, still sobbing, reaches out tentatively and takes it. Him in one hand and my board in the other, we walk out into City's piercing light.

I put the board on the ground. "Climb up on my shoulders."

He does. "Where we going?"

"A church. I promise it'll be safe. I won't let anything bad happen to you, okay?"

"What's your name?" he asks.

I push off down the street. "Grey."

"Why?"

"It's the name I got after I got here. I don't remember my real name."

"Oh."

It's harder to dodge street detritus and potholes with Mario around my shoulders, but I manage.

"Grey, why are you bald?" Mario asks.

I actually smile at that. "I shave it off."

"Why?"

"Don't like the color of it."

"It looks silver," Mario says.

"Yeah. I know." I'm still actually smiling. Huh.

City, you're something else.

Unhinged

((before))

It's so hard carrying all the groceries alone. I wish Mary would pull her own weight now and then, but she's really quite useless, especially when it comes to menial labor.

It was just like me, too, doing what I did. I'd gotten myself so worked up about having a dinner to prepare and the house being a mess and it was already three—the children would be home very shortly and then my husband, you see—that I didn't realize what had happened until I'd been walking in a straight line for, oh, I don't know, maybe four or five minutes or more.

That's what I noticed first—that I wasn't turning or weaving. I could see all the way to the horizon, five blocks away.

Mary didn't say anything about it, of course. Just let me keep on walking like a plain fool. It is so like her. I don't know why I keep her as a friend sometimes.

"Negative Second Avenue?" I read aloud from a decrepit signpost. I would have put my hands on my hips if I wasn't carrying all these groceries. She catches my indignant gaze certainly, though. I hope she'll at least pay attention to that. "Really, Mary. You could have said something."

Mary feigns indifference. And that gets me really worked up.

"I can't believe that they've done this. Can you? How will we get home in time now? My husband and children will be so upset if they don't get dinner in time."

Now, the thing about Mary is, she has this deep-seated envy of my family life. She was never married, you see. Her fiancee came out as gay and ran off with her best friend from college. When I bring up my husband or my two beautiful children, a boy of ten and a girl of eight, it really gets her goat.

Mary makes a sarcastic remark about how City can do whatever it pleases and rolls her eyes.

"Yes, I know," I say. "City *will* do as it pleases. I wish it would consult us though. You know, when I was younger, I thought I would make a point of writing a letter once a week. That's how democracy is supposed to work, you know. Our representatives are supposed to hear what we think. They're supposed to know that they'll be kicked out of their jobs if their actions stray too far from the will of their electorate."

I've struck a chord with Mary now. Politics simply incenses her. Perhaps I'm doing this on purpose. Yes. I think, subconsciously, I wanted to rile her up today. She bunches up her forehead and recites her usual tirade about oppression of and by the masses, about how constant struggle for community, goodwill and trust is the only way out. The masses, indeed! As if one can talk of masses in City.

"Of course," I reply. "City is clearly anarchy. Or a despotism. But listen! One minute I'm on Filemot Way and I know exactly where I am, and the next I'm on a street with a negative number for its name. It's just not right, I tell you. This is not a healthy way for a society to run. My husband runs a strict household, but it's an ordered household. Everything in its place, as he says. I know you think he's too strict, but this is the lesson we all learn as we get older. We learn the value of stability and order. It's the young and impetuous who want anarchy. They don't know what it's like, Mary."

Mary's looking at me now as though I'm too stupid to be talking to. I'll bet she's even reconsidering our friendship. I suppose it's my fault. I've pushed her too far.

She makes a hard left onto Negative First Avenue, and I follow her. I have no idea where I am, but I suppose following her can't hurt anything. I just hope I find my home soon. The groceries seem to be getting heavier and heavier.

"Mary," I try again, adopting a conciliatory tone. "I'm sorry if I upset you. You know I respect your political opinions. I just disagree, that's all. Certainly, we can agree that City is poorly run, can't we?"

Mary agrees with a curt nod. Our pace slows.

I'm glad for that, but as I watch the buildings pass, new worries well up in place of the old. I recognize an abandoned bookstore that's supposed to be halfway across City and next to it lies a power substation that's supposed to be a few blocks from my house. The substation hums ominously as we pass.

At least someone in City is keeping the lights on, even if they don't have the courtesy to acknowledge our presence here.

Mary asks me my name.

I jolt.

The paper bags drop to the ground.

I twist around and point a finger at her. "You know my name, Mary! You know it! I know you know it! Mary, I apologized to you, so if you're really going to be this way, then maybe it's time—!"

I pause. I consider my next words carefully.

I stomp forward one step.

"Maybe you should go home, Mary! I'll find my own way back."

I pull up the paper bags, turn and march away.

Mary calls out, asking my name again.

I throw the bags back down. Glass jars within the right one clank precariously against the concrete.

I turn around, hold out my hands.

"What do you want, Mary? Is this really how you want to leave a month of friendship? In pieces?"

Mary asks for my name.

I close my eyes. Bite my tongue. Unspeakable epithets lie on the tip of it. My hands flail down toward the grocery bags. I jerk the right one up, but the handle tears off the left one. The bag falls and cabbage and potatoes spill out onto the pavement.

"Now look what you've done, Mary!" I screech, but she's looking at me and shaking her head. She looks almost sad, but that just makes me angrier. I shuffle the produce back into the bag, haul the broken one up against my side, and scurry away down the street as fast as I'm able. I picked a bad day to wear my nicest shoes. But appearances must be maintained, even in City.

I'm proud of myself for being able to hold back tears. I walk with dignity, despite carrying one bag up against my chest, its torn handle hanging limply over the edge. I'm sure that looks rather silly, but otherwise I am composed, calm even.

Good riddance to Mary.

She was always something of a nuisance.

I continue down the street many more blocks, and worries about finding my house quickly shove away thoughts of Mary. Not moments after worry turns to despair, I spot my house. It has been relocated to the corner of Negative First Avenue and Negative Fifty-Eighth Street.

"Oh!" I exclaim.

It occurs to me that Mary has led me in the correct direction after all. I bite my lip and feel incredibly silly and ashamed. Oh, I've behaved no better than my daughter during one of her tantrums. I will make it up to Mary. I will call her this evening and apologize. Yes, that's the right thing to do.

I take a deep breath and head inside.

I'm so proud of our place. A short flight of four steps leads up to our front porch, where we have a rocking chair, a small table, and a potted plant. Actually, someone ran off with our potted plant. I worry about tribals sometimes, being as close as I am to the Amaranthine District.

I feel a pang of fear, realizing that City's reconfiguration could have put them even closer to my house. I hope it hasn't.

I head inside and take the groceries to the kitchen, eager to be rid of them. My arms and back ache from the strain of carrying them so far. These damn negative streets! Probably added half a kilometer to my journey.

The dishes are done. Good, good. I decide to check the laundry, even though I suspect the dryer is still running, and it is.

I stretch my fatigued muscles and then begin to prepare dinner. Always so much work to do. My husband and children will be home soon. I take furtive glances at the door throughout the afternoon, watching.

The meat is cooked. The potatoes are ready. The salad is divine! I nibbled it a bit. I outdid myself with the dressing. I take the laundry upstairs, begin folding, and still no one is home.

I finish the laundry, put all the children's clothes away in their upstairs bedrooms.

It's too quiet downstairs. I don't want to go down there. I'm afraid of what I'll find. It's already five. How could no one be home?

The children! What if something's happened to them? I have to call the police! There are no police. This is City. This is City.

This is City.

I am downstairs. I—I don't know how I got here, but I'm standing next to the phone.

I pick up the receiver and dial.

"Mary?" I say.

No response.

"Mary?" I try again.

"Please, Mary. I'm so sorry. Will you forgive me?"

Silence.

"My husband and children…" I sob. I can't keep my composure this time. My hand covers my face. I weep freely.

"Mary," I whisper into the phone receiver. "Please… can you tell me my name?"

City is Amalgam

(( ))

A great philosopher once tried using mathematics to deconstruct God.
In broad strokes, here is an account of what transpired.

He decided first to define all of God's creation in terms of substances and their properties. Human substance. Cat substance. Tree substance. And so on. Humans have properties: skin color, height, weight, muscle mass, intellect. More or less the same with cats and trees. Some differences. Minor. Inconsequential.

So, we have substances, and substances have properties.

The philosopher looked at all the many substances with their proliferation of properties and realized that many properties were shared, and further, that the substances interacted and their properties morphed in response. The substances could change.

But wait!

By definition, God is unchanging. God is perfection incarnate.

But surely—surely—God must exist within the universe. Could he create a universe and live outside it? How could such meager substances as humans have a conception of him if that were the case?

And so God must exist within the universe. God is a substance.

Oh dear.

Now the philosopher is in quite a predicament. As a substance, God has properties. If God interacts with mankind—other substances, which surely He does—then their properties must necessarily change.

Gasp!

God cannot change for He is perfection, and perfection is intrinsically immutable.

Our philosopher has done it now. He has reasoned himself into a metaphysical corner. No escape, it seems.

Until...

The philosopher comes to realize that if the differences between substances were an illusion, *and that if all the different substances humans perceive were just one mutable property of one giant, mega-cosmic whole...*

Aha!

The philosopher has found his loophole, his way out: God and the universe are one and the same.

We have said before that City and its citizens are as one, it is part of their being, they come and go, they leave their mark.

Such a unique relationship is not without its costs. The cost of time. The emotional toll. Even a person's name is consumed in the process.

But from the ashes of a great conflagration may rise something greater, stronger, more resilient than before.

Even in the wake of Naim's unique departure, the shockwave he sent hurtling through all of City's substance and properties, City goes on. It will take more than transcendental scientific philosophy to wreck a god.

Indistinct

((after))

"What city?" the man in the overalls asked.

Gwei had just met him and already she was sick of him. She knew, deep down, that she shouldn't blame him. It wasn't his fault, after all. It was City. But still… Naim was gone, and now this big ugly man covered in dirt was here. His eyes were dim. Not bright, like Naim's.

She perked up, her own eyes wide. She blinked, stared down the long, straight street to the horizon and the swirling blue beyond; her focus moved beyond that.

But how? Naim left City. I can remember his name. I can remember all of our conversations. I remember meeting him. I remember him showing me around City. I remember him introducing me to everyone. All of it. Not like the others…

Of the others who had left City, she could remember no names or particular conversations. She could recall interactions only vaguely, no words formed remembered conversations, only the general sense of what had been said, what had been done, like an after echo in an empty room after someone had shut the door.

But Naim…

Somehow, he remained. Even though he was gone.

Her cheek muscles twitched. Anger rose up within her. That *bastard*! He hadn't even had the decency to erase himself from her memory properly! Of all the people she might not forget here—

"Miss?" The man reached out a hand toward her shoulder. "You okay?"

She flinched, and he retracted his hand sharply in kind. "I'm sorry—"

Gwei shook her head. "No, it's all right—"

His metal box clanged the ground, and he ran his hands through his hair, looking up at the sky, a twisting azure-teal-aquamarine soup. "What *is* this place?"

Gwei took a deep breath so that, hopefully, she would sound more calm than annoyed. "It's called City."

He turned a harsh gaze toward her. "*What* city?"

Right. He'd asked that already.

"Not *a* city," Gwei said. "Just City."

"City…" he gazed off toward the five-intersections distant horizon. His eyes followed the tops of a few skyscrapers jutting up at a forty-five-degree angle from just over it. "How did I get here?"

"No one knows. We only know that we're here now." Gwei kicked at the pavement and sighed. Her own gaze drifted up to a nearby sign. The streets were still in this new configuration. With the numbers. Weird. Only in City…

She began down Negative Sixth Street.

"Hey!" the man called out. The sound of his clattering metal box rushed up behind her. "Where you going?"

"I honestly don't know."

"Is something wrong?"

"Nothing you should worry about."

"Is this… um… is any part of City dangerous?"

"Here? No. I don't think so. But yes, some parts are."

"You know where it's safe then?"

She stopped and turned, looked up at him, making direct eye contact for the first time since meeting him. "I know the safest place. Someone's there who keeps it safe. If I take you there, will you leave me alone?"

He frowned. Blinked a few times. Frowned deeper. "Sure," he mumbled.

Gwei began back down Negative Sixth Street, watching the buildings intently. It was just like back at that intersection with Naim, when the streets had suddenly changed—the greengrocer's, the apothecary and the arcade—all of which were supposed to be kilometers apart, but now they were crammed together on the same block. She recognized many more homes, offices, restaurants, parks, and monuments too, but all haphazardly reassembled into this new configuration.

She gulped. Did she even know where the Amaranthine District was anymore? Could it be scattered and jumbled as well? Could she wander into a tribal, going on as she was?

Gwei stuffed her fear away and strode onward.

"Who's this someone?" the man asked.

"Someone?" Gwei spotted the huge mall, just peaking over the horizon a few blocks over.

"You said you're taking me to someone. Someone in a safe place."

"Oh," Gwei said, still scanning the horizon. "Just Yessel."

"Who's he?"

Gwei bunched up her brow. "Why do you assume he's a man?"

"Err... I don't—"

"Because you don't trust a woman to keep you safe?"

"I never said that!" His metal box rattled irritably.

This wasn't a fight she needed to fight. She was just upset, she reminded herself. "Yessel's a man," she admitted. "A priest. Well, he calls himself a philosopher."

"You don't think he is?"

"He's smart, sure. Naim was the real philosopher."

"Who was he?" the man asked quietly.

Gwei shook her head, and they marched onward.

They continued east, passing through Thirty-First Avenue, then Thirtieth. Not trusting herself to make any changes to their trajectory, Gwei hurried faster down Negative Sixth, and the avenue numbers continued their descent. They walked and walked, passing through the twenties, then the teens, and there remained no sign of Yessel's cathedral.

"You don't know where it is, do you?" The man stopped and crossed his arms.

Gwei stopped and crossed her own arms in retort. "I would normally. The streets have changed."

"What do you mean?"

"Just before you arrived. Yessel's cathedral is on Claret Crossing. But that street is... missing, I guess. There are just these numbered signs now, and these long, thin roads are all the same."

"And how come it's just you and me, huh?" The man narrowed his eyes. "Isn't a city supposed to have lots of people in it?"

Gwei let out a small laugh. "This isn't a normal city—"

Both of their ears perked up and they turned to look down Eleventh Avenue. Gwei winced. She spotted Ward tugging and yanking at Grey's shoulder, determined to restrain him. Grey's obscenities rang out loud and clear.

"Speak of the devil…" the man said.

"C'mon." Gwei motioned to him.

As they approached, she was able to make out more than just Grey's profanity.

"No!" Ward shouted. "Absolutely not. He's your responsibility, Grey."

"Get the fuck off me!" Grey tugged at the other man's hands. Ward was tall, probably the tallest man in City. Wide frame, too. Naim had said Ward had arrived in a policeman's uniform, but apparently he'd shed it the moment he'd found other clothes in an abandoned department store. He'd formed a group called The Collective, one Naim and his girl-friend had been invited into, but they'd declined. The group had since fragmented and disbanded.

Ward's heart seemed to be in the right place, but he was too intense for Gwei's liking. And he gave in to despair far too easily for a place like City.

"You cannot go in there!" Ward shook Grey's arm.

"Fuck off, you old geezer!"

Ward bunched up his face. "Get it into your head that some of us might know a thing or two better than you do."

"You're just butt hurt because you couldn't protect your precious Aria!" Ward's face fell. He released his grip. "Now let me—" Grey stumbled, suddenly free but still struggling. "—go."

"What's going on—?" Gwei's companion took a step toward Grey.

"Fuck you, too!" Grey shouted. He snatched up his skateboard, tossed it on the ground, and sped away, the wheels trundling down the pavement.

Ward stumbled into the side of the nearest building and wrapped his arms around his head, covering his face.

Gwei ran to his side. Naim had told her that Ward had seemed more put-together before Aria's death, but that was before Gwei had arrived. She had only ever known him to be emotionally volatile.

"Hey!" Gwei walked toward a retreating Ward. "Snap out of it!"

Ward lost his footing and slid down the wall supporting him. Gwei crouched at his side. His face was dry, but shuddering fear wracked his body. Gwei took a deep breath. This couldn't all be a result of Aria's death. What had happened to this man before he'd come to City?

"Ward?" Gwei tried.

Her companion crouched beside Ward as well.

"I can't stop it..." Ward mumbled. "It just keeps happening." He shook his head, still trembling. "It just keeps happening."

"I recognize this," Gwei's companion said.

Gwei looked up at his dirt-smeared face, surprised to find herself free of annoyance with him. He set his box down and nodded away from Ward. They stood and she followed him away from the wall.

"The war," the man said. "Do you remember the war?"

Gwei shook her head. "The worlds people remember are all different. Some very different."

The man bunched up his face, exasperated. "There was a war. Some guys on my crew were in it. Some of them couldn't do the work and had to quit. I even had to let one go. They couldn't... things happened to them, and their emotions were all... shot-through. Though they're the sane ones, if you ask me. No sane person could come out of a war and still be normal."

"You think Ward was in a war?" Gwei asked. His logic made a kind of sense, but she remained skeptical.

The man shook his head. "I don't know. But something traumatic. Really traumatic." His eyes shot through with intensity. "If he's like the guys I know... he could be dangerous if we don't get him help. You know, a head doctor."

Gwei took a deep breath. "Our doctor was helping him. But she died. That's who Grey mentioned before he ran off. A new doctor could show up, but I wouldn't count on it."

"People show up here... just out of nowhere?"

"Mm hmm. Just like you did."

A rattling sounded from the wall. Gwei and her companion turned their attention back to Ward. He sat, rummaging through the metal box and pulling out various tools. A hammer, a screwdriver, a wrench. He tossed each one on the ground.

They walked carefully, cautiously toward him.

Ward pulled out a bolt, held it between his fingers, angled it up to the sky, closed one eye and peered at it, turning it in his fingers.

"Ward...?" Gwei tried.

Ward looked down, his eyes locking on the construction worker. He scooped the bolt up in his palm and held it forward.

"This is you," Ward said to the man.

The man eyed Gwei before turning his attention to Ward. "That's... me?"

"Don't you hear it?" Ward smiled. "Bolt."

Gwei's companion cast her a confused stare, but Gwei's eyes lit up and she nodded. "Bolt."

The construction worker knit his brow. "What about it—?"

"Your name," Ward said, "is Bolt."

Bolt blinked, turned away from Ward, moved closer to Gwei. "Sure. Um— Come to think of it, I still don't know your name..."

"Gwei," she said.

"So, um, Gwei..."

"Yeah?"

"If there's nothing more we can do for Ward, I'd like to go meet Yessel."

Gwei put a hand on Ward's shoulder. "You okay, Ward?"

He took a deep breath. "I'll be fine." He picked himself up. "Gotta go talk some sense into that idiot kid."

And Gwei had thought she'd overcome exasperation. She put her hands on her hips. "Leave him alone, Ward."

"I can't!" Ward roared, fists clenched, fuming. Gwei sprinted to Bolt's side, hands clenched behind her back, suddenly sweating. She gulped.

Ward marched off, mumbling to himself. Gwei and Bolt watched him retreat, waiting with consternation and apprehension for him to leave earshot.

Bolt put a hand on Gwei's shoulder. She thought to shrug it off, but she decided to let it stay. It wasn't every day that someone of Bolt's character dropped into City. She found her hatred of him dwindling, but he still annoyed her. She realized she resented him, though he'd proved helpful, protective and loyal. Very rare in City.

How ungrateful I am, she thought. And how juvenile, sometimes.

She shrugged his hand off, and watched his smile fall to a frown.

And why won't these damned streets fix themselves?

Bolt scrambled to put everything back into his box somewhere behind her. He joined up at her side as she stood and huffed and stared down the five-block-long causeway to nothing.

She took a deep breath and strode away. Bolt followed.

They marched in silence for what seemed like forever. Bolt remained stoic. She found herself going over his features. Big. Burly. He probably had a lot of hair under that shirt. Forthright, protective. The exact opposite of Naim. City was mocking her. It had taken Naim from her and given her his polar opposite. Bolt might as well have been named Not-Naim.

"There." Bolt pointed over the rusty-edged sign demarcating the intersection of Negative Sixth Street and Negative Nineteenth Avenue. A spire poked out just overtop a dreary brick apartment building. Atop the spire stood a cross.

Gwei broke the faintest smile. "That's Yessel's cathedral."

She turned them down Negative Nineteenth.

Bolt nodded. "I'm getting kind of hungry and thirsty. What do you do for food and water here?"

"A supermarket showed up last week, so there'll be food to go around for a few more days. But the tribals will discover it soon."

"Tribals?"

Why did everything have to be so damn confusing for him? "The people who let the Amaranthine District into them."

"The district... gets into them?"

"Yeah."

"What does that mean?"

"Hope you never have to see it." Gwei gulped. Speaking of trauma, there was a memory she would happily have expunged. "You'll know Amaranthine architecture when you see it. The angles are all wrong. Lots of frames, scaffolds. The beams bend and twist at weird angles and everything glows purple—"

Bolt was shaking his head. "I'm not an architect, but I've put up enough buildings to know that you can't have weird angles and twisting supports. Nothing would stand. The supports have to be arranged in triangles, and you need load-bearing pillars, or it'll all collapse."

"Amaranthine architecture doesn't collapse. And it can get inside you. If you see the purple glow, just run the other direction."

Bolt continued alongside her. She got the distinct impression that he didn't believe her, that if a glowing, purple lattice appeared before them, he'd go up to it and try to figure out how it stayed upright. Very dangerous. She should keep Bolt far away from the tribals and their toxic district, at least until he learned better.

They rounded the corner of Negative Ninth Street and Negative Twenty-Third Avenue, coming face to face with the cathedral. Gwei remembered cathedrals from before City. They were old and decaying on her world, most of her peers having shunned religion for unrestrained secularism. But these stone facades harkened back to her childhood, the one time she'd left the country with her parents, traveling through ancient lands and seeing the magnificent stonework artifacts of a time when worshipping an almighty had been communion with the highest good. In the present, her peers mocked belief openly. So sad. She'd loved those faraway places.

Yessel's cathedral reminded her of that. It was the one place in City that felt truly safe in Naim's absence.

She and Bolt walked up the stone steps. Gwei grabbed the black, metal ring of a handle and pulled open the pewter-hued doors.

Bolt looked about the stone arches, the stained glass, the burning candles, the enormous iconostasis along the back wall. Organ music erupted around them. They walked around the right side of the central row of pews and came to the front row, looking down the center of the transept. The apse rose up, barricaded, the chapels radiating around behind it.

Gwei smiled, and looked to Bolt. He seemed nervous.

"This is the safest place in City," Gwei said.

Bolt nodded slightly, rubbing his hands together. She sat in the front pew and patted the seat beside her. He gulped and sat, his metal box clanking down beside him.

"Don't you like churches?" Gwei asked.

Bolt shook his head.

After a time, Bolt turned to her. "So, where's Yessel?"

"He'll come out when he's done playing."

The writhing, melancholy tones reached a crescendo, then fell to their denouement, lingered. And then… silence. Gwei loved the silence after the song. She held her eyes closed.

Maybe this is what Naim found. A way to live in this mindset, to be in this frame of mind forever.

"Gwei." Bolt shook her shoulder.

Yessel strode toward them, wearing his long, white robes with blue and red edges. And that silly hat. She thought it looked absurd, but there was no disliking Yessel. His face showed the creases of age. He had to be at least sixty-five. No doubt Bolt was wondering how such a frail old man could secure the safest stronghold in City. The only fearful thought that crossed Gwei's mind concerning Yessel was that City might steal him away just as easily as anyone else, at any time.

Yessel smiled widely. "My daughter."

"D-daughter…?" Bolt stumbled to his feet.

Gwei stood, hugged Yessel. She turned to Bolt. "It's a euphemism."

His expression remained confused.

"An idiom. An expression." She felt her annoyance rising up again, but tamped it down for Yessel's sake.

Yessel turned his attention to Bolt. "My son. Welcome. Have you found your name?"

"Uh…" Bolt stuffed his hands behind his back. "Yes, sir. I guess my name is Bolt."

"How did you get it?" Yessel asked.

"A man named Ward gave it to me." Bolt's eyes lost their fear, grew wide with interest.

"Ah." Yessel nodded and smiled back.

Gwei knew that look. Yessel had become fascinated.

The priest continued. "And in your life before City, you built things, from the looks of it."

"Yes."

"But not just buildings… something else."

Bolt frowned. "No. Just the buildings. Fancy architects in high rent offices come up with the designs. Me and my crew just do the building."

Yessel nodded solemnly. "You will be safe here, my son."

"Thank you," Bolt said. His stomach growled. Gwei had to admit, she was hungry and thirsty, too. Time to raid Naim's old storage area. But first…

"Yessel?" Gwei asked.

He turned slowly to meet her gaze "Yes?"

"Something's wrong. Naim's gone, but I remember his name and everything we did together. It's not supposed to be like that."

Yessel frowned and nodded slowly.

Gwei found herself growing frustrated. She'd hoped Yessel would know. She considered him to be the most knowledgeable person in City, even if Naim had seemed wiser in many regards. Yessel had been here the longest, too, over a decade.

"Has that ever happened before? With anyone else?"

"No," Yessel said. "I've always forgotten them."

"But you remember Naim, too?"

"Yes."

"And…?"

The priest shook his head slowly, meticulously. "I'm sorry, my daughter. I don't know what to make of it."

Such was Yessel. Always honest to a fault.

"I am interested though…" Yessel turned and began walking toward the sanctuary. Gwei followed. Bolt trailed behind, grabbing up his metal box from the pew. "…When was the first time that you remember the streets changing into their grid configuration?"

Gwei thought back.

"They've been a grid the whole time I've been here," Bolt said.

Yessel came to a stop at the wooden barricade guarding the sanctuary. He turned to Bolt. "And how long that has been?"

Bolt shrugged. "About one… two hours, maybe?"

Gwei nodded. "The first time I saw it was just before Bolt arrived. I mean, Naim talked about it endlessly, his 'great mistake,' but I'd never seen it until Naim and I came to that intersection. Perhaps that journey of his is related somehow? You know, his journey to the—"

"No," Yessel interjected. "I am quite sure that there is nothing relevant *there*."

Gwei frowned, remembering how Naim had introduced her to Yessel, and that was how she had discovered about his ruinous relationship with City. No wonder his search for answers had led him elsewhere. He'd discovered his truth, apparently. Or he was dead.

"Do the changing streets have something to do with Naim disappearing?" Bolt asked.

Yessel nodded introspectively. "Perhaps. I think Naim's disappearance has caused something to go wrong with City. I feel what you feel, Gwei. City's rhythm is off. Tell me: what configuration do you think the streets are in right now?"

Gwei shrugged. "I could go check."

Yessel raised a hand, a stream of white trailing from it. "No. Without checking. Right now. How could we discover what configuration they're in?"

Bolt shrugged. "They only way to know would be to open the doors and look outside."

"And then City would choose," Yessel said. "One or the other. Until someone looks, who knows what lies just on the other sides of these walls. The cloister, or Amaranthine hell?"

Gwei gulped.

Bolt took a step forward, his chest puffed out. "If something's wrong with City, then we'll fix it. Tell me what to do, and I'll help. What's our next step?"

Hadn't he just minutes ago been more concerned with food and water, Gwei wondered. She was growing weary of his intensity, honestly. She needed an hour to catch her breath and think over everything that had happened. Some food and water wouldn't hurt, either.

Yessel smiled widely at the construction worker, a wider smile than Gwei had ever seen from Yessel. From anyone else, such a smile might have been frightening.

"That," Yessel said, "is why your name is Bolt."

Bolt deflated. "Huh?"

Yessel shrugged it off with a wave of his hand and turned to Gwei. "I can think of only one thing that will help, and I do not like it. Not after everything that's happened."

Gwei groaned. "You *still* don't have them?"

"Have what?" Bolt asked.

"There used to be a scientist in City," Yessel said. "He's gone-away now."

"City took him," Gwei explained before Bolt could ask.

Yessel continued. "While he was here, he invented bracelets that can repel the Amaranthine District from a person, prevent it from taking them over."

Gwei started to ask about the software engineer who had said two days ago that he would retrieve the bracelets, then realized that she couldn't remember his name. He'd been taken before he could finish his task.

"Is there anyone else left from The Collective?" Gwei asked.

Yessel shook his head.

"I'll help." Bolt's answer rang out loud and clear, and echoed through-out the cathedral hall.

Gwei looked up at him. "Really? You're going to risk getting tribalized on your first day in City?"

Bolt put a hand on her shoulder and smiled. This time, she didn't flinch away.

Embittered

Even in City, she appears in my dreams every night without fail. I see the terrified look on her face, which fades to confusion, which turns to pain and fear as her torso implodes with red and she crumbles. Whirring zips of metal slice through her abdomen, then another through her neck, a spray, and she's collapsed, gone.

I don't know how many times I've played through it in my mind, awake or asleep. I've lost track of which are the dreams and which are the intrusions into reality.

The worst part is, since my arrival in City, I can't remember her name.

I've said it so many times, but it's not there. I've forgotten my own sister's name. The memory's all I've got of her now. It wasn't enough that my fear and cowardice stripped me of her presence, City had to strip away her name, too.

I suppose I deserve it.

What was it Aria used to say—?

No. No. No.

I won't go down that rabbit hole again.

I push thoughts of Aria from my head, but the images of my sister, running, exploding, crumpling, dying. Red. Fill my head. Fill my head. Fill my head.

I laugh, meekly, timidly.

They all ran away. Aria died, and they all went away.

I wonder what my state might be if Aria had been taken instead of killed. If you're taken, no one else remembers your name. If you die, you're stuck here forever.

I wonder what happens to the people that knew you in your real life? Were there all sorts of people—friends, family, coworkers—back in Aria's home who woke up one day to discover she'd vanished? They might have sent out cops to look for her, or posted a missing persons report, like the ones that used to come across my desk.

I worked a beat in a city once. A real city. Not like this place. This is a fraud, a pathetic failure of a city. Can't even keep its own inhabitants safe. Needs order. Guidance. I tried that, didn't I? Didn't work out any better here than at home.

I pull my head out from between my legs and look about my apartment. I swear the mold streaks are longer than when I looked down. I shift my weight, and my cot groans. The festering stench rising off the sink is visible; dirty dishes pile upward, occluding the small window. The thought of washing them makes me sick. I'm not even sure if the faucet works anymore.

A kitchen, a bedroom, a living room, a dining room, all in one. And the door, a pale wood painted white. Ghostly. The metal handle stands out, a silver that would look bright and shiny in contrast to any other door, but against this blaring, luminescent portal it is dark. Its grimy film of rot is all too apparent.

I decide to spend today inside, too. Like most days. If I think of my sister in here, I can bear it. Best not to burden others with my problems.

A knock at the door.

Now that's unexpected. There are only a couple of people it could be. Naim, possibly. But a remote possibility. I suspect it to be either Yessel or Gwei. Or perhaps the tribals have decided to raid my humble abode and fill my blood with their purple effluence.

I wonder if that would stop me from thinking about my sister. And Aria.

I shake my head slowly. No.

Another knock. "Ward? Ward!"

The voice surprises me. Young. Very young. Male. Where have I met— of course! One of the boys trailing at Grey's side. I think of Grey, and my facial muscles twitch, an automatic reaction. What a rotten influence. And to think Yessel had *defended* him. Beyond ludicrous.

"Mario?" I call out. "Is that you?"

"Ward! Help me, please."

I bolt from my cot. The rot in the sink and on the walls and in my bed jolts to the far periphery of my senses, as though someone placed a magnet in my vision and everything negative jumped away in response.

I open the door.

Mario stands there, about three feet tall, light brown skin, curly black hair, a battered yellow t-shirt and jeans. He deserves so much better than City.

"What's wrong?" I ask him.

He fidgets. "Fero and Hyra and Grey ran off and tribals, he's gonna get turned into a tribal, and—" He starts bawling.

I kneel down and put a hand on his shoulder. "Calm down. It's going to be alright. Yessel's not going to become a tribal, right?"

"I guess."

"The cathedral's okay, right?"

"Yeah."

"So, you're going to be safe, okay?"

"Yeah."

"Okay. Now take a deep breath."

He breathes in and out. I grin a bit.

"Now start at the beginning. What happened to Fero and Hyra and Grey?"

"A building showed up. We were on, um, Zinn-bur Street and Grey said it was a food building. And Fero and Hyra were with us. And they agreed. And we saw it pop. Like, it just appeared. So we thought it was new and we were the first ones. But there was tribals inside and their faces were purple and scary and their skin moved and I can't remember I was ever more scared than that, Ward."

He starts sobbing again, and I have to calm him down. Eventually, after some cajoling, I get him to continue.

"Grey grabbed my arm and we all ran out of the building, but they caught up with us near the entrance, and Grey and me got out onto the street, but the tribals took Fero and Hyra away. To Am-er-thine."

I'm careful to keep my face flat for the kid. Maybe I twitch a bit. Can't help that. But I don't bite my lip or blink or any of those kinds of things.

This is not good. Police instinct. There are situations where you can go in and do something drastic, sure. That can work. This is not one of those situations.

My mind wraps back around to how Mario started this conversation. I squeeze his arm, gently. I look at him with wide eyes. "Mario, where's Grey?"

He wells up with tears and his lips tremble, and I know.

"He's going after Fero and Hyra, isn't he?"

Mario shakes his head up and down as he bawls.

Internally, I scoff. That self-righteous, immature, vigilante idiot. Doesn't he care that someone else is going to be scarred when he gets himself killed or worse?

Memories claw at my carefully constructed defenses, breaking through in places, but I shove them away. I think of the magnet effect.

Not now.

I have to be strong for Mario.

"C'mon." I stand upright.

"Where you taking me?" Mario sniffles.

"To Yessel."

"Church is boring. I want Grey back."

"Yessel's cathedral is very *safe*."

"'K." Mario trudges alongside me.

We walk down the narrow causeway of the apartment building past drab door after drab door. To my knowledge, mine is the only apartment that's occupied in this complex. And my door is the only one bright white. I found a paint store when I arrived. It was one of the first things I did.

We reach the elevator, and I glance down beyond the railing only momentarily. I start. The trees down the center and edges of the parkway are gone. Evermore Public Park is gone. In its place are dim, chipped stone walls topped with whorls of barbed wire. Beyond them, smokestacks and rectangles of concrete with little meager windows. It all lies dead, unelectrified, which is weird in City. Most buildings arrive connected to the grid.

I might believe the park had been replaced, but what of the street? Its four lanes have become two.

I squeeze Mario's hand and point to the ground. "What road is that?"

"Dunno," Mario says. "The streets changed again."

I'd only seen that once before, and then I'd been sure it was an effect that Naim or the gone-away scientist had created. This 'change of the streets' apparently persisted even when they weren't around.

The elevator bell dinged and we stepped inside.

"Do you know how to get to the cathedral from here?" I ask. "With the roads changed?"

Mario nods.

"Then you're going to lead the way. Can you do that?"

Another nod.

"Just…" Mario fidgets, trying to pull his hand free of mine. "We should find Grey. I don't want anything to happen to him."

"I won't let anything happen to him," I say, trying to keep despondence out of my voice. Mario can almost certainly sense it. He was a smart kid to seek me out, but he must know I don't like Grey. He trusts Yessel, sure, but Yessel's in no position to go running after and restraining Grey. I wonder why he didn't try to find Naim.

The elevator dings and the doors trundle open. The lighting fizzles and blinks, like usual.

We exit out into the new streets, which are much more dismal and decrepit than the streets I know. I take a moment to look down the one I stand upon. Five blocks away, the twirling blue of the sky meets the road. Such a close horizon. I'm used to the way that the buildings bend and arc in the distance, sure, but the roads curved and twisted so much that the horizon was never visible. Seeing it sets my heart aflutter.

And I thought I was beyond fear.

The vision jolts me. My sister tumbles. A spray of blood. Her contorted, fearful, yearning face, eyes locked on me; the vision pierces my mind.

"Ow! Ward!"

Mario's shout jolts me to my senses. I release his hand, realizing I'd squeezed it too hard.

A hand on my shoulder. I realize my eyes are clenched shut and I'm crouched on the ground.

"It's okay, Ward," Mario says. "Let's go find Grey, okay? I think I know where he went."

I stand up. "The cathedral. Take me to Yessel, then we'll go find Grey. Okay?"

Mario nods. I offer my hand, and Mario takes it.

We walk down the street.

I gawk at the grimy green sign at the right-angled intersection, hanging precariously from a rusted perch. Negative Fifteenth Street meets

Negative First Avenue.

Mario leads me down Negative Fifteenth Street and the avenue numbers descend as we pass through the intersections. Mostly I gawk at the buildings. I recognize a restaurant here, a hotel there, but all of the familiar structures used to be on different streets, some miles apart.

Mario has one up on me in this regard. He's been running these streets with Grey. I wonder how many times he's seen the altered configuration. Perhaps the gone-away scientist knew something about the streets that the rest of us don't. It might be worth searching his lab. Yessel's probably already thought of that, though. It's not like I've been much use to anyone recently.

At Negative Twenty-Third Avenue, Mario tugs anxiously at my hand, turning us north. It's a brisk walk for me, but he's practically running. His chest is heaving up and down and he's gasping for breath. He looks so worried. He thinks he's going to lose Grey. He doesn't understand that Grey and the twins were already lost before he showed up at my door.

The cathedral spire peaks up over the horizon.

I start to worry Mario won't have enough sense to stay put with Yessel. The priest won't be in any position to restrain Mario should he decide to run away.

We approach the enormous doors, and Mario grabs at the metal ring handle with both hands, tugs it open, and runs inside.

I follow.

"Yessel!" he shouts.

The kid must not have cathedrals in his world. He doesn't understand there's a way you're supposed to behave inside one. Or he doesn't care.

"Yessel!" he shouts again, further away.

I follow at a subdued, respectful pace, around the pews.

"Yes, my son?" My eyes haven't adjusted to the candlelight yet, but Yessel's voice is unmistakable.

"Tribals took Fero and Hyra, and Grey went after them, but Ward said we could bring Grey back if I came here." I'm near them now, and I see Mario's face turn back to me, eyes pleading. "We're going to bring Grey back, right?"

"Yes," I say. "I will. As long as you stay here."

Mario furrows his brow. "But I want to help!"

"Calm yourself," Yessel tells the boy gently. "Ward is a man of his word. You'll do everything you can, won't you, Ward?"

I nod. "Yes. I will."

If I can find my way to the Amaranthine District in this new street configuration. I consider asking Yessel, but I don't dare do so in front of Mario, nor should I take him aside and ask him. Mario's in just the state that he'd run away.

I crouch down and beckon Mario to me. He walks over meekly.

"You really gonna bring him back?" Mario asks the floor.

"I will. I promise. Hey." I shake his shoulder. "I won't let you down. Okay?"

Mario nods dejectedly and scampers away into the cathedral.

Yessel nods to me, a slight frown set into his face. Very slight.

I turn and exit the cathedral.

I walk the streets with purpose. Purpose tends to keep the visions away; like poles repelling. But purpose won't be enough. If I don't know where the Amaranthine District is anymore, I won't know where Grey could have gone. And City's big. The gone-away scientist once said that City's area is about three hundred ten square kilometers. Give or take.

No way to know exactly how many people. Especially with the tribals being the way they are. I had once thought it to be in the dozens, but now… probably more than a hundred. That's nowhere near city-scale population density.

And none of us remembers our real names. Or the real names of anyone important to us.

I stop and close my eyes—a flash of blood before my vision. My sister's face.

I take deep breaths and push the thoughts away.

A scuttling, trundling sound edges into the periphery of my perceptions, and I latch onto it. It becomes my magnet pole.

I hear a distant voice—"Motherfucking potholes!"—and I recognize it immediately. The profanity alone…

I take off into a sprint. It feels good to run. Purpose makes everything better. My magnet. I've found Grey. I'll get him back to the cathedral and we'll come up with a plan to help Fero and Hyra together. It'll be just like Aria said, all of us united. The tribals can't win if we're united, because our side is right.

But Aria's not here anymore. I let her—

And I don't let myself proceed further with that thought. I direct my energy into the jog. The clatter of wheels against pavement grows closer.

I turn a corner and spot him. His shirt hangs idiotically from the back of his pants. I can see the top half of his boxer briefs, for crying out loud. And yet he's covered his head with that red bandana. Everyone knows why he's named Grey, after all, but no one dares mention it around him.

"Grey!" I shout.

He grinds to a halt, turns, eyes me. "Whaddya want, Ward?"

"Mario found me. He's worried about you."

"Did he tell you about Fero and Hyra?"

"Yeah."

"Well, then fucking help me get them back or get lost."

Regret wells up within me and I tamp it down. "Think about how Mario must feel."

Grey eyes me scornfully. He's annoyed. "I'll come back and get him. I'm not abandoning no one."

"You go to the Amaranthine District alone and you might not get a choice about that. Have you ever seen someone go tribal?"

"No. But I'm sure as hell not letting it happen to Fero and Hyra!"

"Then come back to the cathedral. We'll find others. We'll figure out a plan together. If not for me, then do it for Mario."

Grey scoffs and crouches slightly. He's going to skate away, so I jump forward and grab his arm. "Don't do this, Grey! You want to leave Mario all alone here? You want him fending for himself in City?"

"Fuck off!" Grey struggles against my grip.

"Come back to the cathedral, Grey."

"You take care of Mario, if you care so much."

This incites something within me I can't quite describe. Rage, at myself, at Grey, at everything. Perhaps the reason I hate this young man so much is because he reminds me of myself at his age, but right now, it's hard to keep my thoughts straight. Anger's short-circuiting every coherent train of thought.

"No!" I shout. "Absolutely not. He's your responsibility, Grey!"

"Get the fuck off me!" He claws at my hand with his free hand, but he's unstable on his skateboard and I can apply more force than him because he also has to balance himself.

"You cannot go in there!" I say. I'm trying to be less angry, firmer, but my normal mechanisms for calm and control don't seem to be working. Aria's hanging there, in the back of my mind, staring me down. Judging me. For not being able to save her. For not doing anything when it mattered. A flash of self-reproach smacks me, and—

"Fuck you, you old geezer!"

Anger and regret consume my common sense completely. "Get it into your head that some of us might know a thing or two better than you do," I find myself saying.

"You're just butt hurt because you couldn't protect your precious Aria! Now let me—" His voice falls away. I see the blood and the gore—a purple pistol in a purple hand and Aria, hands raised, defenseless. Blood. So much blood. Drenched. The images wash over my view of Grey and City. The streets that flow away toward the nothing-horizon all turn red. I'm stumbling, falling, ebbing away. My face is wet. My sister's torso explodes onto the streets and her gore is everywhere and I'm tumbling, wet with her blood. I cry out, howl even, and she's dying, over and over, a hail of bullets to the chest and neck.

God help me. Please.

"Hey," a woman's voice says. Is it Aria's? My sister's? It can't be. They're dead. But it sounds a bit like them.

No.

Recognition washes over me, mixing with the blood, sure, but I remember. It's Gwei, Naim's friend. Reluctant friend. He never seemed to like her much.

"Ward!" Her voice is piercing. "Snap out of it!"

Something hard hits my back. My world is still spinning, so I let myself slide down the scratchy surface until my butt hits the concrete. I take deep breaths. Let something wash the blood away, please... Make it go away...

"Ward?" she asks again. That's right. Gwei's insistent. I remember that about her.

I want to answer her properly, and I open my mouth to, but some gibberish comes out instead. I need a purpose, but I've let Grey get away. I've broken my promise to Mario. It's too much.

I look up. Aria stands over me, looking down. I know there's no sun in City, but the sun is behind her head, darkening her features, spikes of light radiating out from behind her like some kind of twisted halo effect. She's angry, and I don't blame her.

I can make this stop. They used to teach me how to control this. I'm not insane. I can make it stop. I'm in control.

I keep telling myself that, but it doesn't feel that way. Aria's there, glaring down at me still. Or is it my sister? The two of them have become blended, and I can't tell the difference anymore.

Something Aria said once drifts back to me. "You're so perceptive. So passionate. It's your gift and your strength, but also your... Oh, darn. There's a phrase I need, but it's got a name in it. A famous character's heel. It means a weak spot."

I look down. A metal box lies at my feet.

I pull at it. There's a tiny latch in the front. My fingers flick it open with a hollow click. The lid opens slowly, gracefully. I pull out a hammer.

Aria is gone. Gwei has her back to me. A man stands beside her, big, burly, overalls, white t-shirt, covered in dirt, brownish skin, orange plastic helmet. Construction. The box must be his.

I hold the hammer up so he lies beside it in my field of vision. No.

The two of them turn all at once and look at me.

I throw the hammer down and grab up a screwdriver. No. Wrench. No. I toss it.

I go through a few other tools, then I spot it.

I pick it up and hold it beside him. Perfect match.

"Ward...?" Gwei crosses her arms.

I extend my hand forward toward the man. "This is you."

He looks perplexed. "That's... me?"

I smile. "Don't you hear it? Bolt."

Gwei understands. "Bolt."

He gapes at us, just like a new arrival would. "What about the bolt—?"

"Your name," I chuckle, "is Bolt."

He frowns at me, that superior frown that someone who thinks they're sane gives someone like me. Anger for him wells up. Can't he be more appreciative? I mean, I know this place is confusing, but he doesn't have to treat me this way. Just because I see— Stop it, Ward.

A hand on my shoulder. "You okay, Ward?"

I take a deep breath. At least someone understands. I rise. "I'll be fine. Gotta go talk some sense into that idiot kid."

Gwei puts her hands on her hips, condescension oozing off her. "Leave him alone, Ward."

I surge forward. "I can't!" I stop myself just as I think my actions might get away from me. She runs for Bolt. Aria is standing beside me now, casting her accusatory glare over my shoulder. Behind her, my sister falls, bleeding, dying on the pavement. An enormous red splotch adorns Aria's chest, oozing down her blouse. But she just stands there, looking at me like I'm the world's biggest failure.

And I am, aren't I?

I turn from the scene and forcibly push myself down the street. I focus all my attention on my feet. One leg after the other. I have to find Grey. I keep my mind focused on Grey. And Mario. He deserves a much better guardian than either me or the skater punk.

That's my problem. Deep down, I know I'm no better than him. I'm still an arrogant teen of the streets who got a job, who got old.

I can't keep anyone safe.

"Grey?" I yell at the top of my lungs. My voice echoes down the street toward the horizon.

City responds with silence.

Righteous

This man doesn't see my cathedral. Not really.

Ward sees patterns and shapes. Pews are for sitting. The strip of velvet cushions before the apse is for kneeling. My robes are for people with the title of 'priest' to wear. Everything in his world has its place and its purpose. Nothing is done to express a sentiment deeper than base materialism.

To him, this is a stone room.

"Yessel!" Mario runs up and tugs at my robes.

I smile down at him. "Yes, my son?"

"Tribals took Fero and Hyra, and Grey went after them, but Ward said we could bring Grey back if I came here." He turns to gaze pleadingly at Ward. "You'll bring Grey back, right?"

Poor boy. If only I could calm his heart. I've watched it flutter from guardian to guardian. A shame that it was Grey he latched onto upon his arrival. The only worse choice of caretaker would have been a tribal. The Collective had, unfortunately, encouraged it.

"Yes," Ward says. "As long as you stay here."

Mario fumes. "But I want to help!"

"Calm yourself," I say, projecting my calm as best I can. "Ward is a man of his word. You'll do everything you can, won't you, Ward?"

Ward nods. "Yes." He beckons Mario toward him, and the boy scampers away from my side. The two converse in hushed tones.

Mario will not stay with me for very long. We've been down this road before. He runs off with Grey's posse, something happens that hurts his feelings, Naim or Ward inevitably directs him here, he stays until he gets bored, then he runs off in search of a new adventure.

Such is youth.

Only the young presume that to become old and wise is to lose some special magic that only the youthful comprehend. We elderly folk smile back for a reason.

Wisdom has great perks.

Ward looks up to me, and I nod to him. He must be certain of my conviction that Mario will remain, or Ward will fall victim to his own trauma. There is a man that would do well to seek wisdom. It lessens the pain of living, and does Ward ever have pain.

Ward strides out the door, the heavy stone crunching shut behind him.

Mario sighs, walks to a nearby pew, and curls himself up in its corner.

I walk slowly toward him and sit.

"Your hat's funny," he says.

I smile. "A great many things about the world are funny. A person can go about jibing them, or he can embrace them. I prefer the latter."

"You talk funny," Mario says.

"You're upset."

"Duh!"

"Calm yourself."

"How can I be calm?" He stands on the pew and bunches up his fists. "Grey's going into the Amaranthine District and Fero and Hyra are prolly already there, and— and—"

"Ward will help them."

"I want to do something. I want to be strong like Ward."

Ward is not strong. Not emotionally.

"Be careful what you wish for," I say.

He looks at me like I'm stupid.

"There was a writer. From my home. I can't remember his name, of course, but in his play he wrote, 'When god wishes to punish us, he answers our prayers.'"

Mario gives me a look. He thinks the playwright is stupid, too.

He's fidgeting, agitated. He jumps down from the pew and walks up to the apse.

I guess that he's about ten minutes away from sneaking out of the cathedral.

A plan hatches within my mind. It's incredibly risky. I've only shown the catacombs to a couple of people. And there's always the chance that this could backfire and make Mario more likely to run off. A risk like this… perhaps all these impetuous young people are wearing off on me.

"Mario?" I say.

He looks up.

"Come with me."

I walk down the north transept, and bend over very carefully. I run my hand between two slabs of stone and pull up a metal ring from between the crevices. Mario runs to my side and adds his strength to my effort.

"Careful," I say.

The slab, actually a trap door, hauls itself up over its hinge and crashes down onto the floor, revealing a descending spiral stair of stone.

"It's slippery," I add, but Mario shoots downward. Torches light the cavern. Rivulets of water slide down moist stone.

I take the steps one at a time, my hands braced against the wall for support. By the time I reach the last one, I am slightly winded. Mario stands before me in a long hallway, the sound of dripping water echoing about the cavern.

"There's nothing here." Mario shrugs.

"There is more here than a hallway," I say. Mario perks up at this. "But if we are to proceed, you must take hold of my hand, and you must not run, let go, or bolt forward. Such behavior could be deadly. Do you understand?"

He nods slowly up and down, his eyes wide. I certainly have his attention.

I shuffle down the corridor counting stones. At the seventeenth stone on my left, I stop. I beckon Mario closer to me, and extend my hand. He takes hold.

"We're going to take one step through the wall," I say. "Exactly one step. No more. Any more and your life will be in jeopardy. Are you ready?"

Mario nods.

"On three," I say. "One, two, three!"

We each take a step forward into the grey stone. It morphs and twists, reconfigures itself into a room. The walls are metallic. Purple lines trace their way across the ceiling, zig-zagging. Their pulsing glow fills the space.

Mario screeches, and I apply as much pressure as I dare to his hand.

There are two others in the room with us, but they don't look up. One stands at a worktable, crafting something with an implement that looks like a handsaw. Another sits at a desk, poking buttons on an apparatus that looks vaguely like a computer terminal but lacks any kind of visual display. Neither looks toward us.

"Stay absolutely still!" I say in my sternest voice. "One more step forward and you will really be in this room."

"Where—?" Mario looks up at me.

I hold my gaze on the room. "Somewhere in the Amaranthine District."

"Their faces…" Mario's voice is trembling. "They look like the ones who attacked us. Facepaint moving under their skin. And their eyes… It's— it's— Why can't they hear us?"

"I don't know," I admit. "I know that so long as we stand in this spot, we are not really here. They will neither see nor hear us."

As Mario observed, the tribals' skin glows with twisting lines of color, deep reds, purple, violet, down to indigo. The lines twist and morph, bursting every so often like stars and coalescing into new configurations. Their eyes glow a solid purple. No pupils or irises. And they're naked, too. City contains more clothing stores at any given time than its inhabitants could ever need, and yet the tribals go about completely nude, men and women both.

The two in this room continue their work, oblivious to our presence.

"Why didn't you tell Ward?" Mario asks. "He could have come directly here."

"Anyone who enters the Amaranthine District this way will either be killed or converted."

Mario gulps.

"Mario, do you see Fero and Hyra here?"

"No."

"We cannot help them, you and I. I know it is frustrating to be powerless. I have been, and am, in that very position myself. To know and understand, to see and observe, but not be able to do. However, sometimes it's not the doing that's important, it's the being."

Now he's angry again. And not listening. I frown. Very slightly. I catch myself doing it and turn my head so he won't see.

"We're going to step backward now. Back into the hall. On three again, okay?"

I see him nod in my peripheral vision.

I count to three, and we step backward. As expected, the room shimmers and morphs back into the stone hallway below my cathedral.

Mario's hand starts to struggle away from mine, but I hold it tight.

"Back up the stairs," I say.

He casts me a cruel glare, and I lead him back to the stairwell. I decide that this didn't have the desired effect. Had I let him go, he would have thrown himself back through the wall. I mentally walk through all the people to whom the boy might tell about the catacombs, and how much of a problem that would be. Most of the worst are no longer with us—most especially that scientist. I wonder when the next scientist will show up.

I let go of Mario's hand as soon as I am safely between him and the hallway in the stairwell. He looks at me as though he's considering hurtling into me, then runs up the stairwell instead. I follow.

At the top, Mario sprints away into the cathedral. I close the stone slab and walk to the facade at the end of the transept where a button lies hidden between two frescos. I press it and a sizzling sound emanates from the trap door. It is now sealed. I am the only person who knows where the unsealing mechanism is, and I never share that secret.

"Mario?" I call out. I walk down the transept. The pews and velvet cushions lie empty. The stone door to the cathedral shuts with an audible groan.

Mario is gone.

I shake my head.

You can give a person heaps of knowledge, but only experience seems to teach wisdom. In older cultures the young were taught to look to us for guidance, for advice. But too often, our power corrupted us. Too many of us became lazy, seeking reverence for reverence's sake rather than in exchange for true virtue.

You cannot tell Mario that the Amaranthine District is toxic and dangerous. You cannot even show him how awful it is up close. I fear he must truly experience the danger for it to be real. I gulp as I imagine those glowing purple lines tracing their way beneath his skin, changing his eyes, his mind…

I open a gate in the barrier before the apse, and I enter the ambulatory. I take a seat at my organ. It takes a long time to sit. It's been hard to take care of myself properly in City, but I make do. There never seems to be a surfeit of truly kind and generous people, just as there is no surfeit of the cruel and the selfish. Those with good hearts have always managed to find me.

I decide on a tune, and I play.

So soothing. As my hands eke out the melody, my mind is drawn back to the hundreds of people I've met in my decade here. So many of them have names I can't remember, though I remember our interactions with uncanny clarity.

I should not mind to die in City, though I would be immensely sad should my husband never know what became of me. I want him to know. I desperately want him to know of my time here, of the difference I made in people's lives, and that I never stopped loving him. Not for a moment.

The melody ends. I take a moment for that pain. Ten years without his touch. And without my congregation.

I take a deep breath. I rise, and I turn.

Gwei sits in the front pew. Beside her is a man I've never seen. I walk toward them slowly, smiling. I must project calm. I must be strong. For all of them.

City is my congregation now.

Gwei stands.

"My daughter," I say, and I smile.

City is Merciless

(( ))

Some think that City has a "soul."

Presuming that we allow for the existence of such a thing in humans, to say that City has one would be imprecise.

Some are wont to think of City as a kind of endlessly forgiving, benevolent entity, who bestows wisdom upon those it deems worthy of joining its unique intersection of time and space.

City has no such "mind." It does not "care" about its citizens in the way that a human might care for a cat or a dog.

And so the opposite view results. There are those who think of City as a perpetually dreary place, an uncaring, lifeless configuration of material entities. Structures appear here. People appear there. City, under this view, is a vast mechanism, reducible to its component parts.

There is no "life," but rather a collection of complex biological and physical processes. The rules are inherent to City itself, there for anyone to discover who has the intellect and the appropriate tools.

But neither view is entirely correct.

While it is true that City cannot care if a person hurts, it is also true that, as a part of City, every individual is endowed with the ability to care about the suffering of others… or to ignore it.

Whether City is heaven or hell is up to its citizens to decide. The coming and going of people and structures may follow mechanical principles, but digging into the depths of those secrets is a journey that will never end, just as the philosopher can endlessly argue the exception that disproves the rule should he be diligent in seeking it out.

What a vast spectrum of hues humanity comes in! And not just skin color, but emotional hues. Red is anger, yellow cowardice, green envy, blue melancholy. And what of purple? What of purple, indeed.

The scientists wished to understand City by picking apart its clockwork. Its clockwork continued endlessly.

The philosophers wished to understand City by exploring the emotional dynamics of its citizens. Its citizens are, emotionally speaking, as infinitely complex as its mechanics.

And now we meet a third group.

The tribals say simply, "The way you are, City, is wrong. We hate everything you represent. We are not a part of you. We are superior. We can remake you better than you are."

Infected with smug, purple delusion, they toil in their district of supposed perfection.

City may not be "alive." It may not "feel." But the Amaranthine plague cannot be tolerated forever. Unhealthy systems inevitably fail. The question is: how many innocents will fall victim to the cleansing?

Disingenuous

((before))

The spools clanked on the metal counter as Kaia pulled them from her sack. "Three accelerator spools," she said, ticking a row off the holographic list with her free hand. "One ream of printer paper. A book of matches. Two bottles of soda, unopened. Five skeins of yarn."

Naim chuckled and raised an eyebrow at Taum. "What's the yarn for?"

Taum returned the gaze with cold superiority. "It would take too long to explain."

Naim regarded Taum even more coldly than usual. One should never imply to an academic that he won't comprehend an explanation.

Kaia raised the volume of her voice and set the next item down heavily. "Ten meters of wire, plastic coated. And twenty ballpoint pens. That's all of it." She ticked the last box off her interface and closed out the display.

"Thank you." Taum remained fixated on the computer he held. "I've added fourteen days of access to each of your respective storage areas."

Naim glared at him. "Anything else?"

"I'll contact you when I need more supplies." Taum's gaze remained fixed on his computer screen.

Kaia fidgeted and twitched her head. The two of them had been doing this more and more recently, ribbing at one another. At first it had seemed moderately jovial, but over the last week or so, the jibing had taken on a darker tone.

"Thank you, Taum." Kaia took Naim's hand. "C'mon."

The couple left Taum's laboratory and its buzzes and whirs receded. They passed beneath the light-dark staccato of the hallway and toward the exit.

No sooner had the door slid open than a siren blared. Kaia and Naim threw their hands over their ears, ran outside and looked up. Enormous red holograms erupted from the laboratory complex's haphazard walls: "street reconfiguration detected."

"Thank you!" Naim yelled up at the fortress. "We can see that!" He turned to Kaia. "He's got cameras or something, doesn't he?"

Kaia winced. "Why does it have to be so loud?"

"Maybe his hearing is as impaired as his—" Naim stopped his utterance and blinked a few times. Kaia felt a sick feeling welling up within her. She'd told him she didn't like it when he was mean to people behind their backs. She didn't like it at all.

The sirens dimmed, but the red holograms remained.

"Street reconfiguration…?!" A woman's shrill voice pierced the new silence.

Kaia and Naim both jumped and turned around to see a new arrival standing tall, prim and proper, wearing a dark blue dress with big, beady buttons running down the middle. Her shoes were gorgeous. Gemstones lined the toes and fancy lacework the edges. A pair of glasses with thin, immaculate frames donned her narrow face. Eagle eyes pierced the glass.

"What is this place?" the woman demanded.

"You're in City." Kaia gulped. Her disappointment with Naim was forgotten. Disdain for this new arrival had taken its place.

Naim reached out for Kaia's hand and she took it eagerly.

"What city?" The woman asked. She furrowed her brow, looking immensely distressed, then righted her features and returned to glaring imperiously and silently at the couple.

"It's just City," Naim said. "And you can't remember your name, or anyone else's—"

"I most certainly can!" the woman roared.

Kaia rolled her eyes, and Naim stifled a small laugh.

"And you shall not mock me! Have you any idea who I am?"

"No." Naim grinned. "Why don't you tell us."

"Why, I am the event coordinator for—" Her mouth remained open, stultified, only momentarily. She clamped it shut and her entire face tensed and twitched. A moment of confused silence, then blind anger mashed her facial features further together, and Kaia was sure she could spot fear in the mix, too.

"Your proper nouns are gone," Kaia said. "All of them."

The woman twisted her lips together, muttering raspily. "That would seem to be the case."

"C'mon, Kaia." Naim tugged at her arm. "I want to get a move on. There's no telling how long the streets are going to stay this way, and we haven't seen a reconfiguration in weeks."

"What about her?" Kaia asked.

Naim raised an eyebrow incredulously.

"Do not worry about me." The woman had somehow moved closer to them. "I shall determine the best way home myself."

Kaia thought maybe to tell her that City would decide when and to where she would leave, but she didn't feel like absorbing more of the newcomer's hostility.

Naim and Kaia walked away down the avenue labeled Zero.

"Oh," Kaia stopped, turned, and called back. "Just a word of warning. If you see a purple glow, stay away from it."

The woman blinked, her face unmoving. She turned and walked the other direction down the street called Zero.

Kaia watched her retreat, while Naim continued on down the street, eyeing the buildings carefully. It was as if he had forgotten about the imperious newcomer already. He even seemed oblivious to Kaia's presence. He'd been talking about this ever since Grey had hurtled out of that building at them. He wanted to map the grid-City and compare it to his nearly complete map of City-as-usual, which was immaculately detailed except for the empty blob of the Amaranthine District.

Kaia ran to him and put a hand on his shoulder. "You know, that's the fourth new arrival in three days."

"Didn't Yessel say that arrivals and departures happen in clusters?" His gaze continued to dart from facade to facade.

"He did," Kaia admitted. "I'd like to talk to him about all the new people showing up. Find out if he's worried."

Naim perked to attention. "Kaia, I have to do this. We know where the cathedral is already."

Kaia frowned. "Then I'm going alone."

"Kaia…" Naim's tone grew a tinge whiny, and she drew away from him.

"I'll meet you back at Evermore," she said. "In our grove."

"Kaia." Now he sounded genuinely worried, and that gave her pause. "We could do this together. Wouldn't that be nice, to team up?"

No. It wouldn't. She knew it from deep within her gut. City's organization held no deep secrets. But the people she'd met here, they mattered. Every soul mattered deeply. The proportion that ended up as tribals versus those that joined the Collective, that mattered.

But Naim mattered too, right? Why did she have to keep convincing herself of that?

"I'm just going to run to the cathedral. I'll keep track of the buildings as I go. Tell you what, I'll meet you at Evermore, and after that, we'll go to Umber Eleven together and I'll help you build out the map, okay?"

Naim smirked that gloriously cute little smirk of his. "One hour?"

"It's a date." She smiled.

"See you then." Naim nodded and turned back to the buildings.

Kaia took off down the streets. A breeze hit her as she ran, skirting around the right-angled intersections, off toward the cathedral. Under normal circumstances, it towered prominently over Claret Crossing. But now… the grid configuration. She let her eyes scan the buildings as she passed, built the names of prominent architecture into a kind of story, so she'd remember it later: Little alligator pond goes splash, water springs up into the most fashionable of department stores. Drips down into families shopping for their next Sunday best, but the University campus next door doesn't approve of the capitalist machinery fueling their frenzy. They sit in their lecture halls and talk of sociological paradigms and a crass consumer culture, evidenced by the jewelry shop, but its windows have been bashed in. Food is more valuable than stones in City, so I wonder—

Then she spotted it. The cathedral spire.

Her mnemonic game forgotten, she turned a corner and came to the monolithic complex, a bright, stone structure, its stained glass windows ablaze against the ambient City luminescence.

She ran up the steps, grasped the handle, and—

A shriek from behind her, then another, the first female, the second male, in quick succession. She pivoted, braced her back against the stone door.

A boy and girl, just barely teens, perhaps twelve or thirteen, stood, clutching one another.

"My— wha—?"

"Brother…? What's your *name?*"

Both began sobbing.

They looked up at Kaia and jumped. The boy jolted back, pulling his sister with him.

So many new arrivals.

Kaia held up her hands. "It's all right." She walked carefully down the steps. "You're going to be all right."

They continued sobbing, looking at one another, looking at Kaia.

"Why can't I remember *my sister's name?!*" the boy yelled.

"You're in City now." She reached the bottom of the stair and proceeded ever so carefully closer. "People have new names here. I'm not going to hurt you. You're safe."

"What is this?" The girl looked up into the twisting sky and wailed.

"It's just City." Kaia stopped a couple of meters from them.

A sound from down the street. Kaia turned toward it. Voices too.

"How come there's no turtle with a yellow mask?"

"Dunno. You'd make a good ninja though."

"Really?"

"Uh huh."

Grey had such a penchant for showing up when he was least wanted. At least he'd kept his profanity *mostly* in check since adopting Mario. The new arrivals seemed to calm somewhat. Their eyes darted between Kaia and the approaching duo. Grey wore his red bandana, while Mario's yellow t-shirt had been tied up over his head. The shirtless pair swaggered down the street, Grey with one foot on his skateboard and the other pushing him along at Mario's pace.

"What would my ninja turtle name be?"

"Well." Grey bit his lip. "They all have names of famous artists."

"But we can only remember the ones in the game. 'Cause it's written there, right?"

"Yeah." Grey punched the air in front of him, clasping his left fist in his right hand. "So we find a library and raid its art section."

Kaia cleared her throat.

The duo, nearly upon them, came to an abrupt halt. Grey flipped up his skateboard with his foot and pulled it to his side.

Kaia tapped her foot, eyeing Grey.

Grey sighed and slouched. "What'd I do now?"

"We've got new arrivals scared out of their minds."

"Oh, what." Grey threw up his free arm. "It's up to me to take care of every single underage arrival now? Do I look like a fuckin' babysitter?"

Mario cowered and his head drooped. The new arrivals murmured anew. Kaia intensified the gaze she'd fixated on Grey, hoping it might bore some common sense into his thick skull.

"All right, all right." Grey relented. "You two have your names yet?"

"Can't remember," the girl muttered.

"Your City names." Grey tried.

The siblings shook their heads.

"Let's all go inside," Kaia suggested. She turned to the siblings. "It's the safest place in City."

Kaia extended her hand toward the boy, and slowly, he unclasped from his sister, reached out tentatively, albeit trembling, and took her hand. Kaia put her free hand on the sister's back and led them all toward the cathedral.

"C'mon, Mario," Grey said. "Let's get our dinner."

"Fuck yeah!" Mario shouted happily, causing Kaia to wince.

The girl released a giggle, and Kaia realized she wasn't trembling anymore.

They entered the cathedral, where numerous members of the Collective stood about, chatting solemnly. Kaia recognized a red-haired new arrival talking to Elya. Brin, Echo and Skylir sat beside one another on the pews chatting amicably, Brin's arms wrapped around both Echo and Skylir's shoulders. And at the far end, near the apse, stood Ward and Aria talking to Yessel. Ward was speaking with his hands, as usual, while Aria had her arms folded, her focus trained on Ward.

Grey and Mario shot past Kaia and the siblings, careened around the right transept and disappeared, probably off to raid the cloister. Mario was allowed to eat his fill because he was a child, but Yessel often had to remind Grey that his use of the cathedral's resources was contingent upon his sharing half his gains from helping Taum.

Yessel was kind and calm around everyone, but Kaia noticed the telltale signs of strain even from Yessel when he interacted with Grey.

Kaia led the siblings around the pews and toward the transept.

Aria's gaze broke from Ward, darted to Kaia, who wore an expression of worry, then to the siblings, and before Kaia could have another thought, Aria was marching toward them.

Aria squatted down and looked up at the trembling siblings. She reached out and held one of the girl's hands in her own.

"I'm Aria," she said. "Don't worry. It's going to be okay." She looked between them. "Are you hungry?"

They shook their heads.

"Are you thirsty?"

"Yeah," the boy said. "A bit."

"Come on." She took Kaia's place effortlessly and led them down the transept the way that Grey and Mario had gone.

Kaia wasn't sure whether she liked or disliked how effortlessly Aria had taken over her role as care provider. She smirked a bit and strode toward Yessel and Ward.

"My daughter." Yessel smiled. "Welcome."

Ward nodded. "Hi, Kaia."

"Hi," Kaia said. "How are things?"

Ward clapped his hands together and smiled. "Couldn't be better. The Collective's up to thirty-eight members. We signed up Fresco *and* Enigma."

Kaia wondered who'd been responsible for those City names. Sometimes she wasn't sure if names were given *truly*, like everyone said, or just made up. She'd picked her own from a carton of laundry detergent at the first grocery store she and Naim had raided.

Kaia nodded. "Good work. Any idea how many of the new arrivals have ended up with the tribals though?"

"We can never be sure of that," Yessel said solemnly.

"I think we're really strengthening our position," Ward said. "We control eighty-five percent of City's total area. Taum said so. And we've been placing people strategically, getting the majority of arrivals to come back here. And once they're here, we take care of them, teach them. Hard to stumble into a bunch of purple poison after that."

Kaia nodded and gulped. "The streets have changed again."

Ward furrowed his brow. "Every time *I've* checked the streets—"

Kaia released a sigh. "I just followed a straight road here called Zero. The streets have changed."

Ward sighed and walked away, toward the door of the cathedral.

As soon as he was out of earshot, Kaia turned back to Yessel. "I'm worried about the number of new arrivals. One appeared just as Naim and I left Taum's, and another two just as I arrived here."

Yessel nodded and smiled slightly. "It happens like this. You arrived at the tail end of the last wave, as I recall."

Relief washed over Kaia. "I'm glad to hear you say so." She glanced at his expression—slight furrow to the brow, slight droop to the eyelids—and was suddenly slightly less than relieved.

"What is it?" Kaia asked.

"What does concern me," Yessel said mutedly, "is how large the Collective has grown. Ward seems to desire conflict with the tribals. That would not end well. The purpose of the Collective is supposed to be safety."

"Aria will make sure it stays that way," Kaia said reflexively. Then, realizing that Yessel was concerned, second-guessed the reflex. "Right?"

"It is just that misalignment that is the source of my concern. Aria will choose defense above all else. Ward will go on the offense if he senses strategic victory."

Kaia nodded in understanding. "There is no strategic victory against the tribals."

"Only slaughter or conversion."

A tumult of emotions assaulted Kaia. She and Naim had promised each other that they would stay out of the Collective, but the opportunity to weight the group in Aria's favor tugged at her. Without the Collective, what would happen to other new arrivals like Mario and the siblings?

"I'll talk to Naim about it," Kaia said.

Yessel nodded, seeming to understand. She could sense that he knew, that he could tell exactly her frustration, her fear, her love. She didn't need to tell him anything. He'd met Naim only the once, and that was enough. So wise. Did he have love in his past, she wondered?

Warm feelings for Naim rushed back to her. She said goodbye to Yessel and hurried out of the cathedral.

Ward entered just as she left.

"Nothing wrong with the streets, by the way," he said as he passed.

She strode out onto Avenue Zero, checked the sign, then looked back toward the door just as it closed.

Kaia released a sigh, shook her head, and hurried down the grid of streets. Now to find Evermore. Naim would be waiting. Where did that lie? She reached back into her memory, to the last time this had happened. They'd found Taum's laboratory at Negative Forty-Fifth Street and Zero. The park had been some blocks away, a different avenue... Negative Forth! And the Cathedral was on Zero, too. She looked up at the sign looming over the intersection: Eleventh Street.

Fifteen blocks. She could sprint that.

She took off down Zero, playing back her story about the buildings in reverse order. As she passed Taum's she could see his red "street configuration" lights still flashing. She was glad that he'd silenced the siren.

Four blocks later, she came to Evermore. She broke a smile and took off down the path, through the bright, golden tree leaves, and toward the grove enclosed in orange flowers.

She burst through the petals, and her glee turned to horror. Naim sat hunched in the center of the grove, shuddering.

"Naim!" She ran to his side.

He shot to a stance. "Oh! Oh, Kaia!" Relief washed over his fear- and tear-streaked face. He rushed to her, and they embraced.

He squeezed. "Oh, I'm so glad, so glad you're safe. I was so stupid. I won't do that again."

"What happened?" she asked. "I wasn't gone long."

"But you were taken by the street change. I thought you were gone-away. I thought I'd lost you for good."

She pulled him just enough away, held him at arm's length, and looked into his puffy, red eyes. "What are you talking about?"

"Right after you said you were going to go to the Cathedral, and I said I was going to stay and catalogue the buildings, the streets changed back. The road changed back to Cesious Boulevard, right in front of me, I turned to you, and the change of the streets rippled over everything, and that ripple—" Tears erupted from his eyes, and he hugged her so tightly. He sniffled and looked into her eyes once more. "—The ripple dissolved you. You just flickered, and then you were gone. I thought… I thought you were gone for good."

He hugged her again, shuddering. "I'm so glad it wasn't real. I'm so glad you're still here."

"I'm here," Kaia hugged him back. "Everything's fine."

"No," Naim squeezed harder. "I'll never leave again. I promise. We do everything together. No exceptions."

Kaia's gut wrenched up. She loved Naim. She really did. But then… why did she suddenly feel as though everything wasn't quite so fine anymore?

Vainglorious

((before))

A street appears before me. Dingy. Slummish.

How did I arrive in a slum?

The building before me is unusual in the extreme. Spires of metal, antennas, computer screens, eruptions like smokestacks.

Where am I?

I walk myself back through my recent memory. I was in my office. I'd just had the most hideous phone call with an incommunicative little faggot of a self-published author whom I'd made the mistake of allowing to push his homo trash upon my store. It was bad enough that in recent years I'd been forced to allow fruitcakes onto my staff in the name of "diversity" and "tolerance." Now they wanted to fill my shelves with their homoerotic swill.

Don't they know who I am?

I'm—

Now that's a peculiar feeling.

A blaring fills the air. Sirens and bright red lights erupt from the monstrous structure in front of me. At the same moment, its front door opens, and a brown man and white woman emerge.

I wince at the cacophony and wonder if the man planted a bomb inside the building and has just been caught. Unfortunately for that theory, the man and woman both clap their hands over their ears, appearing just as surprised as I am.

Well, he'll probably plant a bomb in something sooner or later.

"Street reconfiguration detected." A monotone voice erupts from the structure.

"Street reconfiguration—?!" I yell at the blaring speakers, just as the noise ceases.

All of sudden, the two of them are looking at me. I look back at them, wondering whether or not they'll own up to some proper manners. They just stare at me instead, so I decide to at least get information out of them, if not respect.

"What is this place?" I ask.

"You're in City," the woman says. She grabs for her terrorist boyfriend's hand.

I furrow my brow, disliking her and the vapidity of her answer. "What City?"

"It's just City," the terrorist says, as though he's allowed to talk to me in such a manner. "And you can't remember your name, or anyone else's—"

"I most certainly can!" I wish this conversation had never started.

The woman rolls her eyes, and the terrorist chortles at me. What nerve!

"And you shall not mock me!" I demand. "Have you any idea who I am?"

"No," the terrorist says with an indignant smile. "Why don't you tell us."

"Why, I am the event coordinator for—"

My brain stops dead in its tracks. Most perplexing. I recall that I am the event coordinator for my bookstore. I recall where it is, the color and texture of the wood panelling, the configuration of the shelves, the faces of my staff—but no names. Not their names, not the name of the bookstore, not the name of the city, not the name of my country—

"Your proper nouns are gone," the woman says. "All of them."

I purse my lips. I do not make a habit of allowing degenerates to position themselves at an advantage to me. But, the statement arriving from the lips of this vapid little tart appears to be factually true. I am, quite unfortunately, at a severe disadvantage.

"That would seem to be the case," I allow.

The statement has its desired effect. They mutter amongst themselves about leaving.

"What about her?" I hear the woman say.

I cross my arms. "You need not worry about me. I shall determine the best way home myself."

That gets them leaving. I smile at a job well done.

"Oh." The woman turns abruptly and calls back. "Just a word of warning. If you see a purple glow, stay away from it."

I grant her my smile of reproach, turn, and walk away. I shake my head. I hope there is someone here who will respect my superior skills and abilities, in whatever this strange place is that can steal away my proper nouns.

I am—

I try to finish the thought multiple times and stumble over each and every predicate.

I am the event coordinator for the most prestigious bookstore in the most literate city of the most powerful country on my planet.

Not exactly a name that demands respect. Not exactly a name at all.

I release a sigh. I decide to turn.

The streets remain dismal and dingy, though the sky is swirling in shades of blue I had no idea existed and there's no sun, but light seems to come from everywhere regardless.

I wonder if I have been drugged and this is some kind of delusion. I have never tried drugs. I saw people smoke marijuana once during my undergraduate studies. The dopers all sat around looking rather morose. I have a vision of myself catatonic in my office, of someone on my staff, one of the annoying faggots, finding me that way—taking pictures—uploading them to the internet. Or email blackmail.

I shake the horrific thoughts away.

My mind turns to more pressing concerns. I am walking through what is clearly a slum. Should I be worried about getting mugged? The streets seem empty enough. And it's not like I have anything worth taking. My purse is conspicuously absent from my person. There are the gems in my shoes, though. My worry turns to the possibility of a sexual assault. The heel of my shoe would make a good weapon.

Horrific thoughts all around.

I wonder if it was a tactical mistake to have sent the terrorist and his girlfriend away. This is not my city, wherever it is, and I am most certainly lost.

"No, no," a voice says, in the distance. "Like this."

Early twenties, male. Poor white trash from his dialect.

"'K." A child's voice. "Lemme try again."

I sigh and walk toward them. It has come time to work with the natives on their terms if I am to survive this, whatever this is.

I turn the corner and a beastly duo comes into view. The early twenties male is indeed poor white trash, as is evinced by the grimy, red rag wrapped around his idiot skull, the dirty shirt hanging out of his baggy jeans, and his slouched, drooping demeanor. The child is perhaps eight, at a guess. He's wrapped his t-shirt around his head and might have been respectable at one time, but all of his companion lowlife's bad manners have infected him.

The child stands atop a skateboard and attempts to push the back up with his heel, stumbles, and falls forward.

"Don't worry," the delinquent says. "You'll get it."

The boy spots me and points. "Grey!"

The delinquent's eyes meet mine. "Hey! You new, lady?"

My frown grows deeper as I fight back my repulsion. How vile that I must debase myself by speaking with such cretins.

"Yes." I take a few careful steps toward them. "I am new."

"You have your name yet?" The boy calls out.

I remain silent. What is it with these people and names?

"Whoa!" The delinquent's eyes go wide and he frames me with his hands, making an L shape with each thumb and forefinger.

I raise an eyebrow.

The delinquent turns to the boy. "You see it?"

The boy grins and nods. "Uh huh. The car, right?"

I turn half my gaze to my right, noticing that indeed, a run down, silver, antique automobile with rusted edges and two deflated tires sits in the street beside me.

"Uh huh," the delinquent says. "Car... Karr!"

I take a few careful steps back. I wonder how quickly I could pull off one of my shoes.

"That's your name!" The boy hops up and down excitedly. "Karr!"

I scoff. "That is not my name."

"Sorry, Karr." The delinquent shrugs. "We don't make City's rules."

"You will not call me that!"

Now he's scowling at me. "Well fuck you too, you uppity bitch! You should be thanking me."

The boy breaks a wicked grin. "Oh, snap."

The two of them slap their palms together.

I am incensed. Anger clouds my vision. I turn and storm away, I don't care where to, just away from the two degenerate children who presumed to name *me*, the event coordinator for the preeminent bookstore in the most literate city of the most powerful country on my planet!

Stupid city.

When my anger subsides and my vision clears, I find I am back where this began, standing before the odd building of metallic spires, computer screens, and flashing red lights. I furrow my brow, walk to the door, and press a button on the panel set into the wall.

The door hisses open.

"Yes?" the voice of a man, perhaps my age, erupts from within, though the hall is empty, just a row of intermittent ceiling lights.

"Who are you?" I call out.

"My name's Taum. I'm a scientist. Who are you?"

I pause. I will *not* use the name those delinquents gave me. "I don't remember."

"New arrival?"

I mull that over momentarily. "I suppose."

"Are you hungry or thirsty?"

Now this interests me. He is trying to establish what is of value to me. This is a game I know how to play.

"Perhaps. And what would you want in exchange for food and water?"

"Fifty minutes of your time and the answers to some questions."

I don't like the inside of his complex. I have no guarantee that it's safe. But then, I don't have any guarantee that the rest of this city is safe, either. I decide I should be happy that the delinquent and his sidekick were merely rude and annoying. I also decide to enter Taum's complex.

The door hisses shut behind me, and I jump slightly.

"Come down the hall," Taum's voice says. "Third door on the right."

I walk down the hall, through alternating patches of light and dark. I nearly miss a door. I reach the third and it slides open.

Taum's lab is filled with all manner of instruments I can't comprehend. There's a wall of cubes in the back, each containing a different substance. Computer monitors display scientific formulae and programming code, both incomprehensible gibberish to me. However, none of his instruments looks dangerous, and I allow myself a bit of relief.

Taum himself wears a white lab coat, looks older than his voice makes him sound, and hobbles across the room toward me, limping on his left leg. I am even more relieved.

He hands me a tablet computer.

I take it. "What is this?"

"A questionnaire. Your answers for two liters of water and a hamburger."

"A... hamburger?"

"A fast food restaurant appeared a few days ago just down Cesious Boulevard. We can't be picky in City."

I cross my arms. "I am a strict vegetarian."

He shoots me a wan smile and nods. I believe I catch his drift. I understand this Taum better than any of the others I have met so far. He has manners and he may even be my intellectual superior.

"I have a few other questions," I try. "Then I will fill out your questionnaire. Will those terms be acceptable?"

"How many questions are a few?" Taum is good.

"Let's say three."

Taum nods. "A fair enough number."

"How did I arrive here?"

Taum shakes his head. "No one yet knows the answer to that question. I've dedicated my entire time here to finding a way to send people home. That's the purpose of that questionnaire, by the way."

I frown. I was hoping for something more definitive. "Everyone here is obsessed with names and a pair of delinquents 'named' me Karr. Why can't I remember my real name?"

"Again, no one knows. To the best of my knowledge, the process that brings people to City affects brain chemistry and memory engrams. Details of your past life survive, but the names of things are repressed or destroyed. I've tried bringing them back in a few individuals, but I've never been successful. Oh, and if you see Grey and Mario again, please tell them I have more work for them."

I scowl. "You employ them?"

Taum smiles. "Is that your third question?"

Damn it. This situation has drained all my usual emotional resources. I am normally much better than this.

"No," I say.

He makes a rolling motion with his hand.

"I want out of this city. What is the best way to achieve that?"

Taum's smile turns to a frown. His eyes radiate intensity from behind his glasses. He pulls his arms behind his back and makes himself as tall as he can. He's evaluating me. I can tell. I do the same thing myself.

After a time, he speaks softly and precisely. "First you will fill out the questionnaire. Then I will tell you about two opposed factions within City and how they relate to my research on leaving this place."

"What are these factions?"

"The Collective and the Amaranthine District."

I imagine him manipulating me like some puppet to bring these two groups together. Love and harmony and friendship and all that insipid bile. I don't like being used. I keep my face flat, but I'm ready to put down his questionnaire and leave.

"I suppose you want me to bring them together," I say.

"On the contrary." Taum stands taller. "For my next experiment to yield useful data, I need to bring them into direct conflict, a situation certain elements are keen to avoid."

I slowly begin to nod. "We could talk about how I might be involved in that."

Taum's frown turns into an inquisitive smile.

I spend the next fifty minutes filling out his questionnaire.

Jejune

((before))

"Oh, snap!" I shout.

Grey holds out his hand, and we high five.

The mean lady makes an unhappy face, turns, and goes away. I laugh, and Grey smiles.

"What was her problem?" I ask.

"Dunno." Grey motions for his skateboard, and I jump off it. He picks it up and leans into it. "Probably had a stick up her butt."

Wow. That's pretty gross. I bunch up my face, wondering why anyone would do that.

"Oh shit," Grey says.

"What?" I look up at him.

"The streets."

I look around. The streets don't turn anymore. They go straight out until they touch the sky. And there are holes and rocks everywhere, too.

"They changed, didn't they?" I say.

Grey nods. He doesn't look happy. I'll bet it's hard to find stuff now, because none of the buildings are in their right places either.

My stomach grumbles at me.

"Hey Grey?"

"Yeah?"

"I'm hungry."

"Well." He throws down his board. "Let's go find the cathedral and get some food then."

"We don't need to help Taum first, do we?" The last time we helped

Taum was two days ago.

"Nah." Grey pushes off down the street. I follow at his side. Grey is stable when he rides the board. Not like me. I have to hold my arms out or I lose my balance. Grey said the place where he got his board is gone now, but we're still looking for another place that has boards. He says it'll be easier to teach me on a lighter board. His board's heavy because it's for adults, but when I get bigger, I'm gonna have a board just like his.

If City will let me stay here, anyway. I hope I'll get to hang out with Grey for a long time. I miss my home and my parents and my friends from school, except for that kid who sits behind me and is always whispering for me to let him copy off my test. He's a jerk, but I'm not sure I'm ready for City to send me back.

"Do you know where the cathedral is?" I ask.

Grey shakes his head. "We'll watch the skyline. The steeple's really tall, so we'll see it if we get close."

I think about how all the buildings are all mixed up and what Grey said before, about the bad buildings in City, and I get worried. "Hey Grey?"

"Yeah?"

"If the buildings got all mixed up, then where did the tribal buildings go? Are they all mixed up, too?"

"Don't worry about that," Grey says. "The Amaranthine buildings glow purple. You can see them from far away. I won't let us get too close."

I feel safe with Grey around. I miss my mom and dad, sure, but Grey's a lot more fun to hang out with than them. And he doesn't make me go to bed at 8:30, or eat stupid vegetables, or turn off my cartoons, either. Well, there's no TV here, but I don't really care 'cause me and Grey ride his skateboard and explore buildings all day.

Recently, a Burnet Burger appeared near Taum's lab, and we've been eating out of there. Grey and I even snuck a bunch of the burgers and chicken nuggets back to the freezer in the underground kitchen in Grey's apartment building. I'm the only one who knows about the freezer. It's our secret. But we try not to eat that stuff too often. Grey says it's backup for emergencies.

Grey's so smart. Not like stupid Kaia and stupid Yessel. Just blah blah blah responsibility, and blah blah blah teamwork. Grey's a badass, and I'm a badass too. We don't need any stupid teamwork.

"There!" Grey points at the sky. I don't see anything, but I'm sure

Grey's found the cathedral. He turns us down a road called Zero.

Before long, I can see the front of the cathedral with its stone steps, big stone door and windows like a finished page in a coloring book. The steeple rises up so high, tilting from its weird angle to straight up toward the sky as we get closer.

I think of food. Then of fun.

"Hey Grey?"

"Yeah?"

"You want to go to Ochre Arcade after dinner?"

"Sure. What do you want to play?"

"Ninja turtles."

He grins.

Grey always plays Donatello. I like Raphael. But I think about how the colors are all wrong. Grey's turtle should be grey, and mine should be yellow. "How come there's no turtle with a yellow mask?"

"Dunno. You'd make a good ninja though."

"Really?"

"Uh huh."

We're close enough now that I spot something else—Kaia is standing over two kids I've never seen before, a boy and girl. They're a lot bigger than me, sixth graders probably. They look scared, but they're not as interesting as ninja turtles.

"What would my ninja turtle name be?" I ask.

"Well." Grey bit his lip. "They all have names of famous artists."

"But we can only remember the ones in the game. 'Cause it's written there, right?"

"Yeah." Grey clapped his hands together. "So we find a library and raid its art section."

We're standing next to Kaia now, and she makes a noise with her throat. Grey pulls up his skateboard, leans into it, and lets out a sigh. He thinks Naim and Kaia are annoying because they constantly bug him to take more responsibility, but not having any responsibility is the whole reason City is awesome. Why mess that up with responsibility? That's what Grey says.

"What'd I do now?" Grey asks Kaia.

She hugs the trembling, sniffling kids. "We've got new arrivals scared out of their minds."

"Oh, what." Grey throws up his free arm. "It's up to me to take care of every single underage arrival now? Do I look like a fuckin' babysitter?"

Wait.

What?

I thought Grey liked how we hang out. I thought we were friends. He doesn't think that about me, does he? Maybe he's just mad at Kaia. He doesn't like these other kids, right? But I can't help but feel like he kind of meant me when he said that.

"All right, all right," Grey says. "You two have your names yet?"

"Can't remember," the girl mutters.

"Your City names."

The siblings just shake their heads. Geez, they're annoying.

"Let's all go inside." Kaia turns to the siblings. "It's the safest place in City."

"C'mon, Mario." Grey sounds happy again. "Let's get our dinner."

I surge with pride. "Fuck yeah!"

We run up to the cathedral, and Grey and I pull open the big stone doors. I follow Grey around the pews. We hang a right before we get too close to the part with the cushions, and we exit through the small door at the end of the hallway into the garden that everyone calls the cloister. It's got big stone pillar walls and vines and tree branches overhead. But everyone says it's weird that you can't see the trees from outside the cathedral.

I don't think it's that weird. Why do grownups insist that everything other than themselves has to make sense all the time?

Yessel always wants the dried stuff, and the stuff that doesn't go bad too easily, like fruit and bread. Right after I showed up, we found a grocery store and we took all the breads and fruits to the cathedral, but then brought all the meat and cheese back to Grey's big fridge.

I open up a bushel of pears, grab one, and chow down. Some of the grownups are walking around and picking out food, but most sit at picnic tables in the center of the cloister.

"Catch." Grey tosses me a roll and I grab it. I wish we could take these back and get out our butter, but that would make people ask questions. Besides, we'll probably grill something later back at our place.

Aria's voice makes me turn. "There's water over here if you're thirsty, and there's food in the barrels against the walls." She's near the entrance helping the two new kids. I'm still kind of annoyed that they made Grey say something bad, but seeing them helpless makes me feel something else. I feel bad about being annoyed with them earlier. Not sure why that is though.

"Hey!" Grey calls out as I stuff the pear in my mouth and sprint toward them.

I take the pear out just long enough to call back to him. "I'll be right back."

I come up to Aria and she looks down at me warily. The siblings look at me kind of scared. They tower over me, and normally, I might be kinda scared of them, but I know City and they just got here. I also remember what it was like when I first showed up.

The pear still stuffed in my mouth, I take my roll, break it in half, and offer a half to each of the siblings.

The girl snatches up the one in my left hand. Her brother nudges her with his elbow, and takes his half more carefully.

"Thank you," he says.

"Thank you," his sister tells the ground.

"Mmmph meph-mumm," I say.

Aria crosses her arms. "Mario. Take that out of your mouth."

I remove the sticky pear half. "You're welcome."

They eat the bread. Aria looks pleased.

"You should come play with me and Grey later," I say.

Aria looks less than pleased. "Maybe later," she says.

"Sure. Well, um, see you."

I run back to Grey.

"What was that?" Grey says.

"I don't know!" Now I'm confused. It's not bad to be nice to people. "They were hungry and scared."

"You coming for ninja turtles?"

"Sure," I say.

We pass them again as we leave. Aria watches us like a hawk as we walk by. The siblings watch us go like they want to come with us. I pump my eyebrows at them and smile.

We walk through the crowded cathedral and exit back onto the weird road.

"You're cool, Mario," Grey says, "but I don't know about those other kids yet. We gotta watch 'em and see if they're cool, too. I don't want to end up being the Collective's go-to parent. I don't want to be the Collective's anything. We're badass. Got it?"

"Got it," I say.

I'm glad I'm still badass.

"Now," Grey says. "Do you remember how to get to Ochre Arcade with the streets like this?"

I bite my lip. "Uhh… Nope. Do you?"

Grey sighs.

City is Cyclic

(( ))

Time is a funny thing.

The everyday experience of human beings suggests to them that time is linear. Events proceed from A to B to C. C is different from B is different from A. There is change, a form of progress or evolution. This change is consistent with the scientist's model.

But, there are some human peoples with a different view of time. Under this other model, time is cyclic. Under this model, A leads to B, and B leads to C, just as before, but crucially, C and A are merely different configurations of the exact same thing. Any perceived progress or evolution is an illusion.

When a person enters City, they lose the names of all the places and people that have come before, and they must discover all the new names for the places and people in City. When they leave, so is that name wrenched away from those who remain.

But crucially, the memories of their behaviors, the emotions they generated, the life and light, or death and gloom—whatever they carried with them—that remains. The quality of each cycle is up to its citizens.

Citizens are approaching a point of no return. Hard decisions must be made. They cannot break the cycle; the wheel of time will hold no matter what trials might come. But what will the quality of that configuration be at the end of the next rotation?

Open a door, speak a word, make a choice.

City ticks a notch forward, awaiting its saviors and its destroyers and its multitudes in between.

Innovative

((after))

Gwei released a sigh and threw up her hands.

Bolt turned to one side, his eyes jerking back the other way, following a shimmering ripple that hurtled through the streets and buildings, changing them.

"Wow." Just when he thought that City couldn't surprise him anymore... "That's what it looks like, huh?"

Gwei nodded morosely. Bolt wondered for about the dozenth time if he might ask what irritated her so much, but the time never seemed right. She was too anxious, too fidgety. They both needed a chance to calm down and talk things through, but Gwei just had to keep pushing forward, and Bolt had yet to understand why. Something was driving her. What was it?

"And now we're in the grid," Gwei said. "Naim figured it out, you know."

Bolt quirked an eyebrow, intrigued. "Figured what out?"

"The grid streets go more places than the regular streets."

"You mean, to different buildings?"

Gwei shook her head. "Not exactly. He was so smart. Too smart for his own good. He named me, too."

Bolt caught it—the sadness in her voice. She missed him. And the way she talked about how he left... She was bitter that he'd left her here. Now it made more sense. Bolt had unintentionally taken up the role of the unwelcome 'replacement.' Well, that could be fixed as soon as he completed the task he'd promised to help with back at the cathedral.

They continued down the street.

Gwei's head darted from side to side, her eyes scanning the buildings and her skirt twirling frenetically.

"Damn it!" she shouted, clenching her fists.

Bolt reached out for her automatically, and she threw his hands away, anger swarming within her eyes. Bolt frowned. The thought to leave her company crossed his mind.

No. He couldn't do that. He'd promised.

"Why are you angry, Gwei?"

"Because!"

"Because we can't find Zen's now?"

"Yes!"

"And that's it?"

"Yes, that's it."

Bolt darted in front of her. She crashed into him and tried to push him aside, but her effort was futile. He held his ground.

"Gwei!"

"Get out of my way!"

"Gwei!"

She closed her eyes, took a deep breath.

"It's okay to miss him, Gwei. I—" He paused and sighed, collecting himself. "I know what it's like to lose someone."

She opened her eyes and looked up into his, for the first time beholding him with something other than disappointment and frustration. Faint traces of hope were visible within her features. "You… who…?"

"My wife."

"I'm sorry." Gwei took a step back, rubbed her hand along the back of her opposite arm, looked away. "I only knew Naim for a week or so. Hardly seems…"

"Sometimes we meet people, and we know right away how special they are." Bolt took a careful step closer. "They treat us well, teach us things. It was like that with—" Bolt smirked and let out a small laugh. "—her."

Gwei nodded. "Naim did that for me all right. Well… after he'd named me, anyway."

At that, Bolt turned inquisitive. "What, you don't like your name? I think you got a good one. Better than mine, for sure."

Gwei twisted up her face and chortled, then ducked and darted around him and continued marching down the street.

He followed alongside in silence.

"I'm sorry," Gwei said, after a time.

"Don't worry about it."

From behind an abandoned bowling alley on their right, a faint rumbling sounded, and the ground beneath them shook ever so slightly. The rusted sign announcing the intersection of Seventeenth Street and Second Avenue tumbled to the pavement. A shattering of glass sounded from somewhere in the distance.

Bolt gulped and looked to Gwei.

Gwei frowned and shook her head. "Don't ask me what that was."

"City's never had an earthquake before?"

"No… not since I got here."

They stood momentarily, listening, but the rumbling had ceased and no further sounds punctuated City's empty silence.

"Maybe we should go back and ask Yessel," Bolt suggested.

Gwei rolled back her shoulders and continued down the street. "I guess if we end up back there before finding Zen's, we could stop by." They strode along, around potholes and past rundown facades. "Tell me about your wife," Gwei murmured.

Bolt broke a light smile. "She was so kind. If I'd had a bad day at work, she would sit me down, and we'd talk through whatever had happened. She was patient, too. She taught me a lot about noticing people, noticing details. Before her, when I was younger, I was all into myself. I really loved that, how just listening to her seemed to make me a better person. And she had the most beautiful smile."

"You must have really loved each other."

Bolt smiled wider. "Yeah."

"What happened?" Gwei asked, her voice even quieter.

Bolt gulped. "I came home one day, and she was on the floor in the living room. She had a pulse but wouldn't wake up. I called an ambulance, but it was too late. She'd slipped into a coma. The doctors said it was— oh god, really?" Bolt bunched up his face. "I can't remember the name of the disease."

Gwei reached out and put her hand on Bolt's arm. "It's not just people's names. All proper nouns."

Bolt looked at Gwei's hand on his bicep and smiled. Seeming self-conscious, she jerked it away and strode down the dismal street faster with Bolt in tow, their feet crunching across the gravel.

"You must miss her a lot."

"The first couple of years after it happened were the worst," Bolt admitted, remembering how he'd allowed his life to pass by in a cloud of guilt and despair for months on end. "It's been almost a decade now."

"How long were you married?"

"A year and a half."

They walked in silence some time more, Gwei seeming lost in thought.

"When you met her," she said abruptly, "did you know immediately how special she was?"

Bolt nodded, fond memories washing over him. "Yeah."

"A week, a month, a year." Gwei stared into the strange horizon. "Why do we get so little time with the really special ones?"

Bolt shrugged. "We should be happy for the time we do get, I guess."

He chastised himself mentally, reminding himself that his wife's death wasn't really his fault, even though deep inside he still blamed himself. If only he hadn't stayed late at work that day. If only he'd gotten home at the usual time. What had really been so important about doing all that paperwork for the foreman? The promotion he'd been shooting for had eventually been offered to him, but he'd turned it down.

Gwei stopped, and Bolt turned to face her. Her eyes were wide, darting between spots on the ground, then up to the dingy sign adorning the nearby intersection.

"Of course!" Gwei shouted. "Why didn't I think of it before?"

"What is it?"

"Zen's apothecary! It was at the intersection where Naim… left. Where I met you. It was… Negative Seventh Street and Twenty-Fourth Avenue! Come on."

Gwei turned and broke into a sprint. Bolt sighed and ran to catch up, his toolbox rattling as he swung it at his side. They turned multiple times, the street numbers descending while the avenue numbers rose.

They arrived, winded, at Negative Seventh and Twenty-Fourth, an intersection much like the others, except for a small, old-timey grocery store next to a structure of red pillars and ornate, curving clay tiles with worm-like dragons erupting from inset metallic ornamentation.

Gwei darted toward the structure, and Bolt followed.

The building had no door, just an open entryway with strings of beads draped over it. Bolt pushed his way through them after Gwei. Powerful incense assaulted his nose. He stood in a room, incredibly bright, with large, circular lamps beaming upon potted plants, stacked up shelf after shelf. The hum of fans filled the room, along with streams of incense smoke, which erupted from dozens of sticks, interspersed amongst the greenery.

Bolt coughed and pounded at his chest.

"Zen?" Gwei called out, disappearing behind a fan of finely articulated fern leaves.

Bolt coughed again, but pressed forward, following Gwei through the maze of shelving and haze of smoke. He came to a desk in the far corner of the room, where Gwei stood, her arms folded against her chest.

At the desk sat a young woman, perhaps in her late twenties, leaning back into a reclining chair, a joint sending up its own stream of smoke in an ashtray atop her desk. She was extremely thin, had dark black hair, a narrow face, and wore a concerted, even hostile, expression upon it. Her clothing consisted of a t-shirt, jean shorts, and sneakers. She held a pile of papers in one hand and fountain pen in the other.

Bolt spotted an inkwell on the desk, amongst piles of white papers covered in fine, cursive prose. Most were... his language, which he couldn't remember the name of, but he recognized other languages too, languages he'd seen on signs in buses and in other parts of his home city, a place where multilingual communication was crucial.

Zen sighed and waved the hand with the fountain pen, sending drops of black ink splattering onto the wall beside her. "Come back later. I'm in the middle of something."

"No," Gwei said. "We need some of the delving herb. It's important."

Zen expelled another sigh, tossed the fountain pen onto the desk and threw the pile of papers on her lap to the floor. Her mouth formed a tiny frown, but was it ever cruel. "*Kak zhe oni menja dostali.*"

Bolt cast Gwei a sidelong glance and raised an eyebrow.

She widened her eyes, tilted her head slightly and pursed her lips, a 'this is just what we have to deal with' look if there ever was one.

Gwei turned back to Zen, who was now studiously scowling at the wall, muttering in a different language than the one she'd just used. "Please," Gwei said, quiet but firm.

Zen took a deep breath in and out, her eyes closed.

Bolt noted the smoke rising up off the joint on her desk and remarked mentally on the fact that Zen seemed rather tense and agitated for a user of relaxation drugs. At least he assumed it was a relaxation drug.

"*Hao.*" Zen rose with a jolt, her wheeled chair careening into the ink-spattered wall behind her. She strode off into the flowing haze, Gwei following in her wake, and Bolt trailing in hers.

With another wave of beads, Bolt found himself outdoors. He looked back to see wisps of smoke flowing up through the bead strings, out of the doorway, dispersing.

Empty concrete basins filled the outdoor space, but Gwei and Zen wound around them with ease, and Bolt hurried to follow. Beyond the last basin, the ground rose abruptly, trees and plants finding precarious patches of the incline in which to grow.

They crossed a wooden bridge and began up a path woven into the hillside with squared wooden beams for steps.

"I didn't see this mountain from outside," Bolt remarked.

"Lots of City is like this," Zen said. "You should check out more of Yessel's cathedral. How new are you?"

Bolt shrugged. "About four, five hours maybe."

"Got your name yet?" Zen rounded a post.

"Bolt."

Zen bobbed her head back and forth and blinked a few times, seeming to evaluate it. "Not bad."

"What's it matter?" Bolt said, instantly wondering what it was about Zen that made him so defensive.

"*Ach,*" Zen said. "*Es heisst Namenstärke.* Names have power in City."

"It's the one weakness of the tribals," Gwei added.

Bolt nodded. "That's the Amaranthine District people we're trying to avoid, right?"

"Right," Gwei said. "When someone turns tribal, they take a new name, because if someone uses their real City name, we can turn that purple miasma against them. It happened once. Just before the gone-away scientist got here. Yessel told me about it. The tribals tried to spread the Amaranthine District, but a gone-away diplomat learned the City identity of the tribal leader. All the tribals just fell flat on their faces and the purple mist retreated. Yessel says it set them back months."

"Huh. Everyone's so scared of them. But their weakness is just a name? One word—?"

"*Kalimna u a-haida tahamil que lu tusadequ.*"

"Sorry?" Bolt spat out.

Gwei grabbed his arm, looked him directly in the eyes, and shook her head vigorously back and forth. Behind her shoulder, Zen climbed faster, still muttering to herself in whatever language she'd slipped into.

Bolt nodded, and they continued after Zen.

At the top of the small mountain, they came to an enormous garden with immaculately tended rows of plants. Birds chirped and danced amongst carefully tended branches, and cool breezes wafted through the hilltop glen. If Bolt hadn't known this place to be part of City, he'd have thought it serene.

Zen led them to a particular row at the far side of the glen, one whose plants bore fanning, razor-edged leaves and tiny blue buds. She crouched down, retrieved a pocket knife from her jean shorts and began sawing into one of the plants. A few moments later, she'd palmed about a dozen buds. Without a word, she stood and took off down the hill.

Bolt looked at Gwei, who shrugged again, her 'just deal with it' face having reached its most exaggerated form, and the two followed Zen back down the mountain, descending in rushed silence.

Back in her hazy workplace, Zen walked to a worktable beside her desk lined with all manner of ceramic bowls, pestles, thin papers, and slabs of stone. She took a bowl, dropped the buds inside, then scooped up a pestle and began to grind. A few moments later, she dumped the fine, blue powder onto a pair of papers and wrapped up her creations. She marched up to Gwei, joints in hand, and wrapped Gwei's fingers around them without a word.

"Light?" Gwei asked.

Zen retreated to her desk, procured a lighter from an audibly rusty drawer and tossed it to Gwei. Gwei caught it, lit the joint, took a puff, and handed the lighter to Bolt, who set his toolbox on the floor.

"What is this?" he asked, holding up his joint.

"I don't remember its name," she said.

He looked at the thing with suspicion, it in the one hand and the lighter in the other, even as Gwei took a second puff.

"What's going on? What does this have to do with the gone-away scientist's lab?"

"The Amaranthine District is growing," Gwei said quietly. "We should be fine, but if the district gets close to the lab, we can't waste any time getting out. This drug will make us sensitive to air pressure changes.

That's how we'll know if we're in danger."

Bolt looked at the joint, then at Gwei. She was absolutely serious. He looked to Zen, but she seemed to have taken up her position again at her desk, her back turned to them, the papers in her lap, scribbling furiously with her ink-stained fingers.

He sighed, lit the joint, and smoked.

A peculiar feeling washed over him. Interestingly, he was still aware of Gwei standing in front of him, the joint in her mouth, and the dingy, smoky, green cave that Zen called home. He glanced over Gwei's shoulder, where Zen sat writing, and as much as he was aware of all that, he was also aware of other things as well.

Reality was still there, before him, perfectly sensical, but it also melted, goopy at the edges. He wanted to laugh and cry at the same time. He pulled the joint from his mouth, and the paper against his lips felt electric. The joint seemed to glow.

He blinked, and he reeled.

His wife stood before him.

"Oh… my…" His lips moved but no further words came out.

"Bolt!" his wife said.

No.

Not his wife.

Gwei.

It was Gwei standing before him.

"Bolt!" Gwei's hand lay on his shoulder. She stood close. Her eyes were streaked with tears. He realized he was crying, too.

"It's okay, Bolt," she said.

"I saw her…" he said.

"Oh, god…" Gwei winced. "Bolt, I'm sorry. But you can see me now, right?"

"Yeah. I-I know it's you."

She took a deep puff. "Maybe you should stay here. Or I could take you back to the cathedral."

"How long does this stuff last?"

"About an hour. Maybe two."

He took another drag, much longer than the first, and the room's colors performed a supernova of hue. His wife's voice drifted in on the breezes from the hill beyond the back door, but he ignored the sound of her voice, difficult as that was, grounding himself in Gwei's face, her eyes, which he realized shone just as brightly under the influence of the berries.

"Bolt?" Gwei asked carefully.

"I'm fine," he said. "Let's go."

She nodded slightly, and led him out onto the street.

As if City hadn't seemed surreal enough before. The streets twisted and turned, despite being in a grid. He knew they were in a grid. He could see that, but he also saw how they twisted and wove between one another, an elegant dance, like a prince and princess waltzing amongst members of their high society. One couldn't help but behold the patterns amongst the chaos, order impossibly superimposed over insanity.

The blue of the sky shot down in bright bursts, luminescence shimmering brightly in some places while others seemed darker, a stark contrast from the omnipresent, evenly distributed light of before.

"Bolt?" Gwei tugged at his shoulder.

"Yeah…" He realized he'd been staring and scurried after her. "I'm fine."

He walked the streets as though in a daze, this time not from anxiety or nerves, but rather the reverse. Whole chunks of his memory of their passage seemed to flit away. He'd find himself noticing Fifteenth Avenue, then Eighth, then Second. Their journey became a staccato blur of sensations.

"You're sure you know where the scientist's place is?" Bolt found the presence of mind to ask.

"I'm sure enough."

They rounded a corner, the intersection itself seeming to twist and swoop with them, and a structure came into view. Tall, gray metallic spires jutted toward the sky. Lighting apparatuses and screens lay dormant on its surface. Its door hung open, a dark black precipice into the frightening cavern of a place. The curving, domed walls of dank metallic gray made Bolt shiver, even under the influence of the drug. The brilliant haze of the rest of City and the bursts of sky-on-the-ground disappeared near the scientist's structure, as though it were a sinkhole for the drug's effect.

"There," Gwei said, her voice betraying fear.

Bolt caught the sight of her outstretched finger, and at first he thought she was pointing to the laboratory, but then he realized she was pointing beyond it, down the street, toward a faint haze of purple. Some three or four blocks beyond, just before the street dipped below the horizon, wisps of lavender whipped up into the air, almost like smoke, before coalescing and whipping themselves back toward the earth. They twisted around the buildings, pulling, spinning, twisting, shaping. The further his eyes went, the more chaotic the structures became, round in some places, forming domes and bowls, and rectilinear in others, forming pentagons, hexagons, and other shapes unnatural for architecture. Even the street bulged and twisted, gaping holes dilating and oozing purple magma pus.

"That's—?" Bolt started to ask.

"Don't say it," Gwei said. She broke into a run, right for the laboratory. Bolt followed, keeping a careful eye on the encroaching purple haze in the distance. He spotted no people amongst that insanity, and ducked into the pitch black depths of the laboratory after his companion.

Lacking visual stimuli, the drug took over, reinventing his auditory input into works of abstract insanity. Amongst the awkward chorus, Bolt could make out the faint traces of real sounds. Distant drips and plunks echoed and reverberated while the groans and clanks of dilapidating machinery rang and rebounded amongst walls he couldn't see.

"Gwei?" Bolt shouted a whisper, groping blindly about the dark space.

All at once, lighting pierced the blackness, and Bolt winced. He instinctively pulled his hands up to shield his eyes, but caught a glimpse of Gwei at a wall, her fingers flying across a computer screen made of projected light. What a technology—!

"We have to hurry," Gwei said without turning to him.

She ran down the narrow hall and disappeared around a corner. Bolt gulped and followed. What had he gotten himself into? He'd been so adamant about seeing this through, but he felt the foundation of his trust in Gwei beginning to buckle. Why did she have to be so erratic? So nervous?

Perhaps he wouldn't truly understand the danger of the tribals until he confronted them. Given Gwei's fear and the fact that she had yet to lead him astray, he decided it best not to test his hypothesis.

And he felt the beginnings of something else unfolding within his mind. They weren't so much memories or thoughts as they were feelings and impressions. Fondness and simultaneous distress, intense longing, and memory, something about memory—Gwei was supposed to remember something. That feeling came to the forefront.

Perhaps it was just the drug.

He scrambled down the corridor after her, for the first time realizing that he'd left his toolbox at Zen's. He grimaced and scolded himself, all while hurrying after Gwei. The fleeting worry entered his mind that the drug might be wearing off. He had no idea how much time had passed since Zen's. Thankfully, he could still see the twisting, curving walls superimposed over the straight, angular features. Good. At least he was still a little high. He allowed himself a slight chuckle at that thought.

"Here." Gwei came to a halt and began tugging at a metallic door to no effect.

Bolt took his place at her side, and wrapped his fingers around the edge of the door. This he could help with.

"Really hard on three," he said.

Gwei nodded.

"One. Two. Three!"

They pulled, and at first nothing, then with a grunt and a creak and a rusty grating screech, the door slid open.

A room appeared, its space well lit. Computer screens of projected light displayed error messages and stuttered in the dank air. A wall of glass cubes lay mostly broken against the back wall. A few held plants and mineral matter. Groans and creaks emanated from all around.

Gwei moved to one of the computers and began tapping at its keyboard, also made of projected light.

"Where did you keep them…?" Gwei muttered.

"What do the bracelets do again, exactly?"

"They keep that purple shit off you."

"So, then, if enough people get these bracelets, why can't we reason with the tribals, get them to share—?"

Gwei held up a palm. "Not now, please. I need to concentrate."

She returned her attention to the computer, and so Bolt began scouring the room: boxes of disused junk speckled the floor, not even all of it technical. Amongst computer parts and circuit boards and other techno-rubbish lay skeins of yarn and pens and mustard bottles and other such paraphernalia.

One computer in particular caught his interest. Its screen depicted the outline of a human being, and above it, the title 'Holographic Amaranthine Infiltration System.' Over the course of many seconds, the human figure morphed, first gaining purple tattoos, then purple eyes, then finally, a flurry of purple wisps about its body.

Bolt marveled at the holographic person. Purple eyes and moving purple tattoos? That's what the Amaranthine District did to a person? No wonder everyone was afraid of them.

Another thought struck him: he was noticing details more clearly.

The drug's effect must have been diminishing. When he looked at the walls, the twisty superimposition remained, but it was getting dimmer, more distant. He felt his rational mind regaining its foothold over his senses.

"Over here!" Gwei's shout pierced his thoughts.

She ran to the wall and he followed. A small cubby door in the wall slid partway open, and she and Bolt jerked on it until it gave way completely.

Gwei reached inside and retrieved a box of gray bracelets, each made of a stretchy plasticine material.

"That's it?" Bolt eyed them suspiciously. Gwei took one out and shoved it onto his wrist. "They don't look like much."

Gwei expelled a disapproving grunt as she stretched one around her wrist and clamped the paper box underneath her arm.

"Actually…" Gwei shoved the box into Bolt's chest. "You carry this." Her features lightened momentarily. "Please."

He nodded, his smile slight, but it felt good to be working with Gwei. He couldn't leave her to do all this herself. "Sure."

She allowed herself a small smile back. "Thank you."

"Not a pr—" Bolt started to say.

His ears popped.

He turned toward the door and witnessed a thick, purple miasma pour in at the edges, yanking the rectangular door into a new shape, some parts twisting round, while others jolted into acute and obtuse angles.

Gwei's face turned white.

She gulped, looked up at him. He gaped at her.

"Through the door," she said. "Back out. It's the only way. Go!"

Bolt nodded and ran. Adrenaline led him away, the paper box gripped tightly under his right arm. He approached the dark purple wisps, fearing that the tentacles might reach toward him, but his footfalls seemed to repel them, and he strode more confidently through the mist, turning only briefly to see it turn its maladaptive attention toward the scientist's desk and cabinets.

They ran for the door, through the staccato lights. The clanks and creaks and drips and drops were accompanied by other sounds now, distant (or nearby?) footfalls, voices, terrible voices, synthetic sounding. Unnatural.

"Faster," Gwei hissed.

They ran, their footfalls clanking through the groaning building.

The entrance appeared, a pale gateway of light.

Bolt ran out into the street, and there was a voice and a din, and a blow at his head. He saw the box hit the ground and the gray wristbands scatter. Gwei shrieked, and there was purple everywhere.

He blinked, and saw blood drip to the pavement. He was looking at the pavement, but his hands held him. He was still strong. Gwei was screaming behind him. He moved his hands about, through his dizziness. His fingers met a stone, crumbly, a piece of pavement? Not very big, but he grasped it.

He stood.

A naked person, her clothing made of living, purple fire, her hair a mess of wispy tendrils, her skin a cacophony of slithering tattoos, had Gwei pinned up against the laboratory's outer wall while a naked man pulled at her arm, clearly trying to wrench the wristband off her.

Gwei roared, kicking and clawing at her attackers.

"Calm down! You'll find th'luster most wonderful once I've released th'damn-bracelet!" the male tribal roared.

The female tribal held Gwei firmly against the wall. "We want to help. Let us help you!"

"No!" Gwei shouted.

His body taking over despite his agony, Bolt walked quietly toward the male tribal. He raised the cement hunk in his hand and brought it down on the purple man, who toppled to the ground with a short grunt.

The woman holding Gwei turned and lunged at Bolt, but he pushed her easily away. Gwei jumped away from the building, grabbed the woman by the arm, threw her to the ground and held her in a pincer hold.

"Th'idiots!" the woman shrieked, her face stuck in the dirt. "Th'barbarians!"

The man groaned, convulsing on the ground, his head bleeding where Bolt had bashed him. Bolt felt his own perceptions begin to spin and wondered how much blood he was losing.

"The bracelets!" Gwei's voice pierced his scattered thoughts. "We need those bracelets!"

Bolt ran to where they lay, but it was difficult to make out the brace-lets from the broken asphalt, their color camouflaged against the pave-ment. He scooped up clumps of something, he wasn't sure what, grav-el…? Bracelets? He shoved whatever it was into his pockets.

He heard Gwei approach at his side. His vision had blurred too badly to make out any details of his surroundings "Bolt. Steady. Bolt! We have to run. I'm sorry, you have to run!"

Shouts resounded from behind.

"Th'barbarians!"

"Th'barbarians got th'bracelets!"

"Hurry!"

"I'm not sure…" Bolt felt dizzy and sick, like vomiting and passing out.

"They can't go where the purple doesn't go," Gwei said, her voice seeming distant. "Stay with me Bolt. You have to move a block. Can you move a block with me? Away from the tribals?"

He thought he responded in the affirmative, but he wasn't sure. He pulled his legs, one over the other, blood dripping down and spattering at his feet. He lurched forward in jolts, not unlike when he was under the influence of the drug. Oh, how he wished he could let Zen's drug take him away.

Pain blared against his skull and neck.

"I'm right here, Bolt," Gwei said. "I'm right here. It's going to be okay."

"I'm sorry, my darling." Bolt's wife lay before his eyes. "I'm sorry I wasn't there for you."

"You did great today, Bolt," she said.

"I did?" Bolt asked.

"Yeah. You saved my life."

"Then I made it up to you, I guess."

"How do you mean?"

"Because I wasn't there when you needed me before."

His back hit something soft, and he lay down.

"Close your eyes," she said.

"Okay… I'm really sorry though… So sorry…" The clouds took him away to sleep, and though they were the gray of sorrow and shame, he was glad at least, that they weren't purple.

Repentant

((after))

Zib—

    Zimbo—

    Zob—

It's a country on the central continent. It's drawn at the center of most maps, anyway. I know I'm close, but its name eludes me all the same. I'm not sure if I'm actually getting better at recognizing when I've gone down a phonetic garden path, or if that's just random interference from having done this so many times.

I scrawl a capital letter Z on the page and stare at it. Such an elegant form: hard angles; symmetry over multiple axes. In addition to being the last letter of the alphabet, it *feels* final. I like finality, surety of thought and form. Ironically, I feel more of that here than anywhere else I've lived. And I know I'm not the only one happy to at least be free of my daily toil.

But then I remember what else that capital Z represents. I now inhabit a world without names. I swear, my existence here is a cruel cosmic joke.

I was never nice to him. I was downright mean. And we used to argue about names. Well, words. Meaning and thought and perception. I was so stubborn. And here I am.

Cruel—cosmic—joke.

I scrawl a capital B next. I think his name might have started with B. Probably not. Doesn't feel right. Br—? I think lots of men's names start with Br, but I can't come up with any.

That slight rage I usually feel when I do this lingers in my gut, welling, coalescing into ache, inching toward my heart. My punishment for being so ceaselessly unkind...

To make myself feel better, I reach into my memory for one of the pictographic languages I learned, and I draw one of the most complex characters I can think of: 獨. Pronounced like 'do' with a question intonation, it means 'alone.'

My boyfriend never liked the pictographic languages. Well, mostly he didn't like their cultures. Funny, as half my ancestry is tied up with one of them. I think of other characters I could write, but I seem to have lost the will for it.

I take the pile of papers from my lap, set them on the desk, and take a drag of my nearly depleted joint. I think of maybe hiking up my mountain to collect berries, but despite my rumbling stomach, the notion is unappealing. I start chastising myself mentally, probably the voice of my mother, telling me to stop feeling sorry for myself and do something useful with my time here, but my mind comes back around to forgotten Br—, and all hope of useful activity drains out of me, runs down the chair, and pools on the floor.

I'm not usually so metaphorical, but I'm having a metaphorical kind of day.

Pffft. "Day." Like there are days in City. I can't even remember what darkness feels like. The best you can do is turn off the lights and close the doors and windows. That'll get you most of the way there, but it will always be bright outside. Light will still seep in between the blinds, through the cracks and crevices.

I have a hard time sleeping with all this light. Something about me. I just can't fall asleep very well if it's not dark. And so I get to ponder my mistakes uninterrupted. Just one interminable flow of anguish where sleep should be...

"Yo, Zen!" The familiar voice accompanies its usual scuffling of feet. There should be a word for that man other than his name. I'd have done better if I'd named him, I tell myself.

I roll my eyes and swivel around in my reclining chair, knowing exactly where he'll traipse into view. He's nothing if not consistent.

His lank, exposed torso and red bandana appear between the leaves. He pushes the greenery away and walks up to my desk. He wears an expression of distress, and he's sweating. Did he run here? And I've seen him skateboarding around City without a shirt, but usually he puts one on to visit me.

"Hey Zen." He rubs his hands together.

"Something the matter?" I ask.

"Everything's gone to shit," he mutters.

I look to either side of him, past him, remembering he'd taken charge of three children. "Where are Mario, Fero, and Hyra?"

"Fero and Hyra got taken by the tribals. That's why I'm here. I need some delving weed."

My mouth falls open. I shake my head, and indignation gets the better of me before I can consider my words. "Where did you take them?"

He stands up straighter and puffs out his meager chest at my accusatory tone. "The fuckin' granary! I ain't stupid. That was nowhere near Amaranthine until a few hours ago. They must be expandin' or somethin'."

Now that is interesting.

"Nowhere near here, I hope."

He bunches up his fists. "Thanks for your fucking concern!"

I stand up and meet his gaze. "I can't get you your *fucking* drug if we turn into tribals now, can I?"

His eyes narrow, but he produces no retort to the contrary.

I fold my arms. "Would you like to answer my question now?"

He scoffs. "It's the other direction. They're eating up Cesious Boulevard, probably heading right for the scientist's place, so I need to haul ass. Can I score some drugs? Please."

It strikes me what I have become. I do not have a professorship at a university. I'm not even a graduate student anymore. I don't even hold a respectable job. No. I am the dealer for an undereducated hoodlum-wannabe. I am a linguist who can't remember her words.

My self-reproach ceases at the moment I realize that this particular undereducated hoodlum-wannabe's goals are, in fact, rather noble, and I indeed have my part to play.

I expel a long sigh. "Come on then."

I lead him to the back door. I turn on him, remembering the last time we did this. "And no touching anything this time."

He rolls his eyes at me.

"I mean it!"

"Fine, fine! I won't touch your precious fucking plants. Can we go now?"

I turn and 'haul ass' up my hill, not quite fuming, but getting there. I never asked for this. I never asked to be pulled out of a promising academic career and dropped into a place that could literally sunder words' forms from their meanings. The worst part is that I feel I deserved it.

And so I help Grey, because it seems less cruel than the alternative. I also desperately want to stop feeling like a cruel person.

Dirt and rocks crunch under my feet. I spot about a dozen trees that need pruning. I wonder what will happen to this place after I leave City… if this isn't a life sentence. I have to admit, my garden is beautiful, but all I want right now is to get the buds of the delving plant and send Grey on his way.

We reach the back of the grove and Grey has his hands shoved in his pockets. I manage a small smile. Nothing too conspicuous. I realize I could be nicer to him, too.

No, maybe not.

I cut ten buds from the delving plant and immediately head back down the hill. Grey follows, scratching his head and wiping sweat from his brow with his bandana.

Back in my apothecary, I roll him a few joints and hand them over.

"Thank you," Grey says, almost meekly.

"You're welcome." I gulp.

He turns to go.

"Grey," I say.

He turns back. "Yeah?"

"Be careful, okay?"

The side of his lips turns up into a grin. "It's the tribals who should worry. I'll give 'em hell."

Somehow I find myself smiling. "Do that."

He runs out the door.

I take a deep breath and return to my chair.

My pen sits in its inkwell at an acute angle to the desk. On the top page of my stack of papers, I see the 獨 I scrawled earlier. I take up the page and move it to the bottom of the pile. I'm not sure I like the blank emptiness of the new top page any better, though.

"Zen?"

My heart skips a beat. I shoot up from my chair, but in that instant, I see Mario looking up at me, and I calm.

"Mario…" I gulp. "Please don't sneak up on me like that."

"Sorry." He looks at the ground.

"It's okay. What's wrong? Why aren't you with Grey?"

"He told me to stay in the apartment. But I can't! Fero and Hyra were captured. They're my friends. I'm not gonna just sit around! Grey's not sitting around."

I nod. "What Grey's doing is very dangerous."

Mario fumes. "I don't care! Yessel said I can't help, but I know I can!"

"Have you ever seen a person go tribal?" I try.

His furor diminishes. He stuffs his hands in his pockets and looks at the wall. "No."

"Well, I have. The man's name was Cob. He arrived around the same time as me. We were scouting out an area for supplies and we didn't realize how close we'd come to the Amaranthine District. The purple mist took him, grabbed him like claws or tentacles… or both. It got under his skin, changed his eyes, changed *him*. He's not even named Cob anymore."

Not that anyone, including him, knows his *real* name, I remind myself.

Mario stares silently at the floor.

"Do you want that to happen to you?"

"No…" he mutters. "But- but- but Grey's in trouble!"

We're all in trouble, Mario. "Grey can take care of himself."

"Help me help him!"

"*For the love of…*" I say it in a language he won't understand, but I'm sure my intonation makes the meaning clear. "Mario…" I step out from around the desk, but he turns up his face into a horrid scowl and bolts through the shelves and out the door. Something crashes to the ground near the entrance.

"Mario!" I twist up my own face. I run to the entrance, where a shelving unit lies toppled, soil and incense sticks and my poor plants lie in a heap. I growl as I retrieve my broom and buckets from the back. I spend the next half hour putting the shelf back in order and restoring the plants to their proper containers.

As I re-light the incense sticks, I think back to the stupid things I used to say to Br—. I used to get myself worked up into a bad mood over the most ridiculous things, some chore left undone, or some detail overlooked. I thought it so overwhelmingly annoying at the time, but I miss the way he challenged me. Even when I was being stubborn and arrogant and awful and mean, even then, he was prodding me to think and reflect. I wonder what he's doing right now? Does he miss me, or is he glad to be rid of me? Thanks to my behavior, probably both. And now here I am in a city without names. 獨.

I return to my desk and my joint. I try to take a drag and realize that the thing is spent. I walk to my work bench and roll another. The new joint relaxes me. I fall into my chair. My pen reaches my hand effortlessly. The pages are in my lap, and I become aware of how they got there only after the act of moving them occurred.

I write, letting my six semi-fluent languages mingle on the page, even though I'm likely the only person in existence who will ever make sense of such a conglomeration of codes. Some heavily declined, case-sensitive nouns here, a few picto- and ideograms there. It occurs to me that I haven't tried this before. If I let go completely, can I find my own meaning amongst the senselessness? Paying attention is too difficult, too painful. I don't want to see City's dismal streets and wreck of a sky anymore. It reminds me too much of the wreck that is my life.

A cough sounds from the front of my humble abode, and the sound takes some time to make its way to my senses. I ignore it and continue scrawling.

"Zen?"

I look up and see Gwei pushing her way through the leaves. A man appears behind her, big and burly. I've never seen him before. Must be a new arrival. Perhaps another influx has begun. I suddenly wish for all the inhabitants of this place to leave me alone.

"Come back later," I mutter. "I'm in the middle of something."

Gwei's request for delving herb flits into my senses, and it's almost too much. Delving herb, delving herb, delving herb. Has the whole of City decided to go tribal? She says it's important.

"*Why can't I be left in peace!*" I say in my favorite language for irritation. It's the one I used to scream at Br— in.

I can remember Br— and all our experiences at least. What would he do? I know the answer immediately. He would help. He would do everything in his power, no matter how much nastiness I hurled his way.

"Please," Gwei says.

I nod. I'm frowning, but I nod.

"*Fine,*" I say in yet another language. My brain still hasn't gotten out of polyglot mode. The drugs must have stuck me there, which is fine, I guess, because I like my polyglot self better than any of my other selves.

I lead Gwei and the new arrival out the back door and toward the hill with the glen and the plants and the birds and the trees and the sunless sky. I think of the difference I've made.

I wonder if Br— would be proud of who I've become. I'll keep trying, for him, and pray that someday soon I get to tell him how sorry I am. I wanted to hurt him because I resented his presence, but it's so clear now that in reality, I was hurting myself all along.

Consanguine

((after))

I think about my pain sometimes, even though it's th'one-thing you're never supposed to do. Th'pain is for th'weak. Th'strong absorb th'weak and make them strong, too. I suppose that's what happened to me. It's just, sometimes I don't feel so strong.

It's all I can think about though, since I was promoted to Th'Incandescent. And I worry about th'luster. I can feel it in th'back of my mind, wriggling, squirming, listening. If I think about th'pain too much—

I tell myself to stop that train of th'thought, and I focus on my footsteps. Th'sounds have seemed duller since my ascension. I noticed that right away. Everything muted, and while th'physical-forms grew deeper, richer, and every of th'touches grew sensual, every of th'tastes grew exquisite… th'sounds dampened and muted. It's hard to hear now.

But th'brethren tell me I shouldn't mind because I can hear th'luster.

I walk down th'hallway of Th'Home, toward th'door I have seen but never passed through. I saw Th'Incandescent walk through once, when I was of Th'Luminous. But now I am of Th'Incandescent, and now I must walk through th'door.

My footsteps are soft and seem distant, but th'walls and th'floor and th'ceiling are extraordinary. I never tire of gazing upon our architecture. I vaguely feel that, before my ascension, I found these forms frightening. That is th'memory most distant. Th'moment th'luster touched my skin, I saw truly, wholly. Th'angles, th'shapes, th'forms… all th'chaos I beheld became th'order, and I became whole.

I can't imagine going back.

I recognize bits of th'walls, th'floor, th'ceiling. Part of th'chandelier sticks up out of th'barrel and th'repair-shop-car-post bends elegantly and twists around th'bookshelf upon th'ceiling. Well, half of th'bookshelf, anyway. I wonder where its books went?

I reach th'door.

It's th'thing most sturdy and imposing, all purple of course. It's th'deeper-purple than th'luster. Very regal.

I take th'deep-breath. I know what happens next. I thought I was prepared, but in th'back of my mind, I'm worried. I hope I'm strong enough to keep my worry from th'luster.

I press my finger into th'button set into th'frame at th'door's edge. It slides open, and I do my best to suppress th'gulp. My heart threatens to pound out of my chest.

And there she stands: Th'Resplendent Adema. She has th'desk, which sits atop th'staircase. She stands, resolute, imposing. She places her hands at her hips and bows, our signal of th'respect. I perform th'same-gesture of th'respect, taking th'moment at th'bottom of th'motion to breathe. I see th'luster swirling at my feet, and I wonder if it knows, if it's mocking me being in this rank I don't truly deserve.

"Rise, Th'Incandescent Kin," Adema says.

I pull myself up to th'stance.

"Thank you, Th'Resplendent Adema," I reply. My voice cracks th'bit and I wince. I feel like th'stupid-teenager all over again.

"Please sit." She motions to th'chair before her desk—th'central of th'three—then returns to her own seat.

I walk up th'staircase in th'utter-terror. Th'walls of her office churn with th'complexity most inordinate and beautiful. But also most dangerous. Beyond th'wall behind Th'Resplendent's desk lies Th'Chamber—th'center of Th'Home and all our power. From there, th'luster pours and spreads.

I sit before Th'Resplendent. She looks upon me with th'kind-eyes—I think. She wants me to be calm. But I've seen th'way she talks to Th'Brethren-Incandescent. I wonder what it would take for me to warrant that ire.

"How is th'expansion proceeding?" Adema asks.

"Well," I say, my mind grasping for th'bits of th'knowledge that I have on th'subject. "Th'zone-four-luster is stable and healthy. I measured th'periphery myself at seventy-two of th'PPM three of th'hours ago."

"How close are we to th'lab of th'gone-away-scientist?"

"We will reach it within th'hour."

She nods. I find myself wishing I could read th'eyes. Th'luster absorbs our pupils. It's how we see better, how we see all th'beauty it creates. But I used to be good at reading th'eyes, and I wish I could now. Th'Resplendent Adema is notoriously exacting. Th'brethren never know what will set her off.

"Very good," Adema says. "Are you looking forward to th'incursion?"

"Yes, ma'am."

"I don't need to tell you of th'importance of this mission."

"No, ma'am."

"Good."

I shoot to th'stance. "If that will be all, Th'Resplendent Adema—"

She holds up th'palm and I jolt back into my seat.

"Th'Incandescent Kin, before you go, there is th'thing you must know."

Am I sweating? Damn it all. I'm starting to sweat. I clench my fists to stop my hands from shaking.

Adema continues, either unnoticing or uncaring for my predicament. "You must hear th'true-story of th'luster and th'origin of th'Amaranthine."

"Th'— true-story?" My mind is reeling. "Th'story… isn't true?"

Adema nods. "Th'Incandescent and myself all know th'true story. Th'luster… was created by th'gone-aways of th'long-ago."

I blink th'few-times, my mind reeling. "It wasn't… always here? In Th'City?"

"No."

"How—?"

"We don't know all th'details. Long before, there was th'great-battle between two of th'sides—th'logical-rational clashed with th'philosophical-spiritual. Both formed th'weapons using th'technology most strange and complex. Th'texts that speak of its workings are unparsable by even our greatest minds. Th'Technos and Th'Sophos, as they were called, waged th'war upon each other in Th'City, and nearly destroyed it, but in th'end, Th'City took them all away. It took th'*people* away, but not their weapons. Th'people who came later put th'weapons of th'two-sides together, not knowing how they worked, and created th'beginnings of th'chamber."

"Th'luster… was th'accident?"

"Yes."

I am stultified. I feel glued to my chair, th'rigid-immobile-statue.

"What are you thinking, Th'Incandescent Kin? Tell me your thoughts on this."

I gulp. At once, my mind is clear. Th'part of me struggles. I should keep my mouth shut. I should say what Th'Resplendent Adema wants to hear. But I can't. "What does that mean for us? Are we not Th'Definite-Incarnate? Why do we hide th'truth from th'lower-brethren-ranks?"

Adema nods. "I asked these same questions when I was first initiated. We are indeed Th'Definite-Incarnate. But even amongst us, there are differences between our physical skills and mental capabilities. Th'Caliginous and Th'Somber, of whom there are many, would not fully understand th'true-story as you do, Kin. Many are dull enough that they would grow violent and fearful. They might even rebel against th'luster. That must not happen."

"I see." My mind is reeling. "So... Th'Brethren-Incandescent—?"

"They know." Adema clasps her hands together and rests them on her desk. How I wish I could read her eyes. "They were told when they became Th'Incandescent, just as I am telling you now." She leans forward ever so slightly. "How do you feel about your upcoming assignment?"

"I will guard th'luster's spread with my life." I intend for my voice to sound strong, but it comes out th'whisper most hoarse. Damn it all.

Adema breaks th'wan-smile. "It is good to hear you say that. We will talk more of this when you return."

I start to stand up, very slowly. Adema senses my hesitation and nods her consent. I bolt. At halfway down th'stairs, I think I am free of this embarrassing escapade when she calls down to me.

"Yes?" I turn and call back.

"In securing th'materials and th'research of th'gone-away-scientist, you are to use th'lethal-force against th'barbarians, if th'conversion proves difficult."

I frown and tilt my head, th'confusion roiling in alongside my fear. "Are we not to grow our numbers?"

"Th'bracelets, Kin. None of th'bracelets must leave that lab. They have caused us enough of th'trouble already. You, of all th'brethren, should understand that."

"I do."

"You have your instructions."

"Yes, ma'am."

I hurry away out th'door, th'stupid-stupid-door. I have heard th'muted-grumblings about Adema's appointment to th'rank of Th'Resplendent. I was also against her. Especially I. But she was appointed. I wonder what she remembers from before th'luster took us. It is dim in my mind, but I do get th'occasional-glimpse…

Th'luster stings me.

I decide to distract myself, and so I rub at my right arm until th'luster beneath my skin forms th'information I seek—th'names of Th'Three-Luminous under my command for th'final-stage of th'expansion. Th'letters appear with ease, and I recognize th'names immediately. One is th'new-recruit I converted in our last raid. I brush at my skin, and th'luster contorts into th'different-shapes.

I recall how, as th'barbarian myself, I found it so horrifying, so primitive-seeming that Th'Amaranthines don't wear th'clothing. But to experience th'luster suffusing you, protecting you, is to realize that th'cloth is th'pettier of th'two-options. Th'luster is far nobler.

Thirty-eight of th'meters down th'hall I walk, then knock at th'door to th'Luminous-halls and wait th'many-moments. Finally, I press th'button beside th'door-frame and it slides open. My three recruits jump to th'stance and run to me.

"Th'Incandescent Kin!" They shout in unison. They place their hands on their hips and bow.

I return th'greeting. "At th'ease."

"Twenty-one of th'minutes until th'incursion!" Harrn says. He's th'young-man I converted yesterday. He entered Th'Luminous and will join me as Th'Incandescent by th'end of th'year, I suspect.

"Let's go," I say.

I lead them away without more of th'words. I think that I should say th'things to ease their minds. They are about to go into th'situation most dangerous, but I am wrapped up in my own folly, in th'troubling-story Th'Resplendent told me. Th'luster was th'accident of th'past? Unnatural? What does that make us? What does that make me? Surely Th'Resplendent has grappled with these questions, but th'fact that she has not been more open fills me with th'doubt of her, of our whole rank system.

I pass th'many-halls in th'daze. We move through Th'Luminous-Halls into th'halls of Th'Bright, then Th'Moderate, then th'meager-abodes of Th'Dim, Th'Caliginous, and Th'Somber, who all share th'same-living-spaces. Not really th'halls, they are more th'wreckage-leftovers of th'luster's expansion. Th'luster is thin here, and moves with less effort and grace than in our halls. But its inhabitants are th'brethren, and we care for them all th'same.

We exit out of th'cavernous-mishmash-amalgam that is our home and into th'streets. Th'luster expands outward, eating up Cesious Boulevard, but its brightness dims under Th'City's luminance. For th'first-few-days after I found th'luster, I had th'overwhelming-impulse to wrap myself in it, to surround myself with nothing but th'luster in all th'directions. I'm sure that Harrn feels th'same-way. Right now, he will follow all my orders, all my commands. He will do anything for th'luster.

I find myself wondering about th'purple in my mind. Is its power really worth fighting for?

I feel th'sharp-jab to my senses.

Th'sting of th'luster forces my perceptions outward. I take th'stock of my surroundings. We can see now beyond th'place where th'luster ends, and I realize instantly that th'things there are badly amiss.

I order my vanguard to halt with th'quick-gesture and glance about. They form up beside me.

"Th'street…" I say, looking over th'buildings th'luster has yet to claim.

"They're different," Circa says.

"What happened to them?" Mai asks.

Harrn stands tall. "It just keeps going… And those intersections. Th'streets have formed th'grid."

"Have you ever seen th'streets like this?" Circa asks. Her eyes are all purple, but I can sense her imploring need from her face and body language.

"They have changed," I say. I feel I should reach back into my memory for th'relevant-time from when I was th'barbarian, but I can't quite remember, and th'luster resists my urge.

My vanguard exchanges th'glances most worried.

"Stay calm," I assure them. I draw out th'messages most urgent upon my forearm, tracing strokes of th'luster into letters: "Th'streets have undergone th'transformation most sudden. Request th'full-appraisal of th'integrity of Th'Home. Th'highest-urgency."

Th'message flits away off to its recipients.

"Stay calm," I repeat to my group, mostly for myself.

Th'rumbling sounds in th'distance. Th'abandoned-car near us rattles. We hear th'things inside th'buildings fall and crash. Our street vibrates beneath us. Harrn takes Circa and Mai's hands. I take their others, and we stand in th'circle amongst Th'City's rage. I recall th'dark-tales we learn as th'new-Amaranthines—th'worry that Th'City may learn to take us away, that th'luster will, one day, no longer protect us from Th'City's indecisions most callous.

We are Th'Definite-Incarnate. We will not be taken.

Then, th'rumbling stops, but th'street remains strange.

Th'response from Th'Home appears on my arm: Th'halls are intact. Whatever change has affected Th'City, it has not affected us.

I let go of Circa and Mai's hands and bow to them. They bow back.

"Th'Home is safe. This change does not affect it."

Their relief is visible, though they say nothing.

"Let us continue." I turn and lead them down th'street, th'rest of th'way to th'very-edge of th'luster. It seeps down th'pavement, through th'cracks and th'crannies. Th'City's streets and infrastructure are appalling—th'chaos most random. At Th'Home, we have th'beauty in th'four-dimensions of th'lustrous-purple. I would give my life to protect that beauty. In th'heartbeat.

We walk slowly, following th'luster as it spreads. I can see th'gone-away-scientist's lab. Th'luster is just making its way up th'back-wall. Circa follows it with her eyes. She's older than Harrn, but she has never seen th'expansion before. Only Mai and I were here for th'last.

I remember that th'laboratory has th'back-entrance as well. I motion silently to Mai and Harrn, instructing them to follow th'luster as it consumes th'back of th'lab. Circa and I will guard th'front-entrance. They are only to enter once th'luster has secured th'building. They nod their comprehension and off they run, leaving me with th'nervous-Circa at my side.

We creep to th'front-door of th'lab, following th'luster as it absorbs th'disorderly-building and reshapes it before our eyes.

Circa nods toward th'door, asking silently if there are th'people inside. I motion that we should remain on th'guard on either side of th'door until th'luster has consumed th'entire-building. She takes up her position on th'door's left, still looking nervous. I stand beside th'right.

We wait for eight of th'minutes. I alternate watching th'door and th'luster as it absorbs th'wall beside me. When it reaches th'middle of th'structure, my mood lightens. I begin to think this will be easy. I imagine us going inside and I plan my coordination of th'search for th'bracelets.

I turn back to Circa and her eyes are wide. She scowls at th'door.

I hear it, too: th'feet, shuffling and scuffling, ever closer.

I remember Th'Resplendent Adema's order. I hold out my hand and will th'luster into th'cane. Th'purple forms into th'solid-rod in my hand. Circa holds out her hand and forms her own.

Th'debate most horrific churns within me. I do not want to kill. One of those pairs of th'footfalls sounds most heavy. Th'luster is everywhere. They must already have th'bracelets. Can I really convert th'luster-repelled-person much larger than myself? What do I do?

Th'barbarian emerges before me, large and burly, and in th'split-second, I make my decision. I raise my rod and bring it down on his head before he has th'chance to react. He falls to his hands, his head bleeding.

Circa grabs th'woman in th'skirt as she emerges, and throws her against th'wall. Th'woman claws and kicks, but Circa holds her tight.

"Th'luster!" Circa shouts. "It's repelled!"

I look at th'man, gasping, stunned, bleeding, still on his hands and knees. I should attack him again. I should. Instead, I turn my back on him and look to Circa and th'barbarian-woman. I spot th'bracelet on her wrist. I know I should give th'order—to kill her. But I can't. I know I must, but I can't.

"Tear off th'bracelet!" I shout, but it's all Circa can do to hold her still. Th'woman squirms and screams horribly. I run to them and grab at th'woman's wrist myself.

"Calm down!" I shout at her. "You'll find th'luster most wonderful once I've released th'damn-bracelet!" I know why they are scared. I remember how we seemed. How we looked. How Th'Home looked. But I would not deny anyone its glory.

"We want to help," Circa yells. "Let us help you!"

Amidst her flailing wrists, my fingers catch hold of th'bracelet. Th'victory is mine. I pull at th'stretchy-metallic-ring, and it slides down toward her fingers, even as she twists her wrists, I begin to slip it off, and—

Th'sharp-pain and th'jolt most agonizing and I am on th'ground. I scream and moan. My head spins and spins.

Th'barbarian. Th'damn-burly-barbarian. This is th'thanks for my benevolence. This is why they must die when they cannot be converted.

Through th'horrific pain, I wonder if th'luster will heal me as it has healed so many others of th'injured-brethren, or if it will punish me for my sin, for failing to follow Th'Resplendent Adema's commands. I see my blood, and I know then that I am too weak to be Th'Incandescent. I should have refused th'promotion.

I hear th'footfalls, th'reinforcements, summoned by th'luster upon my massive injury.

"Th'barbarians!" Circa shouts. "Th'barbarians got th'bracelets!"

"Hurry!" Th'new-voices yell.

I already know. I cannot see, but I already know.

Th'barbarians got away.

Perhaps it was th'mistake to become of th'brethren. I should have let Th'City take me away instead.

City is Potential

(( ))

It never ends.

As long as humans have had the capacity for thought, they have had the capacity for ideological conflict. One cannot hide behind 'logic' and 'reason' as the definitive answers to all questions, because they provide only limited shelter and have ambiguous boundaries.

Two plus two?

Logic has an answer.

What is the speed of light?

Logic has an answer.

How many years until City suffuses away into effervescent, particulate nothing-everything?

Logic, one day, will have an answer.

How does one cope with loss? With pain? With mistakes? With regret?

Logic has no answers to questions such as these, yet these latter questions are just as important as their former counterparts, if not more so.

Who are humans? Are humans violent barbarians capable of meting out only pain and misery upon one another, or are humans kind, compassionate, giving, caring people who consider the emotional impact of their behaviors upon their fellow societal members?

Just as with all things in City, humans are neither one nor the other. Humans exist in a superposition between these states, capable of both, but inhabiting neither with any certitude until one analyzes a particular behavior at a particular moment in time.

But neither can humans be reduced to the sum of their component parts.

Even the most broken and distraught have the capacity for empathy. Even the kindest and most faithful have the capacity for capriciousness.

Do humans have free will?

Perhaps. But it is nonetheless bounded.

All that is certain is that City and its humans undergo constant change. Yes, even the Amaranthines, who wish to fix themselves and their structures against City's explicit will. They will change and grow and learn, and absorbing no amount of their 'luster' will halt that process.

City waits. City is patient. City's change can be slow, even glacial, but it moves with the force of the ages, pushing its citizens along with it.

Obsessive

((before))

"We are certain about the number of tribals," Ward said. "Taum has even confirmed for us—"

Kaia shook her head. "Does he have direct footage of the Amaranthine District's interior?"

Ward scowled. "He doesn't need it! People can't be holed up in there for days on end without coming out for air."

Kaia rolled her eyes. "You've clearly never met an academic."

Aria put her hand on Ward's shoulder. "Isn't it enough that we hold our own against the tribals and prevent their numbers from growing?"

"Then we're giving up on them."

"Taum may yet develop his bracelet technology further," Yessel said.

Ward, Aria, and Kaia turned to face him and blinked. Kaia's mouth hung open. Not only had Yessel been silent for the last ten minutes, he'd broken that silence to speak of *Taum*.

Yessel glanced between them and shrugged. "His contraptions do have their uses."

"You're right," Aria said. "It's a good point. Our position is secure. We should use this stability to find the best option."

"I'm sorry," Ward said. "I disagree. The best defense is a good offense."

"If you fully understand your opponent and the game's rules," Yessel said.

Kaia nodded. "And there's a lot we don't know about the tribals."

"Let's send a contingent in, then," Aria said blithely.

The incredulous stares turned her way.

"I'm serious," she continued. "We don't have enough information so let's get it. If we can trade with Taum for four or five of his bracelets, we can actually get people inside the Amaranthine District and gather some real intel. For all we know, Taum might even be able to secure the bracelets to our skin in some way. We should play for time and information."

Ward threw up his arms. "And how many people will get converted in the meantime?"

"None," Kaia said. "You said yourself our coverage is solid. With the influx tapering off, our patrols don't even have much to do."

"Oh no." Aria frowned, her gaze turned toward the entrance to the cathedral, where Naim stood, looking bored. Kaia finally spotted what had drawn Aria's attention: Karr was walking around the rows of pews toward them.

Kaia turned her attention back to the group. "I hope she doesn't want to talk to us."

"My daughter," Yessel said sternly. "That's hardly productive."

"Did you hear what she called Ward?" Aria spat out in a whisper.

Ward wore a face like he was about to wretch.

"Why no." Yessel seemed sad. "She does seem rather aloof, but that's no reason to—"

"*Rather* aloof?" Ward's tone and volume prompted uncomfortable stares from the rest of the group.

Kaia could see the pretentious blue dress getting closer in her peripheral vision and put on her best condescending smile. "Speak of the devil…" she whispered.

Karr's clip-clop high heels came to a halt beside them. "Good to see you all again."

Kaia and Aria responded with simmering silence. Ward walked away in the direction of the transept.

"My daughter," Yessel said. "Welcome back to my cathedral."

"Thank you," Karr said.

"How is your work with Taum going?"

"Quite well."

"That is good to hear."

Karr crossed her arms. "I am here on official business. As you know, Taum has desired components of your cathedral for quite some time. He is wondering, now that he has perfected his bracelet technology, if he might reopen negotiations."

All at once, the noxious disgust for Karr left Kaia's mind. Her eyes met Aria's and she knew instantly that they were thinking the same thing. Both of them turned to Yessel, who smiled that smile of his, the one that spoke volumes before he even opened his mouth.

He let out a sigh. "We could talk about that, yes. Have Taum write up a list, and we'll begin negotiations. I take it Taum wishes to remain in his lab?"

"Yes," Karr said.

"Are you authorized to negotiate on his behalf?"

"I am."

"Good. I await Taum's initial offer."

"Very good speaking to you, Yessel," Karr said, casting superior glances at both Kaia and Aria before turning on her high heels and walking away the same way she'd come.

When she'd walked out the cathedral doors and shut them behind her, Kaia turned to Yessel. "I think you might be the only person in City she treats with a modicum of respect."

Yessel shrugged. "I'm sure she treats Taum well enough."

Aria rolled her eyes and turned her gaze to the boy who'd arrived a few weeks ago. He careened into the cathedral proper atop Grey's skateboard and barely stopped himself before running into a pew. Grey scrambled in after him, shouting and cursing, Mario scampering alongside him. The boy's sister followed them both wearing a bemused expression.

Aria giggled.

"Aww," Kaia said. "They've become a little family."

"The siblings finally got their names, too," Aria said.

"Oh, really?"

"It was Yessel who did the honors."

Kaia turned to him. "Well?"

"Fero and Hyra."

"Pretty good," Kaia said.

The three of them watched Grey subject Fero to a detailed analysis of every single one of the dents and bruises Fero had inflicted upon the skateboard. When Grey finally clopped the thing down on the floor and jumped atop it, by way of demonstration of proper technique, Yessel cleared his throat, loudly. "Your lessons are to be conducted outdoors, Grey."

"Yessir!" Grey shouted back with a wry smile. He flipped up his skateboard and led the kids out through the doors.

Kaia's eyes caught Naim's, and he expelled a long sigh.

"I've got to go," Kaia said.

"Stay safe, my daughter."

"Be careful out there," Aria said. "You and Naim both."

"I'll tell him you said so."

"Oh, and Kaia?" Aria said.

"Can you meet me tomorrow morning, maybe? Here at the cathedral?"

Kaia tilted her head. "Sure. Is something up?"

"Maybe," Aria said with a wry grin.

"Alright," Kaia nodded, wondering what might be the secret. "See you then."

She turned and jogged to the front door. She looked at Naim, but his eyes betrayed the fact that he was miles away from her.

They exited the building, walked down the stone stairway, and found themselves on a long, narrow street that went straight in both directions all the way to the horizon.

Naim smiled. "The grid."

Kaia released a sigh of her own. She would now spend an indefinite number of hours traipsing down street after street alongside Naim as he mapped. She'd lost track of which blocks of which quadrants he'd completed. All of the streets were starting to look the same, too. Not that there was, in fact, much difference.

"Where to?" Kaia asked.

"Somewhere new," Naim said calmly. Too calmly. His gait was different, too. Less nervous. His usual frenetic energy during a City-as-Grid transition was noticeably absent.

"What?" Kaia grabbed his arm. "What's 'somewhere new?'" Fear struck her. "You don't mean the—"

"No." Naim shook his head vigorously. He took up a quick pace down Negative Twenty-Third Avenue. "Not the Amaranthine District. I'm not crazy."

"Where to then?"

"Straight down this road."

"Okay…"

"Do you remember how far we've been down Negative Twenty-Third

Avenue?"

Kaia wracked her brain. She glanced up at the rusty sign announcing the intersection of Negative Twenty-Third Avenue and Negative Tenth Street. "Somewhere in the Negative Fifties, right?"

"Negative Sixty-One."

"Right. I said it felt kind of cold. I think."

"I think you were right. It got a bit colder."

They walked in silence for some time, Naim walking straight ahead, not looking at buildings, not scanning facades. He exuded calm purpose. Kaia had thought so many times that she'd love for Naim not to be so scattered of thought and emotion the way he'd been recently. She'd wished for him to pull himself up out his quagmire any way he could. But now she realized she just wanted him back the way he was before City became his obsession. She liked this new behavior even less.

"Naim?"

"Yeah?"

"Where are we going?"

"As far down this street as we can."

"Why?"

"To prove a theory."

Kaia gathered all her emotional resources to remain calm. She reminded herself that he was an academic. Whatever was in his head, its structure was detailed and its conclusions rigorously cross-analyzed.

"Describe it to me," she said.

"In the other configuration, City-as-Usual, the streets twist and turn. They intersect at weird angles. It keeps us near the equator."

"The *equator?*"

"When we're in City-as-Grid, it's the east-west street called Zero. That's the equator. City's on a sphere, remember? A small one, about ten kilometers in diameter."

"Right. I remember Taum saying that."

"In City-as-Usual, you can't get that far away from the equator. The streets will always curve you back around toward it. Unless the tribals have some special access, but I don't think they do."

"Why?" Why was she still playing this verbal game? Why was she still following Naim around at all?

"Because they're still here. I think the way home, or the way to stay fixed without turning into a freak, the way to be whoever you want, to do whatever you want within City, beyond it, that's at the one place—well, two places—that only City-as-Grid can take you."

"And what places are those?"

"The poles."

She watched the intersection of Negative Thirteenth Street pass by.

"What makes you think there's anything at the poles at all?"

"It's the place where the probabilities would have to converge."

Kaia's heart sank. Now he just sounded crazy. If she hadn't had so many discussions with him about philosophy, she would have thought herself being led around by a truly crazy person. But then maybe not all academics were as put together they liked to pretend they were.

Give him the benefit of the doubt, she told herself, remembering conversations with intellectually hostile extended family members. Having a doctorate in sociology without an academic position meant she'd had to defend her selected line of scientific inquiry at every turn.

She could not help but extend the same courtesy to Naim. "What do you mean by 'the probabilities converge?'"

"Let's back up," Naim said. "Where are the grid streets when we're in City-as-Usual? And where are Cesious Boulevard and Claret Crossing and the others when we're in City-as-Grid?"

"I thought maybe the matter was getting rearranged?"

"Can you imagine the energy required for that? Atomic manipulation on that scale, plus the simultaneous redistribution of all City's buildings?"

"But if they're not getting transmogrified…?"

"I think City is a superposition of two states. Both City-as-Usual and City-as-Grid exist here and now, but something is causing them to flip instantly from one to the other. There was a physicist who talked about this phenomenon on the atomic level. He used a cat as a metaphor."

"Right, I remember that. The cat was in a box with radioactive decay-activated poison. Radiation is based on quantum collapse, so the cat could be both alive and dead until someone opened the box and observed its state. You think that City's poles are where its two states converge in real space?"

Naim nodded. Negative Seventeenth Street drifted by.

Kaia let her mind wrap itself around that for some time. Then finally, she asked. "What do you think causes the two states to flip?"

Naim shook his head. "I don't know. I'm not too worried about that, though. As long as the changes continue we can make as many attempts at the poles as we like. We don't seem to have any control over them anyway, so it's not worth worrying about now."

Kaia had to admit it all sounded logical enough. Logical in a City kind of way. But's Naim's rigid insistence on chasing after the poles wasn't something she could really say she wanted. No. She knew. She didn't want to go there. But ever since the change of the streets had separated them days ago, they'd stayed together, never growing any more distant from one another than the interior space of a building would allow.

She had agreed and promised, and won permission to join the Collective as a reward. But the victory was bittersweet. It had made Naim pursue his investigation of City all the more fervently.

Negative Twenty-Second Street.

"What do we do when we get to the pole?" Kaia asked.

"I don't know. I'm not sure it matters. If I'm right, and the poles lie at the intersection of the superpositions… Well, to extend the cat metaphor, it would be like the cat discovering a latch to open the box and jumping out before the experiment was complete."

"And we're the cats."

"Right. It doesn't matter exactly what the latch is, just that it exists and we can lift it. We might need to make multiple attempts."

Maybe she could reason her way out of this. Maybe she could convince him that there were more important uses of their time and energy. "Yessel's going to trade with Taum for his bracelets. The Collective's going to try to infiltrate Amaranthine and gain more data on them."

"Is Ward still pushing for a confrontation?"

"Yeah. It's an appeasement mechanism. Ward gets more information about the tribals, and Aria and I get peace. For now."

Naim didn't respond. He just continued walking, looking straight ahead. Single purpose. One track. Nothing mattered to him except the damn pole anymore. Did he really care about her, or did he just want the control? What did love matter if it felt this miserable to be in it?

She continued trudging alongside him through the negative thirties, then forties, then fifties. They walked in silence.

As they passed Negative Sixtieth Street, Kaia noticed the air growing colder and drier. Still they walked in silence. By Negative Seventieth, they were shivering, and their exhalations had become visible.

"Naim." She grabbed his shoulder, bringing them to a halt. "It's too cold. We should go back."

"I can go a little further."

"I can't." She closed her eyes momentarily and collected herself. She opened her eyes and looked directly into his. "Let's go back and get proper clothes for this. Then we'll come back. Okay?"

Naim pulled her close. "You're the best. Thank you."

"I love you," Kaia whispered.

"I love you, too."

"Do not move!" A voice from behind them. Male. Young.

Naim held her tighter.

"What should I do?" Naim asked.

"Just stay still!"

Kaia peeked up over Naim's shoulder. A boy came into view, late teens, probably only a bit younger than Grey. He was covered from head to toe in a knit-together patchwork of quilts, clothes, tents, dishcloths, and more. It appeared as though he'd taken every available scrap of cloth and sewn it together. He held forward a makeshift spear, more like a couple of fishing poles tied up to a tree branch with a blade secured to the end.

He remained silent, just huffing and pointing his weapon.

"I'm Naim."

"And I'm Kaia."

His spear remained outstretched at them.

"What's your name?" Kaia asked.

"Ondeck."

"Hi, Ondeck," Naim said. "We're just here exploring. We won't hurt you. In fact, right now, we just want to go back the way we came."

Ondeck gripped his spear tighter. "Once, a long time ago, Milesprint came out here and met a person covered in purple goo. He touched the goo and came back to us. He told us where the body was, then got really sick and died. And because he died in this place, he couldn't be taken back to his home. I want to go back home someday, so you just stay away from me. If you want to go, then just go."

"Did you say purple goo?" Kaia asked.

"Yeah."

"Not a mist or a cloud?" Naim added.

"No. It was a purple slime. That's how everyone describes it."

"The Amaranthines need to stay warm…" Kaia said.

Naim nodded.

"Ondeck," Kaia said. "That person was a tribal, from a place called The Amaranthine District. They're our enemies, too."

Ondeck looked them over, tightening his grip on his spear. He sighed, expelling a cloud into the frigid atmosphere, and dropped his spear to his side.

Kaia remained clasped to Naim, but only because it was so cold. "Have you ever been to the cathedral, Ondeck?"

He shook his head.

"Evermore Park?" She tried. "The observatory?"

"No," he said. "We don't leave the Republic. It's all poison purple outside the cold parts. Isn't it?"

"It's not," Kaia said. "Lots of us live outside the Amaranthine District."

"How far does this street keep going?" Naim nodded further into the cold.

Ondeck twisted up his face. "The streets are weird. They changed when I left the Republic. I was just exploring, I guess. Will they change back?"

Naim chortled. "Eventually, but there's no telling when."

A thought occurred to Kaia. "Does the realm of the purple people, the tribals, touch the border of your Republic?"

Ondeck nodded.

Kaia looked up at Naim. They could both get what they wanted. A reconnaissance trip into Amaranthine would appease Ward, and the same trip could take Naim to his south pole. It could work. Naim nodded his understanding and smiled.

"We'll need to go back," Naim said. "Get some proper clothes."

"We've got lots of stuff you can wear back at home," Ondeck said.

"And say we bring four or five more people?" Kaia asked.

Ondeck bobbed his head up and down. "Hmm. Sure. Should be fine."

"We'll be back," Naim said. "Thank you."

Ondeck saluted, two fingers drawn up to his eyebrows. Unsure whether to return the gesture, Naim and Kaia both nodded and smiled, then turned.

"Uh, hey!" Ondeck shouted.

They turned their heads.

"We're really cold," Naim said.

"Sure, but, um, can I come with you? I want to see these other normal people for myself."

Kaia smiled her consent to Naim. He smiled back.

"Sure," Kaia said. "Come on then."

Ondeck took up position beside them, still holding the fishing pole spear at his side. Kaia and Naim headed quickly northward, teeth chattering, back toward warmth.

Altruistic

I swab the scrape on the side of Fero's face with gauze and disinfectant. He flinches.

"Hold still."

He winces and holds his head steady while I wipe down the rest.

"Perhaps you shouldn't be using Grey's skateboard until you find a helmet," I suggest.

Fero's eyes flutter open and he looks up at me with a stern smile. "Grey says helmets are for pussies."

"Oh, really?" I stand up, cross my arms and lock my eyes onto Grey, who stands near the entrance to the observatory, just across the room. He scratches his head and looks up toward the ceiling. "Well?" I shout to him.

Grey drops his arms. "Hey Fero!"

Fero turns around on the cot. "Yeah?"

"No more skateboarding 'til you find a helmet."

"Aww man. Seriously?"

"Seriously," I say.

He turns back to me, his smile inverted.

I lean down and whisper. "Grey will still think you're cool if you wear a helmet. He just doesn't want to admit it."

"Really?" Fero whispers back.

"Really."

"Okay."

"Let's keep your brains in your head, shall we? I can fix a few scratches, but I don't want to see you come in here with anything worse, okay?"

"'K." He jumps off the cot, runs over to Mario, Grey, and his sister, and they exit out the main observatory entrance. The big, metal double doors shut with a resounding clang. Our seven cots lie empty. Big boxes of medical supplies sit in the corner, disused, alongside a tall stack of cots. At one time, we'd set out all twenty of them.

"Sometimes I kind of miss the old days." Sez stands at my side. She's a young woman, perhaps in her twenties. She wears overalls and holds a wrench. She used to help me run our makeshift clinic, still does really, but recently she's had much more time to play with the telescope's guts, her real passion. Today, she's covered in oil. Must have been down in the basement.

"I don't miss the old days." I frown. We had more patients than we could handle, and every day badly injured newcomers would tell stories of arrivals getting converted by the tribals. "I don't miss people getting hurt."

"I miss feeling useful." Sez turns the wrench around in her hand. "I miss helping people."

"Well." I turn to her. "You could come to the cathedral with me sometime. Help push for non-aggression."

Sez holds up her hands. "I'm not sure the result would be non-aggression."

We both laugh a bit at that. She's right. Her attempts at diplomacy with Ward have all ended in catastrophic failure.

"Have you got it working yet?" I nod up to the door that leads upstairs to her loft, where the big telescope sits.

Sez furrows her brow. "Not sure. I thought I'd finally gotten it yesterday…"

"But?"

She puts her hands on her hips. "Well, first I tested it on a point on the horizon, and that seemed to work just fine, so I turned it up at the sky. But no matter what magnification setting I use, I get the same image. I mean, it's like the sky is the same swirling pattern at any distance from City's surface. But that doesn't make any sense."

The shifting streets story is weirder, honestly. "You've heard about the philosopher, right?"

"Naim?"

"Mm hmm. He's making two maps of City. One he calls City-as-

Usual, and there's another one. Same City, different configuration of streets. All the same buildings, too, but mixed up. He says that City's randomly flipping between them. Grey and Mario say they've seen it, too. Have you ever seen anything like that?"

Sez frowns and shakes her head.

"Didn't think so." I take a glance around the empty observatory. Our voices have been echoing in the enormous chamber, the observatory's auditorium before Ward helped us rip out all the chairs. "I better get back to the cathedral."

Sez salutes. "Roger. Give Ward hell for me."

Thinking of Ward makes me smile. "Will do."

Sez turns and walks to the far door at the back of the room, probably going to work on the telescope again. I head across the room and out the main entrance. City's ambient luminescence blasts my face. I shield my eyes as I walk down the tall stack of observatory steps. The moment my feet hit the sidewalk, I notice it. The street is not the same.

I turn and look down it, straight in both directions, all the way to the horizon. I gasp and stumble sideways into a street light pole. I catch myself just in time, nearly hitting my head.

I wonder—did I do this? Does mentioning Naim or City-as-Grid make it real? If so, what a terrible power to have. It makes me wonder about Kaia as well. Is her role in this something more sinister than the annoyed significant other, dragged along for Naim's crazy ride?

I don't like being suspicious, but as I gaze around—to the nearby clothing store and restaurant, each of which I know to be across town in different directions, now adjacent to the observatory—I can't help but wonder about them.

No. They want to help. I can tell it the moment I look at someone. Even Grey. I mean, yes, he's completely immature, but deep down, he doesn't like seeing people get hurt. Now that new arrival woman, Karr, and the scientist Taum, those two are cold inside. They could let people get hurt, and if they saw some good in it, they'd have no problem letting it happen. They just *feel* different when I look at them.

I spend a lot of time doing that. I listen to myself, inside, when I interact with people. I'm not always right, but I've practiced it enough now that I'm usually close.

I take a deep breath, grasping the pole a little harder for strength, let go, turn myself around—

I let out a yelp and jump back. But it's only Mia.

She stands next to me, her arm outstretched, but she's flinching away now, looking vacantly and dejectedly at the ground.

"Mia." I shake my head at my insensitivity. "I'm so sorry."

"Oh no," Mia says forlornly. "I shouldn't have snuck up on you like that. But the streets changed, and I saw you there, and I—"

"There's really no need to apologize."

Mia is looking sadder than usual. She's had a rough time of it. She dropped into a delusion involving her family shortly after arriving here, which she carried on for a month or more. She finally showed up one day at the cathedral, scared out of her mind. We gave her all the help we could, but really, we're not equipped for psychological trauma. Ward himself could really use more than my care. He told me the story of his sister once and bawled for minutes afterward. Just hair-raising.

Mia still gazes absently beyond me.

"Mia?"

Her eyes jolt to me. "Sorry. I was just— It's so hard to explain, Aria."

"You don't have to explain to me. Life in City is hard. Would you like to walk with me to the cathedral?"

Mia frowns and looks away vacantly again. She clasps her hands behind her back.

I put a hand on her shoulder, and her eyes dart back to me. I give her my warmest smile.

"Actually," Mia says, gently and deliberately, "if you have time, I'd like you to come back to my house with me."

Two feelings hit me at once. My common sense says I should be scared. But my knowledge of Mia combined with her current state of mind and comportment tell me something different. She's not tearing herself up over how she might treat me when we get to her house—she's tearing herself up over how I'll treat her. She's worried I'll betray or belittle her fragile emotional state if she opens up to me. I've seen that often enough to recognize it.

I could be wrong, but I'm rarely wrong about these things.

I nod. "Alright."

Mia turns and leads the way.

I quirk my head. "You know how to get to your house with the streets like this?"

Mia nods vigorously.

"So, you've seen the streets change?"

"Only once, actually."

"Then how do you—?"

Mia bites her lip and walks faster.

She takes me down Sixth Street until the cross street reads Negative Fifty-Eighth Avenue. We turn down that road and the avenue numbers began descending. By the road called Zero, I am grimacing at just how dingy, cragged and disused all of these new streets are. The ones I'm used to are well maintained, though I've never seen maintenance people, of course. These roads are awful. We dodge asphalt detritus and potholes, and the sidewalks bulge and dip, contorted, even torn up in places.

Mia steps gracefully around an upturned sewer grating, and still I follow.

"Here we are," Mia says, sounding almost like she did when we first met and she was still holding herself together with delusion.

She pushes open the door to her modest little two-story home with white siding. A rocking chair on the porch creaks back and forth, stirred to life by a passing breeze.

We both enter.

I scan the surroundings. Everything appears to be in order. Good. If she'd let the place go, that would have been all I would have needed to bolt for the door and run for my life. But Mia has swept, vacuumed, kept the bookshelves in order, even arranged a bouquet and vase on the side table in the front hall. She has maintained her sanity, clearly. Then why is she so worked up about my reaction?

Mia takes me to the kitchen.

The linoleum table is littered with sketch pad papers, torn at the top edge from her sketchbook. Charcoal portraits of some moderate skill depict people, three of them in particular, repeated over and over, each with a different pose and facial expression. Without a doubt, these are her husband and children.

I smile. "You took my advice."

Mia smiles too. "I did. You can't imagine. It feels so good to think about them. I'm sad. But I can keep the sadness in me now. I don't need to pretend to talk to Mary anymore. God."

I wrap an arm around her. "It's okay, Mia. It's alright. I'm sure they're fine. They miss you too, but they'll be okay."

She sniffles and wipes away errant tears.

I turn, grasp her shoulders, and hold her at arm's length. I look her over. There's something else. She's still *worried.*

"Mia…?"

"Yes?"

"What aren't you telling me?"

"This way."

Mia takes me through the other kitchen door into the dining room and flicks on a light switch. The chandelier on the ceiling erupts with luminance, casting its light over an enormous piece of paper stretched over the living room table. Upon its surface lie two circular splotches, each one filling half the table.

I move closer and inspect the splotches. Far from homogenous blobs of graphite gray, I can make out intricate lines. Within the left circle, the lines weave and twist, turning every which way. Small rectangles lie against the lines, filling the interstices entirely. All except one spot. A giant blob in the lower right section is a mess of graphite, as though Mia had jammed the side of a pencil into that area and smeared the tip every which way.

The other circle is much the same, with the same awful, blurred mess in its lower right region. It also contains the little rectangles, but on this one, the lines are straight and intersect one another at right angles. The edges distort that of course. The vertical lines bulge out around the equator. But…

I look up at Mia. "You drew this?"

Mia nods.

"How…?"

Mia bites her lip.

"Really, Mia, it's okay."

Mia exhales, hangs her head, turns it a few times, looks up. "I thought you might get angry."

"Why would I get angry?"

Mia throws up her arms. "I was 'seeing' Mary, wasn't I? Oh, Aria. You have no idea just how people *look* at you once you go and admit something like that. And now I've gone and done *this*…"

"These are maps, right? Of the two street configurations."

"I was just doing what you and Yessel said. In the morning I would draw my husband, at noon I would draw my daughter, and in the evening my son. I went to the cathedral once a week too, just like you told me."

I nod. She insisted on staying in her house, and we told her as long as she visited us once a week to check in, that would be fine. I remember her visiting four days ago, right on time.

"And then!" Mia puts her hands on her hips. "And then three days ago, I woke up, and instead of drawing my husband, I— I—"

She lifts her hands to her face. I put a hand on her shoulder and wait for her to stop sobbing. I tell her it's all right many times, and finally she regains her composure.

"And I went to the art store, and I picked up the enormous paper roll, and I carried it home, and I just started… drawing… this. I don't know, Aria. I don't know what's happening to me anymore. Why does City have to do this to me? Why?"

I hug her. It's all I can do. I look over her shoulder at the two maps of City. It's really quite amazing. A complete map. Naim is going to blow a gasket. I smile at that. If this map ends his little quest to understand City's true nature, it might just save his and Kaia's relationship.

"Am I still crazy?" Mia mumbles.

"No more than the rest of us," I say.

I release her, and Mia wipes away tears anew.

"Where's the cathedral on here?" I point to the grid map.

Mia points to it.

"Join me for a trip."

Mia smiles, quite genuinely. "Yes, I think that would do me some good. Oh, Aria. You're such a good friend. I don't know what I would do without you."

"Don't mention it."

Mia leads the way out of her house.

The streets are, indeed, still a grid. This sudden alteration of something so crucial to City's structure fascinates me. I wonder how long it lasts? I think of Ward, and suddenly I worry. He's been so adamant that City does not change. I wonder if he'll believe me.

"Do you know what causes the streets to change?" I ask.

Mia shakes her head. "I just drew the map. I don't even know how I did that. I remember thinking in the middle of it that I should stop and think about my family, but I just kept drawing that damned map. Oh, you really have no idea how worried I've been about showing it to anyone. If the streets hadn't gone and changed, I might never have. That's what got me out of the house, by the way. I was biting my nails, and I was pacing, and I went to the window, and I saw the street had potholes and only two lanes. I recognized it immediately. I ran for your clinic, actually. I don't know how I knew where it was, I just knew. It was so good to find you there. Oh, it feels so good to be able to say this!"

She goes on for some time. I nod and occasionally recast back to her. It's understandable. She's naturally loquacious and has been bottling all this up for three days, from the sound of it.

I smile when I spot the steeple of the cathedral peeking out at a bent angle over the horizon.

"Almost there," Mia says. She breathes in and out. "I'm not sure I've ever noticed before how fresh the air is in City. No pollution at all. Am I right?"

"I think so."

We enter the cathedral, and Mia hugs me once more.

"I'm going to get some food and water." Mia nods in the direction of the cloister. "Thank you, Aria."

I smile. "I'll come see you in a few hours. Will you be back at home?"

"I think so, yes."

I'll work her up to showing Yessel the map, next a few other trustworthy people, and then it'll be Naim and Kaia's turn. I'll enjoy that. I've felt sorry for Kaia recently. Naim's clearly been driving her nuts.

And speak of the devil. The cathedral doors open inward and the couple enters. Naim's upset to be here, of course. He's opposed to organized religion on ethical grounds. He avoids talking to members of the Collective and stands moping by the door.

Kaia spots me and approaches, her expression morphing from exasperation to solemn fortitude.

"Are you all set?" I ask. No need to admit that I almost didn't make it here on time either.

Kaia nods.

Ward is already talking to Yessel near the barricade of cushions before the apse. I smile at him, and he smiles back. Oh, Ward. You have no idea just how crucial you are to all this tenuous stability. If only you wouldn't try to undermine it. Affection is affection and work is work. I should really learn to separate the two. My biggest strength and my biggest flaw. Just like Ward.

Yessel begins by asking us about the state of City. I give my report of the clinic. Nothing exciting. Ward goes next and starts in on the numbers of The Collective versus the supposed numbers of The Amaranthines. This, of course, gets Kaia's goat and they begin to argue.

My eyes lock with Yessel's while they go at it.

We have an unspoken language, he and I. We observe the same things about people. And about each other. So we don't really have to say anything. Just smirks. I wonder if he too has to remind himself not to be condescending? That was my biggest failing as a young person. It's hard to imagine Yessel doing that.

Finally, Kaia loses her temper and says something typically snarky of her. I can see Ward's rage start to boil over, so I put a hand on his shoulder. "Isn't it enough that we can hold our own against the tribals and prevent their numbers from growing?"

Yessel nods at me.

We'll keep this place together. Somehow. For everyone in City. As long as it's the four of us, and as long as I can talk Ward down from his anger and moderate his worst impulses, everything should be fine.

I keep my worry locked away. I dare not show it. But I know. Deep down, I know. City does not stay the same. One day, one of us will go. And what will happen then, I wonder.

But I don't bother myself with that. I focus on today.

Sophomoric

((before))

"Got another one!" Bell shouts from behind the science building.

I throw my shovel into the snow and take off toward his voice. I'm sure my feet are sending up clouds of white powder behind me as I churn toward the red brick building across the quad.

I turn the corner, careening into the small, dreary courtyard between the science building and the wall. Bell stands with his face craned upward. I look up and spot a guy with blonde hair and blue eyes bulging out of his skull. He's on one of the little balconies against a window three stories up. He's looking around, probably confused and scared out of his mind.

I have a powerful flashback to my arrival in City—I appeared on the catwalk over the stage in the Republic's theater.

"Shit, Bell!" I punch him in the arm. "Why didn't you tell me?"

The guy up on the balcony twists himself around and yanks at the latch of the locked window behind him.

"Hold up!" Bell yells up at him, as I simultaneously shout for him to calm down.

"I'm going up there." I don't wait for Bell's reply. I sprint through the snow and back around to the front. I hit a slick patch of packed snow near the front and slide as I turn. I pull out of it and hurtle into the science building.

It's pretty dark inside. We leave the lights off in here. The lights and heating work great, but it smells. Makes for bad living quarters. And we don't have any need to study science. Chemistry was my second favorite subject before I came here.

I fly up the stairs two steps at a time. I alight the second floor, then the third, panting. In my haste and the multiple roundabouts of the stairs, I've forgotten which way I'm facing relative to everything outdoors. I pause, orient the turns of each staircase to the front door, then I've got it, and I take off down the hall, just as a jarring, metallic scraping and thumping signals my destination.

I hurry into the room and grope for the light switch. Illumination floods the space, emblazoning long, stone desks equipped with metallic spigots and glass beakers.

I run to the window where the new arrival is still yanking at the handle. He's shivering now, and his teeth are visibly chattering. I can hear Bell's muffled yelling below.

The window's old and crusty, but after flipping open two locks, I pull and the frame groans inward.

"C'mon." I hold out my hand.

Our eyes lock for a moment, and I can't help but smile. He's cute. His eyes are just… beautiful.

He's also scared out of his mind. He grabs my arm, and I help him through the window and inside. I shut and latch it behind him.

"Where am I?" he asks helplessly, still shivering.

"Welcome to the Republic of Fuckknowswhere."

He gulps. "Wha—?"

"Hold that question." I hurry to the wall, find the thermostat and turn it to its maximum setting. A clicking resounds from the far wall and a dull hum follows it.

"Why can't I remember my name?" he asks as I walk back toward him.

I bite my lip and shake my head. I've only had to do this once before. "No one does. We all showed up here, just like you did. But the Republic will take care of you. Don't worry about a thing."

"What's your name?" he asks.

"Ondeck."

He quirks his head. "What kind of name is that?"

"The kind of name you're going to get if we don't come up with something for you—"

"Windowdeck!" Bell announces from the room's entrance.

I swoop around and cast my evilest glare at him. "Seriously, Bell?"

He casts me a look.

I exhale in exasperation. "Close the door, already." I turn back to Window. Damn it, I'm already thinking that stupid name. It's too late. Even if we come up with something else, Bell will certainly declare the name at standup, and Ramrod likes him better, so there will be no help there either.

Window's rubbing his upper arms with his hands. He's got nice biceps. It's too bad we're going to have to cover him up in three or four layers of scrap cloth. He casts his eyes between us as Bell walks closer. Finally his eyes land on me, look me up and down. My blood rushes with excitement, but to my chagrin, he turns to Bell without a word. "How about you? What's your name?"

"I'm Bellsquare, but everyone calls me Bell. You know… 'Ondeck' and 'Windowdeck' are pretty similar." He tussles my hair. "That makes you two practically namebrothers."

I slap his hand away. "Quit it!"

"Geez."

"So, um," Window fidgets. "How'd I get here again?"

"No one knows," I say. "We're all just… here."

"Right now's the middle of an influx," Bell says. "Lots of guys showing up."

He casts a wry smile. "Any girls?"

Oh fuck me. Why are the cute ones always straight?

"Nope," Bell says. "Sorry to say, but the Republic's a big sausagefest. Not that Ondeck here minds that too much." He winks at me and I punch him again. He just continues. "All strapping young lads between the ages of fourteen and nineteen. Well, there are women outside of the Republic, but…"

The energy drains out the room. I shoot Bell a look. He can be so tactless sometimes, but even he's probably realized that he shouldn't have broached that topic of conversation.

"But what?" Window looks at us askance.

"They're purple," I say.

"What does that mean?"

"There's something not right with them. Their bodies are poisonous. It's not pretty. *Anyway—*"

I'm pretty sure I know where Bell is going, but I interrupt. I don't at all like the way Window's been looking at me since Bell implied about my orientation. "You should stay here for now, where it's warm. We'll bring back clothes after we're done with standup."

"Standup?"

"It's a daily thing," I explain. "Accountability and all."

Bell is looking at him sternly. "In case you're thinking of doing anything rash, I'd suggest against it. You won't survive very long without clothes, and even if the cold doesn't get you, those purple people will get you, so just don't. Trust me."

Window nods at us morosely. I notice a sheen of sweat has formed on my back. I'm starting to overheat in my three layers of rags. Bell probably is, too.

"We'll be back," I say, and we head out the door.

Once Bell and I are safely outside, he nudges me. "He's a cute one. I bet you two'll have a lot of fun together."

"Shut up, Bell."

His gaze turns hurt, then menacing as we clomp through the snow. Flakes fall around us, the neverending blizzard.

"Why you have to be like that? In case you can't tell, I'm kinda jealous. Stuck here for two years, not a girl in sight. Imagine what it's like for us, will you?"

This is too much. "And imagine what it's like for me knowing that all of these other guys are thinking of tits and pussies when I'm with them. Yeah, sure, it was fun at first. But I'm starting to feel like a sack of meat. Is it too much to ask that maybe one of these guys might actually like *me* for a change?"

"We're all friends in the Republic."

"I know. 'We all watch out for each other.'" And we trudge out into the frozen wilderness and scavenge for food from abandoned stores. And we spend our mornings shoveling. And our afternoons training. And our evenings fucking our brains out with whoever's horny enough to give it up for another guy.

I was going to go to college for linguistics once. No other languages here, or if there are, we're all being translated for each other's benefit. City even had the gall to bring the only half the campus of the university through. We've got the quad, the science building, the humanities building, where most of us live, the bell tower, the cafeteria, the mail room, and the administration building—but not the library. Oh no. City couldn't have me getting a glimpse of the life I'm missing out on.

It's funny. I was something of a loner early in high school. Had a couple of dates that I completely botched. Jerked a few guys off, nothing else. And now—oh now—I'm living a fantasy I'd played through in my head so many times before: living with a bunch of horny, hot straight guys so anxious to get off and deprived of female interaction that they'd settle for another guy. And here I am, victim of my dream come true.

Bell and I march into the plaza in front of the bell tower, right where Bell appeared, actually. He showed up in the same influx as me. I got here first, a day or so earlier. I brought him extra bread at dinner. He was one of the ones who wouldn't talk at first. Just clamped his mouth shut and shook his head yes and no. But I gave him food, and he opened up to me. We've been inseparable ever since.

Bell also happens to be one of the few guys here I've never done it with. Sometimes I think he likes to keep it that way. Sometimes I think he feels I'm keeping him at a distance. I'm never sure with him.

Underneath the giant bell, atop a platform made of torn-up milk crates, stands Glorious Ramrod. "Is that everyone?" he shouts to us.

A few are called out as missing, but I look around and can see them running to join us. All in all we number thirty-four. Thirty-five now with Window.

"Let's get started," Glorious Ramrod announces. He's not particularly good looking, or particularly strong, or particularly smart. I wonder how he came to lead the Republic. He doesn't actually have a ramrod. It's a euphemism for things more carnal. Most accept his advances. And I've heard he always takes the dominant position.

He doesn't force anyone though. And he's strict about making sure that everything's consensual. The few times that someone has complained that they were taken by force, Glorious Ramrod made the perpetrator spend a night naked and alone in the unheated cafeteria building with only a single blanket. Glorious Ramrod always talks about how sex should be as fun as it can be, given our unfortunate circumstances. And that's exactly how he's made it, which is good to a point, I suppose.

Standup begins, and Glorious Ramrod goes first, talking about the food he scavenged with his party yesterday and his work to retrofit the windows in the humanities building to provide better insulation. He motions to Snowface, who stands next to him, and he begins talking about the next bed he's building.

We go around like that, each of us talking about what we did yesterday and what we're planning on working on today.

Glorious Ramrod says it keeps us honest with each other, so we can apply social pressure to anyone who's not doing their share. Seems fair enough, I guess.

Suddenly, I realize Bell is speaking. "We've got another new arrival. We've got him holed up in the science building. He needs clothes."

"What's his name?" Glorious Ramrod asks.

"Windowdeck," I say. All eyes turn to me.

Glorious Ramrod widens his eyes at me. "Is he cute?"

"I guess."

Glorious Ramrod winces.

"Oh, he's cute," Bell says. Glorious Ramrod's eyes grow wide. I want to curl up and die. No, I want to curl up in a warm room with a good book. I want to have a husband of ten years who will come to my side, kiss my forehead, and whisper in my ear that I'm special. I want away from the pathetic sham of a university, of a city, this frigid excuse for debauchery.

"Well," Glorious Ramrod says, "get him some clothes and show him around the campus."

And so shall the hazing begin.

Glorious Ramrod calls an end to standup, and our group disperses.

I find my legs taking me away from Bell and past the science building.

"Hey!" Bell shouts. "Where you going? Who's going to help me take care of Window?"

"I'll be back in a bit."

"Shit, Ondeck. Are you really going to make me do all this alone?"

I'm nearly to the gates.

"I said I'll be back," I shout over my shoulder.

It's too much.

I push open the rusty, screeching brown gates. Its metal grating leaves concentric arcs in the snow, which I pommel my feet through as I run out onto the street—

The street!

I look down the street. All the way down. It's become a straight line. I can actually see to the horizon. Besides the university, where an empty motel should sit, lie huge frozen piles of metal and cardboard and plastic bags topped with snow. Some kind of trash dump. Wait a minute. I've seen that before, about half a mile away from the Republic. Bell and I went exploring in the direction away from where the purple people live. But it had grown even colder, well below freezing, and darker too, so we'd turned back before too long.

The monuments of rubbish are nearly as tall as our Republic's buildings. Why hadn't I seen them peeking out from over the top of the walls?

Exploring could be dangerous. What if the purple people are somehow closer to the Republic now? I look at my footprints and follow them back to the half-open gates. I grimace and stride forward down the new street.

"Ow!" I shout out.

Pain flares through my foot. I rub at it, rather ineffectively, since about six layers of cloth, gloves, and boots lie between them. Scanning my eyes over the road, I realize that there are shallow indentations in the snow. Those must be potholes. And the bulges must be rocks or other detritus. The layer of white has softened the details.

The stories of Milesprint's death assault my memory alongside a gust of wind. I pull the strings of my hoodie tighter and run for the far wall of the university.

I kneel before the red brick at the very corner of the wall and brush away the snow. My hands shuffle about until they land on the long, thin thing that Treeclimb put here. He refuses to go anywhere outside the Republic's walls without a weapon. He was with Milesprint when he died. I wasn't here for that. It happened before my time, but Treeclimb, who's been here almost as long as Glorious Ramrod, does. Few people talk about it, except to tell new arrivals what's what.

I pick up the spear, a cobbled together mess of fishing pole, tree limb, and butcher's knife. It'll do.

I set off down the road anew, dodging bumps and holes in the pavement. The first intersection I come to is a right angle. I'm not sure I've seen a right-angled intersection in City before. That street, too, goes to the horizon, which sends shivers down my spine even though I'm not in the least cold. I grip my spear tighter.

Before setting off, my eye catches a dingy sign atop a lamppost at the far corner. The sign is topped with a small tower of snow, but it's legible. I'm at the intersection of Negative Twenty-Third Avenue and Negative Ninety-Second Street.

I scoff at the idiotic numbers and continue down this supposedly negative avenue.

Part of my brain tells me I should head back to the Republic, that I've had my fun, that every step I take increases my risk of meeting a purple person, or worse, a group of them. But I continue on. There's nothing for me in the Republic, and I've known that for a while. I should be home right now. I should be studying. I should be meeting real people, genuine people, not building igloo forts with a bunch of juvenile delinquents who can imagine nothing more stimulating for their free time than getting their jollies off.

By Negative Eighty-Seventh street, I notice that the falling snow has diminished, and the depressions and bulges in the layer of snow on the ground are getting more pronounced.

I gulp, grip my spear tighter, and continue onward.

I want away from this. I want away from this so bad. Milesprint didn't know any better. He touched the dead purple person. Would the ones I run into be dead or alive? He said it was naked, too. They won't survive long in the cold like that. Maybe they've learned what clothes are by now. If they're even human at all.

Negative Seventy-Eighth Street passes and the snowfall has ceased completely. Patches of white dot the ground, and the plunking of water dripping down drains fills my ears. My boots trudge through brown-black slush.

By Negative Seventy-Third Street my layers are starting to feel gritty, restrictive and gross. I'm starting to sweat.

Voices reach my ear, and I duck into an alley.

Two people stride into view, shivering—a man and a woman. Older, too. They're in their late twenties at least, probably early thirties. They're gripping each other for warmth, and the woman seems anxious. I catch something about going back. The two of them stop.

I don't see any purple about them.

Did Milesprint know? Was the body dead when he found it, or did it keel over from the cold and turn purple when the person died? All I know is, these people can't be from anywhere near the Republic. Our little enclave is too perpetually cold for t-shirts and jeans. They came from somewhere else. I can't decide which evidence to believe—the fact that they are not purple or the fact that they are not the right age and one of them is not the right sex. The only people who show up normal in City are males between fourteen and nineteen and they show up within our walls or nearby.

I gather up all my courage, and with beleaguered steps, hold my spear out before me and march out of the alley. I approach the huddled couple from behind.

I am about to speak, when I hear the woman. She whispers, but I hear her clearly: "I love you," she tells the man.

"I love you, too," he hugs her tightly.

I stand there, holding the spear, fear and courage mixing with dejection, that awful despair at seeing this very human, very frail, very tender thing which I can only dream of. That thing I can't have, because I'm all alone. Alone in a degenerate world run by teenagers, who, unlike me, have no aspirations whatsoever. If these two are purple, so be it. I'll accept my lot. But they're not purple. I know it, because their words feel so genuine and real. Nothing monstrous could speak like that to another human being. Not without—

I stand tall and tighten my grip on my spear.

"Do not move!" I shout in my most confident voice. I'm not sure I believe myself. I am really just a stupid kid, not so much unlike all those others, I guess.

The couple turns around to face me, and I brace myself for whatever my fate may be.

City is Intractable

(( ))

Humans on some planes occasionally develop this notion that art needs to describe what is "real" in order to be genuine. This ideological position invariably fails. It lasts a little longer on some planes of existence than others, but it does fail.

Take the multicosm itself. Infinite possibility spreads itself outward, encompassing every quantum shift for every particle in all of existence. Even the organisms that inhabit quantum space itself strain to understand it all.

And humanity occasionally develops the gall to think that it can describe, let alone define, what is "real."

Take away one layer of reality, and another, equally complex layer will present itself. These layers go on endlessly, just as the scientist can peel back layer after layer of physics, and the philosopher can delve ever deeper into the infinite depths of the human psyche.

The most successful human artists are those who accept the inherent, paradoxical dualism of real and unreal. It is from within that paradox that anything approaching truth actually exists.

Never presume to know all of City. The moment you stop and think there is a Collective here and an Amaranthine District there, is the moment you've reduced City to an overly simplistic and false representation of itself.

Humans are, if nothing, incredibly resilient. They can survive and thrive under even the most adverse of conditions. Even at City's periphery lives brilliant complexity, awaiting its catalyst.

Contemplative

((after))

Gwei sat in the garden, staring at Aria's grave. It was a slab of concrete (no other stone had been readily available; a quarry at the terminus of File-mot Way had abruptly vanished), and so upturned concrete was the best they'd been able to do. Ward had carved her City name into it himself. His hands had bled afterward.

Gwei had still been very new to City at the time, had no stomach for blood, and so had looked away. Sez had mended him.

She looked down at herself now, sitting cross-legged. What to make of all this?

She tilted her head back until she faced the sky.

Naim had found something there, but what? After all this time, she really had no idea. Bolt was here. Newcomers would come and they would have to be taught. It never ended. Nothing ever changed. The Collective that Aria and Ward had started was in ruins, and no one remaining was able to pick up the pieces and start over. Ward himself was a wreck. And here lay Aria.

Gwei looked down at herself again.

Could she really trust her thoughts anymore? What had she become? She still felt like herself. The slab of concrete still looked like a slab of concrete. The grass still looked green. City's gentle breezes still brought her a feeling of comfort and refreshment.

And yet, something else.

The edges of the tombstone felt inarticulate, somehow. The dome of the observatory behind her felt too round, too bulky. Her own body felt both familiar and firm, and yet inflexible and unwieldy, as though she were a teenager all over again, except that she knew she wasn't.

Looking at herself now was worse than when Ward had been covered in his own blood, dripping from his gaping hand wound. The tower of a man had stumbled and fallen, bleeding in more ways than the physical.

There's no patching this up, she thought as she looked at herself.

"I wish I could have known you," Gwei told the grave. "Of all the people in City I've heard of, you're the one person I'd want at my side right now. The ironic thing is, you got shot because you were brave. You protected Ward right to the very end—"

"Gwei?"

Gwei turned her head. Sez stood at the open back door of the observatory.

"I need a minute," Gwei called out. She turned back around, but she knew Sez was lingering there. Gwei knew what she was thinking, too. Sez didn't trust her anymore. No one would trust her now. Maybe not even Bolt.

Perhaps that was why she found such comfort in the thought of Aria. If Aria were here, she would see past this. She would see that Gwei was still herself inside. That it hadn't wrecked her.

But deep down, she wasn't sure she really did trust herself.

The dome of the observatory was too round. What did that even mean? How could a dome be too round? It was bleak and sterile, less than perfection. Perfection was as dynamic as chaos with an equal measure of order. Th'dome was anything but.

Gwei gulped.

"Help me," she whispered to the tomb.

She rose, and with a hobbling gait, meandered back toward the observatory. Halfway there, Sez appeared at the door and held it open for her.

"How are you feeling?"

"Fine," Gwei shot back, more harshly than she'd intended. She lowered her voice and softened her tone. "I feel fine. How's Bolt?"

"We can both go see."

Gwei followed Sez up the stairwell leading away from the door, unable to take her eyes off the dual armbands on Sez's wrists. Two of them. Just in case Gwei managed to rip one off. Another reminder of what everyone would now suspect she'd become capable of. She wouldn't ask, of course, "are you feeling like you want to murder me?" just, "how are you feeling?"

Sez probably wasn't even aware that she'd asked it three times in the last hour.

They continued upward along the edge of the dome, past the door to the auditorium clinic, further on up, toward the loft. The stairwell led them right up into the ceiling, where Sez pushed open a hatch, and the two of them stepped up into the loft.

Bolt lay on Sez's bed, his head wrapped in bandages.

He let out a slight groan and turned himself over.

Gwei ran to his side. This was the first she'd seen him move since bringing him here.

His eyes opened all at once, bleary and red.

"Gwei?"

"I'm here Bolt."

"Are you okay?"

Gwei smiled. This was probably the last time she'd ever hear that question genuinely asked. "I'm… I'll be fine."

"Did we get the bracelets?"

"Five. We got five."

He blinked a few times. "There's something you're not telling me."

She saw his eyes try to focus, and instinctively shoved her hands behind her back, but she was too late. Bolt jumped in his bed, then moaned and fell back onto the sheets and closed his eyes.

Sez ran to his side. "You're still hurt. You need to stay still."

"Gwei!" He roared, his eyes still closed. "What happened? What'd those bastards do to you?"

Tears streaming down her face, Gwei held her hands out before her. Purple miasma licked at the tips of her left fingers, but proceeded no further down her hand. That was the wrist with the bracelet. On her right arm, the purple mist proceeded from her fingers down her forearm, until it nearly touched her elbow. Living, purple tattoos danced across her skin, though they remained relegated to the affected regions of her body.

And there were her feet too. The purple burst out from her shoes angrily, as though trying to rip itself free of her clothing. Oddly enough, there were th'moments in which she felt compelled to strip naked, for no reason other than that it felt wholly unnatural to be wearing anything at all. But shortly after such bouts, she invariably told herself that that was insane.

"What'd they do to you? Gwei?!" Bolt lurched upward and Sez leapt, tackling him back to the bed. Bolt's closed eyes streamed tears and Gwei's lips opened and closed, wordlessly. Her mind felt a million miles away from her body.

"Gwei!" Sez roared.

"I don't know exactly. Somehow, when that tribal was trying to tear the armband off, it must have come off partway and... my left fingers... my right arm... and my feet."

Bolt opened his red eyes, calmly, and Sez drew away from him.

"Are you...?" Bolt blinked a few times. "Is there a way to fix that?"

Gwei shook her head and gulped. "I don't know."

"Gwei..." Bolt shook his head. "I'm sorry."

Gwei took two strong steps forward and found herself kneeling, grabbing Bolt's hands without hesitation. Bolt didn't flinch. Instead he looked into her eyes.

"You saved my life," Gwei said. "Thank you."

He lay back down. He took a deep breath in, his broad chest rising high, then expelled the air. "How long do I have to stay like this?"

Sez shrugged at Gwei.

"We don't have a doctor anymore," Gwei admitted. "That was Aria."

"So you don't know."

"No," Sez said.

"What do we do next?"

"You're going to rest a while. I'm going to talk to Yessel. He might know where Grey has gone. He's kind of an idiot, but I trust him more than Ward at this point."

A small rumble shook the building. The desk near the window shuddered against the floor. Bolt's bed slid toward the wall in stuttering jumps. All at once, the quake ceased. Sez half-stumbled, half-ran to the enormous telescope, her brow furrowed, and ran around to its far side.

"I thought you said that City doesn't usually get earthquakes," Bolt said.

"I did," Gwei replied.

Bolt spoke between spasms, each momentarily locking up his throat. "You and Yessel said something about City being messed up. Maybe the quakes—?"

"I'll ask Yessel about it." Gwei walked to the far end of the room and opened the hatch in the floor. "I'll be back."

She tried to make eye contact with Bolt, but found her eyes straying from his face. She hurried down the stairs, toward the main floor, where she exited into the empty, dark space with domed walls. Cots sat in stacks or lay overturned. Boxes of medical supplies were mostly stacked against the near wall, but many lay open, their contents exposed, in some cases strewn about the floor.

Gwei tried to imagine the space as it had been months ago, as the newly-formed Collective had struggled to bring some semblance of order and community to the haphazard existence that was life in City.

A look at her hands told her that such a form of order was just as futile as the order implied by th'thoughts most bizarre seething within the recesses of her mind.

She strode across the empty room, her footfalls echoing throughout the eerie space. She put her hand on the metallic bar that opened the building's entrance doors.

"Gwei!"

She turned. Sez stood at the far end of the room, gazing across the vacant clinic. She put one hand on her hip, and walked toward her. When she'd come within a meter of Gwei, she halted and let out a long sigh. "You're not going to the cathedral, are you?"

"Of course I am."

"Gwei. Bolt might buy that, but I wish you'd give me more credit. You probably can't even get within a block of the cathedral with your hands and feet like that."

Gwei took a deep breath. "I'm going back to the Amaranthine District. If I meet Grey along the way, all the better. He can get a bracelet."

"They'll completely convert you."

Gwei let out a small empty laugh and held out her hands. "You think I want to go on like *this*? I can already feel it, Sez. In the back of my mind there's this little voice whispering to me. And not just that. I see everything… it's like everything has two forms. The way I've always seen it, and a new way. I think… did you know we seem like children to them? We call them tribals because they go around naked, but they call us barbarians because we can't see the world the way they do. They think those tattoos are *better* than clothes. And that mist is powerful. Whatever it is, it's so incredibly powerful, but it's got th'mind of its own, and it doesn't care about humans. I think maybe it did once, but now it only cares about itself—"

Gwei registered how Sez was looking at her, with narrowed, fearful eyes, and Gwei clamped her mouth shut.

"Why did you say, 'it's got *the* mind of its own?'"

Gwei blinked. "I didn't say that… I said 'a mind of its own,' didn't I?"

"No. You said 'the.'"

"Definite Incarnate…" Gwei whispered.

"Look, Gwei." Sez reached out toward Gwei's shoulder. "Maybe you better stay here. I've got bracelets, and I'm strong enough to— Just in case—"

Gwei pulled away. "No, really, Sez. I need to do this."

"I insist."

"No!" Without thinking, Gwei extended her right arm, cupped her fingers, and watched as the miasma formed into a puffy, purple pistol.

Sez shrieked and jumped backward, nearly stumbling over herself, then scrambled away toward the far stairwell.

Gwei flooded with revulsion and tried to throw the disgusting thing away, but the contraption merely evaporated into purple smoke, which took up its former position, wafting to and fro about her arm.

"Sez, wait, I—"

The door across the room slammed shut with a resounding clang, sealing Sez in the stairwell on the other side.

Gwei gulped, turned, bit her lip, and pushed the exit doors open. Bright light assaulted her eyes. She held her arm up over them as she walked down the steps, one at a time. As she stepped down the last, another rumbling sounded, and the ground shook beneath her feet so violently that she had to grab the metal handrail to steady herself.

It lasted only a moment, and Gwei took a few deep breaths.

City had never felt so empty, and she had never felt so alone. Not even after Naim had left.

She blinked a few times.

Something about the memory of Naim.

The purple, which she could feel in her mind, didn't like her thinking about him. Angry with it, she thought of him again. She thought of how they'd met, how he'd taken her to meet Yessel, how he'd introduced her to Ward and Grey and Mario and the twins and—

A migraine shot through her forehead, down into both eyes and back across her scalp. She held her head with her free hand, still steadying herself against the handrail with the other.

Okay. Fine. She wouldn't think of Naim.

She took a deep breath, pushed off the handrail, and hobbled away down the street. Grid again. Th'damned-grid. But she remembered what Naim had told her—a brief shock of pain from invoking the thought's source—that in both City configurations, the Amaranthine District stays in the same place. The grid makes it even easier to get there, so long as you know where it is.

No drugs this time, she thought. *I'll walk right through the purple and give them a piece of my mind.*

Two blocks, three blocks, four blocks.

Still empty.

Part of her wished that she would run into someone, even if they did react with horror. She was pretty sure she wasn't coming back from the Amaranthine District, not as herself. It would be nice to have one last interaction with someone human, as a human. It would be nice to know she wasn't so far gone.

Another earthquake rumbled through the terrain, this one weaker. Gwei steadied herself and took a few steps forward, but something at the far corner of the intersection caught her eye—a bright green light.

Whatever it was, it lay in the middle of the sidewalk, right in front of the curb, and it was shaped like a rock, about the size of her fist, definitely rock-shaped though, and it was radiating neon-green light so bright that it was difficult to look at.

Gwei approached it, peered down at it, and tilted her head, not sure what to make of the thing.

She scanned her environment, spotted a normal rock of about the same size, picked it up, and tossed it at the green one. It tumbled across the sidewalk, bouncing and clattering, and then—

It contacted the green glow and simply vanished.

The green glow hadn't moved in the slightest either.

Gwei furrowed her brow.

She scanned the buildings—a hardware store, a high-rise, a four-star hotel, aha! She spotted a hovel across the street.

Gwei ran to it, and leveraged all her strength to pry a piece of wood from its dilapidated exterior. It popped off the dilapidated exterior with a hollow crunch. Plank in hand, she returned to the green rock and gently lowered the center of the plank onto the green. Upon contact, the plank wrenched violently to one side; Gwei released it and scurried backward all at once.

She scrambled up and scurried carefully forward to observe what had happened. Two pieces of the plank lay on the ground, broken through the center. The edges of the break were smooth, though. Far too smooth. And they matched the contour of the shape of the neon green rock.

Another earthquake struck, and this one rumbled stronger than the last. Gwei spotted nothing to use as a support, and tumbled down to her hands and knees before she could think to run for cover. The buildings rattled, their interiors tumbling and shattering and exploding. A sound like a shriek erupted from behind her, and Gwei turned. To her horror, the left half of the hovel behind her split open before her eyes and began oozing the same bright green light as the rock. She turned and noticed the same had happened to the lamp post across the intersection, which now sported an enormous green gash.

The earthquake subsided.

Gwei picked herself up, and, gasping and afraid, burst into a sprint.

Purple miasma, destructive green light. It was too much.

She raced down the streets, faster and faster, spotting more incidents of the green light as she ran—a window here, a planter there. Small pieces of City, not just destroyed, but utterly negated with each quake. Yessel had said that something felt wrong. City had changed fundamentally, and not for the better.

And damn it, the catalyst had probably been Naim's stupid departure.

Pain shot through her head.

"Will you stop that?!" she shouted at no one in particular.

"Gwei?" The voice sounded from down the street.

She ground to a stop, and turned toward it. Grey stood half a block away from the intersection she stood in. She looked him over. His shirt hung limply from his baggy jeans, which were falling further down him than usual. Sadness was smeared across his face. He looked like he'd given up. And he'd never admit it, but he was probably scared out of his mind, too.

"Grey!" she called out, her voice lay somewhere between excited and apprehensive.

She ran until she was within ten meters of him, his eyes growing wider and wider as she approached, moving to her hands, then her feet, then finally back to her face. She came to a halt, maintaining the precarious distance.

He took a few careful steps toward her. "What happened to you?"

"We got bracelets out of the scientist's laboratory." She dug into her pockets, produced the last of the bracelets, and threw the ring down the street toward him. "Put that on before you get anywhere near me."

"Is this one of those bracelets the Collective was goin' on about? I thought those things were whack."

"I turned them back on. It'll make you immune to the District."

"How do I know you're not tryin' to trick me?"

"Am I talking like a tribal?"

"No."

"Am I trying to kill you?"

"I dunno. Are you?"

"Very funny. Put on the bracelet."

Grey picked it up and ran his fingers over it. Gwei crossed her arms. "We don't have all day."

Grey nodded at a nearby car, the left half of which was erupting green light. "Think I can't see that? That is some fucked up shit. I'm gettin' pretty sick of tryin' to keep up with all of City's disorders, is all I'm sayin'."

Gwei chuckled. For the first time since she'd met him, the words flowing from his mouth seemed somehow apt.

Grey slipped the bracelet on and looked at his arm, twisting it around a few times. "Don't feel anything."

"You won't."

He walked slowly toward her. "Better keep me safe."

"It'll keep you safe from that purple mist. Now, the tribals themselves, that's another matter." She held up her right arm. "That's how this happened. C'mon."

"You know how to get there?" Grey threw his skateboard down, jumped atop it, rode only a few feet, then ground to a halt and looked around. "Oh shit. The streets changed."

Gwei quirked her head. "They've been this way."

"No," Grey said. "Not 'til you showed up."

They continued down the street.

"You sure?"

"Sure as you got purple hands."

She shot him a nasty look.

"Well, you do."

Gwei rolled her eyes and they continued in silence.

A question struck Gwei, so she voiced it. "What were you planning on doing when you got to Amaranthine?"

"Demand they give Fero and Hyra back."

"Subtle."

"You have a better idea?"

"Nope. My plan's worse. I'm going to try to bargain with them."

Grey trundled along beside her in silence. Then after some time, "Gwei?"

"Yeah?"

"What's that green shit?" He sounded deeply and genuinely scared. "Do you know? Have you ever heard of anything like that?"

"No," Gwei said quietly.

Grey remained silent. He seemed to jerk forward in uneven fits and starts on his board after that.

The streets passed on, empty and silent. The swirling blue sky hung above them, casting down its omnipresent light. Gwei wanted to shout up to it for Naim to undo whatever he did, wherever he was. This wasn't fair to the rest of them. City was bad enough already.

Grey ground to a halt and pointed forward without a word.

Purple mist, in the distance, just four blocks away. And inside that mist stood two figures, too distant to make out, but from their heights…

Without thinking, Gwei reached out and grabbed Grey's arm.

"Get offa me!" He threw her hand away. He broke into a sprint, letting his skateboard clatter to the ground.

Gwei followed after, shouting his name.

"You bastards!" Grey shouted. "You did it! You bastards!"

Two more figures stepped out of the mist, adults, standing alongside the two tribal children.

Grey reached the edge of the purple mist, which licked at their heels as it contorted the asphalt beneath their feet. Gwei followed just behind him, running as fast as she could to keep up.

Grey dropped to his knees before the two children. "Guys… You remember me, right?"

"Don't worry, Grey," Fero said. "We have Th'Home now."

The girl put her hand on her brother's shoulder.

Fero continued excitedly. "If you take off that armband, you can join us. You'll understand it. It's amazing, to be th'—"

"Definite-Incarnate." Gwei spoke the words in unison with him, though the boy garbled the term.

The two adult tribals looked between one another, then turned to Gwei. Grey kept his face to the ground, his back jolting up and down.

The female tribal spoke, staring with her blank purple eyes into Gwei's. "How do you know of Th'Definite-Incarnate?"

Gwei snarled and held up her purple-shrouded hands.

"Interesting," the tribal man said.

A new woman emerged from the mist, very tall, and she walked with extreme precision, even barefoot. She put her hands on the siblings' shoulders. "These are Tyr and Vall now. You shall not use their false names."

Grey shot to a stance. "I'll call them whatever the fuck I want! Fero and Hyra! Fero and Hyra! That's their fucking names!"

The twins shrieked and fell to the ground, the purple tearing itself away from them, taking pieces of their skin with it.

"What have you done to them?!" Grey shouted.

The tall woman stepped forward and glared down at him. "It is what you have done, you miscreant fool! Invoke their false names and they lose th'power bestowed them by th'luster. Do not do so again."

Slowly, the purple wisps receded back toward the twins, and they huffed and panted and convulsed intermittently. Drops of their blood fell to the pavement where they crouched. Grey fell to his knees and reached out to the twins. "Guys…"

Another quake struck, this one even stronger than the last. Everyone standing wobbled on their feet and struggled to steady themselves. A crack tore through the nearby pavement, erupting green, and—Gwei gasped—a gap opened up in a twisted amalgam of metal pipes covered in purple miasma—on the Amaranthine side. It turned green, too.

The quake stopped, but Gwei held her gaze on the Amaranthine construct with the green fissure in its surface. She turned to the tall Amaranthine woman with a broad smile. "It seems you and the rest of the City actually share a problem."

The tall woman bit her lip. "Yes. It is the only reason we are not converting you at this very moment."

"You want to work together, then?" Gwei tried.

The woman stood taller and glared down at Gwei with her full-purple eyes. "You will refer to me as Th'Resplendent Adema, or th'leader of Th'Home. That is 'th'Amaranthine-District' in your imprecise nomenclature."

"Just call me Gwei. And if you can get this purple…" She took a deep breath. "Luster off of me, I'll do whatever I can to help you stop the… green light."

"We will talk more inside Th'Home," Adema said.

"No," Grey said. "Here."

"*You* will speak no further," Adema shot down at him.

"No deal," Gwei said.

"Sorry?" Adema had turned her lips down into an incredulous frown.

"I'll go with you if you bring the rest of the bracelets from the gone-away scientist's lab, give them to Grey, and send him off safely with them."

Grey grabbed her shoulder. "Are you fucking serious?!"

"Yes, Grey, I'm *fucking* serious."

She turned up to Adema. Her scowl had grown deeper, probably hating both Gwei's demand and the fact that she had been forced to agree with Grey.

Gwei met her empty stare coldly and firmly. "I'll walk. I don't mind. I don't know whether I can be taken back home or not now, so sure, I'll disappear in a green flare of non-existence. Why not?"

Adema let out a scoff and began tracing lines on her forearm. Momentarily, she stopped, stood and stared.

They all stood silently, all except Fero and Hyra, who busied themselves rubbing purple mist into the wounds all over their bodies.

"Well?" Gwei asked.

Adema held up a finger, scowling imperiously.

Two or three uncomfortable minutes later a new tribal man appeared, carrying a cardboard box whose edges twisted and warped under the influence of the luster. He handed the box to Grey, who looked at it with a snarl and then grabbed it up.

Gwei took a step toward him. "Is it—?"

"Yeah," Grey said. "Bracelets."

"How many?"

"I dunno."

"Guess."

"Maybe twenty."

Gwei turned to Adema. "I go with you when he's safely beyond th'luster."

The tribals all shot each other curious glances, all except for Fero and Hyra, who shuffled uncomfortably still.

"You sure…?" Grey readjusted his grip on the box.

"Go."

Grey shrugged. "Hope you know what you're doing." He turned and looked at the twins dejectedly. "Guys?"

The twins made a point of looking away from him as they rubbed more purple into their gaping wounds.

Grey slouched, turned and walked away, his back receding down Negative Twentieth Avenue. When he'd gone safely beyond its limits, Gwei turned back to the tribals.

"What now?" she asked.

"Come with us," Adema said. She and her entourage turned on their heels and entered the miasma fully.

Gwei took a deep breath, summoned up every iota of courage she possessed, and followed them into Th'Home.

Methodical

((after))

I feel the sharp warning buzz hit my hip, the little twinge that tells me I'm dying.

They're coming more frequently, now. I don't know how many days have passed since I've been without maintenance. I stopped counting weeks ago. Probably three, four, five months. We're not supposed to go more than forty days. It said so in the manual. Not that I read the whole thing. No one does.

I run halfway back up the stairwell towards my loft, where Bolt lies unconscious. I'm not worried about him quite yet. I look downward to where Gwei would appear if she opened the door to come inside. I'd hear that. I couldn't not hear that.

I take a deep breath, pull up my arm, and activate the holographic display.

Neurological enhancement systems have reached Stage II failure.
Automatic shutdown in 09:32.

The seconds tick away, little green numbers hovering in the air: thirty-one, thirty, twenty-nine, twenty-eight...

I activate the repair routine, which eats up some tiny fraction of a percent of my energy stores. But after a hundred days or more those minute fractions have begun to add up. About a week ago, I finally dropped into a single digit percentage on biocell life, and I haven't looked at the number since.

Although, what's more horrible, I wonder? Watching it tick down and knowing when depletion will occur, or trying to initiate the repair routine one day to discover that it doesn't work? No, the worst part will be the inevitable, painful rejection of my synthetic biosystems. Unless I am pulled away.

Or…

No. I don't like to indulge in that possibility anymore. After so many months, the likelihood of it happening is so remote.

I break a smile. Maybe it's just the tingle running up my spine as nanites fuse metallic strands to my nervous system making me giddy, but I decide to indulge in the thoughts once more. Ever since I got here, I've had my internal computer system ping wireless traffic. I wrote a program to search for medical control systems similar to the ones from my home. The idea is that, if a medical facility from my world were to show up here, I could at least recharge my biocells, and maybe even effect more permanent repairs.

But City is so random. It hasn't happened for months, and the more time that passes, the less likely such an occurrence seems.

I keep the communication system active regardless. Sometimes I wonder how many days of my life that decision represents. To think that my life can now be measured in organic battery power has come to make me nauseous whenever I think about it.

I remember, at home, there was a political group. I can't remember their name, of course. They were against cybernetic enhancement ideologically. We used to laugh about them at work. Some people even whispered words like "moralizers," or worse, "degenerates." I myself never uttered such words, never judged them that harshly, but I admitted privately to my husband that I found their logic flawed and their position absurd.

Were I to return now, I'd happily have my implants torn out and join their ranks.

How many days of life have I traded for the certainty that real help never arrived?

I should never have had to make the trade.

I should never have put myself in this position.

But then, that hardly would have been a rational decision before: 'Well, I better not fill my body with enhancement technology. I might be whisked off against my will to a deranged City-sphere that doesn't have proper medical infrastructure!'

For some reason or another, Gwei jumps to the forefront of my mind. I couldn't believe it when I saw her. There she was, Bolt passed out against the wall of some building, both of them battered and bruised, blood everywhere, but all I could look at was the purple on her hands and feet. That awful, awful purple.

In the depths of my mind, I sometimes wonder whether becoming a tribal would prevent biosystem rejection. And that thought fills me so thoroughly with repulsion that I want to wretch. I'd rather be dead than monstrous.

But then I think back to a week ago, and I can't help but wonder to myself if I'm not monstrous already.

I turn off the computer and lower my wrist. The holographic display fades and the metallic portion of my forearm shimmers and takes on the holographic appearance of skin.

I walk down the stairs, very slowly, and upon reaching the bottom, gaze out the small window in the door. Gwei is sitting, hands in her lap, in front of Aria's tombstone.

Very slowly, I push the door open.

"Gwei?" I call out.

She hesitates, winces, turns.

"I need a minute," Gwei calls back.

My tone is flat. I wonder if she thinks I'm repulsed by her predicament. In a sense, I am. But it's not her. It's me. It's these thoughts churning through my mind that I can't reconcile.

Sometime soon, I am going to die.

What about my husband? And my daughter? Will they ever know what happened to me? What are they doing now? Will they be okay? I want my daughter to have a mother. I don't want to die here. I don't want to become a tribal. And if they could see me these last few months—

Gwei interrupts my thoughts. She stands, turns, and walks to me. I motion for her to come inside.

"How are you feeling?" I ask, to keep from thinking about how I feel.

"Fine," Gwei shoots back defensively. Ah, right. She's worried about the Amaranthine miasma. Of course. If only she knew about me. If only I could tell her. We have much more in common than she thinks.

Gwei takes a deep breath and seems to regain her composure. "I feel fine. How's Bolt?"

Not good, I think. "We can both go see."

I motion up the stairs and we clank upwards toward the observatory loft. The sound of our footfalls echoes inside the empty passageway.

Finally, we come to the top. I throw open the door and we climb inside. Bolt lies on the bed. This man is a mess. Barely a day in City and already he's gotten himself attacked by Amaranthines and a nasty blow to the head. He's pretty bad. I'm no doctor, but I'd bet good money he's got worse than a concussion. He needs the kind of help I used to give when Aria was still here.

No. It was before Aria left, wasn't it? I still remember that first time. I beat myself up so badly over that. Still am beating myself up, I guess, now that the twins have gone missing, presumably captured by tribals.

God help me.

Gwei runs to Bolt's side, and he actually stirs. She forgets her hands, though. They talk about bracelets. Bolt senses there is something amiss. I can see it in his eyes. It won't do him any good to know about Gwei's condition, so I stride across the room and put my hand on his shoulder. "You're still hurt, you need to rest."

That's when I know that he's seen the purple. She pulls her hands behind her back, but even so, she can't hide her feet. I'm not sure what she thinks she'll accomplish.

"Gwei!" He roars. "What happened? What'd those bastards do to you? What'd they do to you? Gwei?!"

He lurches upward, and I grab onto him and hold him down.

Shit. Shit, shit, shit. I shouldn't be able to hold him down. I shouldn't be strong enough, not without my enhanced musculature, but I do it on instinct and now I'm wondering if they'll notice. I'm holding him down, and it's all I can concentrate on through the worry that they will notice that I'm pinning to my bed a man twice my size.

I'm not sure how much they say to one another, but after what seems like an eternity of worry, Bolt's eyes go calm and he falls back into his pillow, and I pull back.

More moments pass. I feel dizzy and my vision is blurry. All I can think of is that I have to keep up the act for these two. If anyone were to find out about the implants— I won't stand anyone's pity. I won't have any of it.

Gwei turns to me with a questioning look on her face. I have no idea what the question is, so I shrug.

"We don't have a doctor anymore," Gwei says. "That was Aria."

"So you don't know," Bolt says in my general direction.

"No," I say. I'm still not sure what the context is, but it seems like the right answer. My thoughts instantly drift elsewhere, away from the conversation.

They're interrupted by an earthquake. The telescope rattles, and tables judder against the floor. The bed even rumbles slightly beneath Bolt's weight.

My breathing has increased, and my heart is pounding out of my chest, so I take the opportunity to run to the telescope, just as the earthquake subsides. It's an enormous contraption that fills more than half the room, its lens opening up through a hole in the ceiling. I dart to the far side of its giant base, throw my back against the cold metal and work to steady my breathing.

Gwei and Bolt's conversation is distant noise.

Why'd they have to invoke Aria? Why? But then, why had I insisted she be buried here? I wanted the reminder. I wanted the memory of failure to haunt me. If my husband and daughter knew, they'd be ashamed of me... God, he was just a boy...

I push the thoughts away, and wipe my eyes.

I walk back around from behind the telescope and discover Gwei is no longer here. I hadn't even heard the door close...

"Bolt?"

"Yeah?"

"Where'd Gwei go?"

"You didn't hear?"

"Sorry. I had to fix the telescope. Where did she go?"

"She says she's going to see Yessel, but I think she's going to the Amaranthine District. Sez?"

"Yes?"

"I'm dying, aren't I?"

I stare. I don't blink.

"It's okay," he says. "You can tell me."

I have to say something to this. If I say nothing, he will think not only that it's true—and it might be; I have no idea—but worse, I would be awful for letting him give up hope. For letting him think that I think that he doesn't matter. For letting him think that there's a little timer inside him counting down numbers, little arbitrary symbols whose only signification is the inevitable breakdown of his bodily functions.

"I don't know." My voice is a whisper.

"Go to Gwei," Bolt says. "Help her."

I throw open the hatch and race downstairs. Let him think I went to go talk to Gwei. I couldn't stand to be in that room. But I know, even as I clatter down the steps, that I can't escape the real source of my anxiety—myself.

I throw open the door from the stairwell into the disheveled central auditorium. Gwei stands at the far end, just before the front entrance. I shout her name, and she pauses, turns. She looks sad, weary, and most of all scared. I gulp and walk across the room as casually as I know how. Inside my own mind, I am screaming.

I stop. We stand face to face. Her eyes are bulging, and she's practically hyperventilating.

"You're not going to the cathedral, are you?" I whisper.

"Of course I am." She's looking over my shoulder.

"Gwei. Bolt might buy that, but I wish you'd give me more credit. You probably can't even get within a block of the cathedral with your hands and feet like that."

Gwei lets out an exasperated sigh. "I'm going back to the Amaranthine District. If I meet Grey along the way, all the better. He can get a bracelet."

So much for logic. "They'll convert you," I try, but at this point I've basically given up on her. That's what I do, isn't it? Give up on people.

Gwei begins speaking, her eyes growing more frantic, and my thoughts become distant from the conversation. What is happening to me? I am not this callous. I'm not. I can't be. I'm a good person. A decent person. I also have a little timer inside me that's counting down to my death. My death is imminent. I'm going to die. Painfully. In horrific, unrelenting pain. And Gwei is worried about purple.

Fine. I decide it then. I'll take her upstairs and I'll heal Bolt thus ending my own life. But would that scar them? What would that do to them? How would Bolt react?

I refocus on my attention on Gwei. She is talking to me after all. "Whatever this stuff is, it's so incredibly powerful, but it's got th'mind of its own, and it doesn't care about humans. I think maybe it did once, but now it only cares about itself—"

Gwei clamps her jaw shut, and is breathing even harder now.

I blink a few times. "Why did you say 'it's got *the* mind of its own?'"

"I didn't say that… I said 'a mind of its own,' didn't I?"

"No. You said 'the.'"

"Definite Incarnate…" She gets a faraway look on her face.

"Look, Gwei." I reach out toward Gwei's arm. "Maybe you better stay here. I've got bracelets, and I'm strong enough to— Just in case—"

"No, really, Sez." She jerks away from me. "I need to do this."

"I insist."

"No!"

The purple around her arms flows into currents, coalesces around her outstretched fingers, and resolves into the shape of a pistol.

Fear strikes me like a knife in my back. I turn and scramble away from her as fast as my legs will take me. I throw open the far door of the auditorium, throw myself inside, and slam the door behind me.

I slide to the floor and I weep. I don't even know who I'm weeping for anymore—myself, or Bolt, or Gwei, or Fero, or all of us, trapped in this damned City against our will. Of all the people to stop with, why Fero? Why did I have to choose him?

I pull myself to a stance, supporting myself against the door. I pull it open a crack. Gwei is gone, of course. I could have guessed that, but I had to be sure.

I shut the door and clamber up the stairwell, wiping away tears. I decide I will put on my best performance for Bolt, but in order to do that, I will need to know. I will need to really know.

I activate the computer screen in my arm and take a deep breath. My finger hesitates over the button for the biocell activity panel. I jab it, and the window maximizes.

1.87%

That's… three or four days? Certainly not more than a week.

At least now I know.

It won't be a surprise.

I turn off the screen and proceed the rest of the way up the stairs. I push the door to the loft open and climb inside. Bolt is lying on his side, his eyes wide open and red, his head wrapped in white linens, a red-stained white, now more of a brown-black.

He raises an arm, wobbling, and points. "It happened just after you left."

Protruding from the center of flipped-open trapdoor is a… something. It shimmers neon green light and hurts my eyes. It's shaped vaguely like a cartridge. Yes, like one of the energy cartridges for the telescope, about the size of my fist.

I pull up the door, slowly, and to my surprise, the green thing stays on the floor, while the door moves through it. It's then I realize that my door now has a cartridge-shaped hole in it.

"What the—?"

"Something's wrong with City." Bolt's voice is weak. "It was Naim."

I turn slowly around and look into his eyes, quivering, bloodshot, fearful.

"I don't know how I know. I think, maybe… I've just been his replacement since I got here. But I'm no good. Not after the things I've done. The ways I've failed. But because it was him and then me, in the same spot, I can tell. He screwed things up. Bad. People aren't supposed to leave City like he did. The purple was bad. It hurts City. But City could handle a little bit of purple. But now there's green, and it's getting worse and worse. Too fast. It's too much. City's—"

He looks up at me. His eyes are so empty.

"I love her."

"Wha—"

I sit down on the floor and look at him. There's something else in his eyes now. A kind of deep sympathy and regret.

"I love her."

"Gwei?"

He nods.

"You've… you've just met her, haven't you?"

He nods and smiles. "Doesn't matter. It was like that with my wife. I was young. It took me longer to figure it out. But I knew right away. Are you married?"

"Yes."

"Did you know right away?"

"Not exactly. I… kind of put up a fight."

"But if you hadn't wanted to fight?"

I smile a bit. It's so good to think about him in that light. First meeting him. God, I was obnoxious in my twenties. "Yeah, I think I see what you mean."

"I need to help her," Bolt said. "I just know that I can't anymore. I've gone and gotten myself bashed in the head, and now, when she needs me by her side the most, I'm helpless."

"You'd go running after her then? To the Amaranthine District?"

"Yes."

"Even knowing what they'll do to you?"

"She needs me there. Because of what Naim did and because of what I am—the Naim substitute. I know it."

He's going to get himself killed. I fill with such awful emotions. How could I possibly give up my own life for someone I know is going to run off and get himself killed? I could be whisked away. The ping could find a facility. He's insane. His plan is absolutely insane.

But then… 1.87%. What the hell kind of chance is that? If I'm going to die anyway… but for a guy who's babbling about loving a woman he hardly knows, who clearly doesn't care nearly as much about himself as he does about her? It's insane!

"Sez?"

"Yes, Bolt?"

"Is something on your mind? You seem distracted."

"I'm—" I stare at him. I'm not sure how to finish that sentence, is what I am.

"What?" he asks gently.

"I'm going to tell a story, if that's alright."

"Okay…" he seems hesitant, but he must also realize he's a captive audience.

"So, once…" My heart is beating so fast. "There was once this woman. She received a bunch of bio-organic computer implants. Now, on her world, this is all perfectly normal. She gets maintenance every month, and her model can run just fine without maintenance for a month and a half. If she needs to go on a long trip, or something like that, and she takes some basic supplies with her, she can extend that to six months. But one day, she finds herself whisked off against her will to a strange place where there are no medical facilities and she has no basic supplies. Just the clothes she was wearing when she was taken."

"So…" Bolt says slowly. "She has a month and a half to live?"

I shake my head. "Not exactly. See, she's fairly good with a computer, and hers can control little molecular repair cells that can be programmed, so she jerry rigs a bio-organic lattice into place and that keeps her alive for about four months."

"But…?" Bolt asks.

I take a deep breath. "But those repair cells use a lot of energy. She eats as much as she can and she gets a lot of sleep, but in the end, every time she activates those cells, her body is getting closer and closer…" Could she actually say it? "To complete rejection of the synthetic systems."

Bolt's voice is a whisper. "That sounds like it would be incredibly painful. And scary."

"It would be. But I haven't told you the worst part."

He lets out a small laugh that's more like a yelp. "There's a worse part?"

I nod in stutters. "You see, this woman somehow found herself helping a doctor run a clinic. And the doctor was good, but without proper equipment and supplies, there was only so much the doctor could do. Now, the woman with the bio-organic systems, no one knows it, but those biocells aren't just capable of healing her. They can leave her body and heal other people, too."

"I'll bet that takes a lot of energy," Bolt says.

"Oh, it does. Now, at first her energy stores were at ninety percent, then eighty, then seventy, but there were so many people crying out in pain, bleeding, and here she was, sitting on a massive technological advantage. She helped every last one of them. Every last one!"

"That was very noble of her."

"Not noble." My voice is harsher than I intend it, and I work to calm myself. "She showed her true colors in time." My eyes are tearing up. "One day, she woke up to discover that her biocell fuel reserves had dropped below ten percent capacity. Below ten percent. It was easy to help when she had so much energy, but in that moment— She didn't realize it, but something within her changed.

"Later that day, the doctor arrived, and there were no patients. They had grown few and far between. It was just the two of them. They talked and talked. The woman with the implants nearly forgot about her low biocell charge.

"And then a boy showed up. He had been playing with a skateboard, and had fallen and hit his head. The woman with the implants thought to herself, 'He's only a boy, and it's not a severe injury. He'll heal on his own with time.'"

Bolt's stare was agony. "And did he?"

"She thinks so, but…" Tears streamed down her face. She bit her fist, momentarily. "He disappeared, and she doesn't know, and if he's a tribal, then she can't tell him— She can't apologize, not that any apology would—"

"I don't think it's fair of the woman—"

"Point zero zero two percent."

"Sorry?"

"The amount of her biocell fuel she would have had to expend to help him. His wellbeing wasn't worth a few minutes of her life. It's so easy for us to talk about nobility and decency when we sit in comfort, but when it really matters, we're selfish creatures through and through."

I am gushing tears, sobbing.

I pull my wrist up and activate the computer.

Bolt's eyes widen. "Sez… what are you doing?"

"Help Gwei. Don't blame yourself for this. And if it's possible, I want my husband and my daughter to know what happened to me, and that I love them."

Bolt is scrambling off the bed as best he's able, but he's falling over himself to crawl across the room toward me. Another quake judders the room, making it harder for him to crawl and for me to type. My computer interface stutters with the shaking.

"And tell Fero I'm sorry. Please."

"Sez!"

The 1.87% of biocell fuel drops to zero. I see a holographic image of Bolt's head. I see reports of biocells staunching hemorrhages and tissue resealing and the carvings of bone fragments sizzling into nothing and the construction of scar tissue.

A pain grows in my spine and shoots up my neck. I topple to the floor and shriek. This is agony. Horrible agony through all my limbs and my chest and my head and my skin burn.

Please God. I did my best.

I am—

Indignant

((after))

"Why do you think he did th'thing so stupid?" Brother asks.

I roll my eyes. "Who knows why th'adults do th'things they do."

We walk down th'corridors of Th'Moderate, our new home. We haven't quite learned th'ways yet. All th'passages twist and turn, and they're made of th'things most strange. Th'typewriter here, th'paint-can there. All this stuff. It's ugly in th'City, because everything's th'discord. But here it's beautiful.

"Sister?"

"Yeah?"

"What would you do if Th'Brethren-Bright told you to hurt me?"

I shoot him th'stare most pointed. "Why would they do that?"

"What if they did? Maybe you'd become th'traitor, too. Or wouldn't you?"

"Let's not talk about th'stupid-things. Okay?"

"Sure."

We walk further down th'hall and come to th'door to th'chamber-hallways of Th'Dim-Caliginous-Somber. We enter, we turn, and we groan.

Th'line to witness th'traitor stretches down th'whole-hallway. We can't even see th'end.

"What did he do again?" I ask Sister.

"Th'More-Lustrous gave him th'order, and he failed to obey it."

I narrow my eyes at her. Th'things don't add up. But... I don't want to talk about them here. Th'adults in th'line in th'front of us would hear. I draw th'message on my arm with th'luster: "Th'Bright are our More-Lustrous, right?"

She nods.

I continue writing. "Yesterday, Th'Bright Prell told me to brush my teeth after th'dinner, and I forgot. Does that make me th'traitor?"

She looks at my arm, scans th'text, and then slaps it away. Almost immediately, she pulls my arm back up and rubs at it until th'words are erased. She huffs and begins writing on her own arm. I tap my toes against th'floor.

Eventually, she extends her arm. "No one cares if you forget to do th'little-thing once in a while. Th'Resplendent told th'traitor to kill th'barbarians in th'lab, and he didn't, and now th'barbarians are running around with th'bracelets."

I write back. "Think one of them is Grey?"

She slaps my arm away again, and th'luster stings my mind in th'same-moment.

We stand in line for many of th'minutes longer. Th'line moves forward at th'pace of th'snail. Th'brethren who walk by, those who have finished with th'traitor are of th'two-kinds: th'angry and th'upset.

I don't like this ritual with th'traitor. Brother seems to think it's all th'game. He thinks most things are th'game. Nothing serious for him. I want to take th'life more seriously. Else we'll end up like our mother.

Brother thinks that Grey is like our father, but I know better. Th'father was always there for us. Grey might be th'man, but he is much more like our mother. It's because of Grey that we're here.

We like being here, th'luster reminds me.

I agree.

Eventually, we can see th'door to th'chamber of th'traitor. We grow close to it. Finally, we stand before it. It opens. Th'pair of th'women leaves, cursing most foul. They spot my brother first, and shut their mouths when they do. They stalk off, leaving us to shuffle into th'room.

Th'room is so dark. There is almost none of th'luster here. It is uncomfortable. Th'shivers run down my spine. Brother has th'gross-look on his face, like he ate th'grapefruit, his least favorite food. Our father loves th'grapefruit, and I think it's alright, but Brother hates it.

We walk toward th'bed where th'traitor lies. He's th'adult, but he's curled up in th'ball like th'child.

He is silent.

"What do we do?" Brother asks.

I shrug.

We stand in silence. Th'eerie-icky-silence.

I poke th'leg of th'traitor with my finger.

Sister reaches out and slaps my hand.

Th'traitor giggles and we both jump back.

His giggle turns into th'laughter most strong.

"Shh!" Sister puts her finger in th'front of her lips and shushes him as loud as she can. "Are you trying to get us in th'trouble?"

He returns to th'giggling. "No. No, I'm sorry. It was just too… funny."

I realize he's looking at me. His face was buried in his legs before. His eyes look so sad, even though they're just purple. I realize I've never been that sad before. The worst was when I fell off th'slide in th'second-grade and hit my head and had to get th'stitches. That hurt so bad. I was sad for th'day. I think I played on th'slide again th'next-day.

Th'traitor looks like he'll be sad for th'very-long-time.

"What happened?" Sister asks.

"I would not kill," th'traitor says.

"Why were you supposed to kill?" I ask.

He shakes his head. "I don't know."

Sister quirks her head. "You were Th'In-ca-des-ent, right?"

"Yes."

She furrows her brow. "Who was your More-Lustrous?"

His voice is a whisper. "Th'Resplendent."

Sister bites her lip.

I open my mouth. "Th'Resplendent Adema ordered you—" Sister grabs my arm and shakes her head back and forth at me with th'wild-wide-eyes. I finish my question with th'whisper. "—to kill?"

He nods his head up and down.

We both gulp.

"We should go," I say, adding in my own mind, *before Brother can ask another of th'questions most stupid.* But he actually looks th'bit scared himself.

We back out of th'room. Th'trio of th'men wait. They look very angry. I worry for th'traitor, but I can do nothing. We hurry away past th'long-line and down th'hall and back to th'safety of Th'Moderate halls, where th'luster is much thicker.

We walk for th'long-time without thinking of where we're going. We cannot enter th'doors that lead into th'halls of Th'Bright, but Th'Moderate have very many of th'halls, and we are still learning all th'ways.

I wonder what Grey is doing right now. Is he sad? Does he miss us? I think that if he were to feel th'luster, then we could be together again, and we could have th'fun again. And th'luster agrees. Th'luster would love to have Grey here, too. I trust th'luster. It feels right.

"What do you think Grey is doing right now?" I ask Sister as we walk th'halls. We're alone.

"I don't know, and I don't really care. I never really liked him."

I sigh, feeling exasperated. I knew as much. "Why not?"

"He only cared about himself."

"That's not true!"

She stops, twists my arm. "He's not like Dad! It's 'cause of him—"

I yank my arm away. We both stare at each other. I know how she wanted to finish that sentence. Th'luster is pinching my mind uncomfortably, but I can feel th'end of that sentence without her saying it: *It's because of him we're in this place where they spit at you and call you th'traitor if you won't kill for them.*

But it's way better than being th'barbarian. We'll grow old with our new family, we won't be taken away, and we have th'luster. We are th— th'Def-nit-In—. Whatever th'adults call it.

Sister flinches and shakes her arm. I feel th'tingle in mine, too. I raise up my forearm and watch as th'luster forms into th'letters on my skin.

Th'Moderate Tyr and Th'Moderate Vall: Report to Th'Central-Corridor immediately. Your presence is required for th'acquisition-training of th'new-brethren.

           — *Th'Bright Argio*

I turn to Sister. "Th'acquisition-training?"

She looks confused, too. Then her eyes brighten. "Remember when we first came to Th'Home? There was that woman. She helped us feel better and showed us th'halls."

"Wait. *We're* supposed to do that? For someone else?"

Sister shrugs.

We go back down th'hall th'way we came.

My mind fills with th'doubt. Brother and I can't help th'new-brethren. We still are th'new-brethren. We've got, what, maybe two of th'days on this guy? Or th'girl. We won't know until we arrive.

And, I love my brother, but I don't know how he will help. He will probably say th'stupid-thing and upset th'new-brethren instead of making them feel better.

My arm tingles again.

"Now what?" Brother pulls up his arm.

I look at mine.

Th'new-order.

Now we are supposed to head outside and meet th'adults of Th'Bright by th'place where th'luster becomes th'street called Cesious Boulevard.

They can order us to kill and to go to th'place and then to th'other-place. Are th'adults stupid? Maybe the th'luster is making them stupid.

Ow!

That sting really hurts.

"You all right?" Brother asks.

"I'm fine."

We walk and walk, and finally come back to th'halls of Th'Dim and Th'Caliginous. We have to pass through their halls to get outside. We see th'line, still there, and decide to take th'long-way around it. It hurts to think of th'traitor, too, just not in th'same way as th'luster hurts when you think th'wrong-things.

Th'roof and th'walls fall away. We are outside.

We spot th'adults of Th'Bright. There are two of them, one of th'men and one of th'women.

They beckon us.

"Why were we called?" Brother asks, trying to sound tough. I think he probably sounds ridiculous to them.

"You are to stand at th'edge of th'luster," th'man says, "down this street, Cesious Boulevard, or whatever street it becomes—"

"Th'grid-streets?" Brother asks.

"Yes," th'woman says. "Stand at th'edge of th'luster and beckon to th'barbarians that arrive."

Brother and I exchange th'glances.

I look up at th'woman. "Will they arrive?"

"We believe so," th'man says.

"Will they hurt us?" I ask.

Th'man and th'woman share a smile. "We are sure they will not. You know them from before."

Brother's eyes light up. "Grey?"

I roll mine.

Th'man and th'woman nod. "Do you understand your task?"

"Yes."

"Good. Go."

They part, and we pass between them, out down th'street that has been shaped by th'luster. Like th'play-dough. Th'City is like th'putty to th'luster. It plays with Th'City like we play with th'blocks and th'clay.

We walk and walk.

"I'm tired of th'walking," I say.

"Almost there," Brother says excitedly.

I grab his arm, th'nasty-scowl certainly on my face. "He will hurt us. Again."

He yanks his arm away. "Shut up."

We walk in silence. We reach th'edge. Th'straight-street forms in front of us. Not Cesious Boulevard, but th'different-street.

Brother crosses his arms and pretends I'm not here. I wish he'd grow up and act his age.

I watch th'street. There's th'nothing at first. Just th'buildings, all gray, th'holes in th'pavement, th'abandoned-cars. There are no sounds. Th'light everywhere. Th'stupid-sky.

I miss our parents. So much.

Th'luster reminds me that I have th'new-parents now.

I tell th'luster to shut up and it pinches me again.

I love you, I tell it. I love you. Don't hurt me, please.

"There!" Brother shouts.

It's th'shadow in th'distance— two of th'shadows.

Th'one moves toward us very quickly.

"You bastards!" th'figure shouts. "I can't believe you did it! You bastards!"

Brother smiles. "Grey is back."

I level my sternest gaze at him, even though it never works. "He. Will. Hurt. Us."

Grey is at our feet.

We look at him.

Sister doesn't know how wonderful it will be. She'll see. Grey will be with us and we'll all have th'fun again. Just like before. He looks so sad right now. But once he gets th'luster, everything will be okay. Just like before.

City is Imminent

(( ))

You have seen the many faces of City.

You have seen its many wards, districts, boroughs, neighborhoods, nooks, crannies, coves and vales.

Purple and green wait for resolution.

Naim and Gwei wait for comprehension.

Kaia waits for absolution.

Bolt waits for redemption.

Taum waits for enlightenment.

All of City's inhabitants, strapped into immobility, not because of their physical limitations, but because of their emotional ties.

Who will be the first to overcome the hurdle?

Who will save City from its imminence?

City cannot help but continue.

City waits for nothing.

Divisive

((before))

Sirens blared.

"Street reconfiguration detected!"

Naim jerked to a stance. He looked to his side and smiled at Kaia. She returned only a wan smile.

"This is it." Naim tried to sound encouraging.

Kaia nodded slightly, still trying too hard to smile, stood, and pulled up her backpack. He pulled his own over his shoulders. Heavier than he'd expected, but he'd need the extra layers where they were going.

He led Kaia around to the front of Taum's complex, and just as he approached the entrance, Taum exited, riding a wheeled contraption upon which he stood. It made him just a hair taller than Karr, who strode out alongside him, obviously uncomfortable at having someone else loom over her for a change. The sight made Naim smile.

"So, we must get those others?" Karr adjusted her weight, obviously disliking her backpack. And seeing her in regular shoes instead of her high heels was another delight.

"Yes," Naim replied. "Let's get going."

He grew less and less sure with each change of the streets how long the interval of the grid configuration would be. And what would happen if a change occurred as they neared the south pole? None of the streets led there. Would they be trapped in that frigid region for days? He hoped that it wouldn't matter. The fold between the states, the ultimate comprehension of their predicament, the ability to leave or fix oneself, fix others, change the Amaranthine District, everything—it lay there, waiting.

They walked in silence.

It was clear that Taum and Karr had nothing they wanted to say to each other than Naim and Kaia would overhear. Naim wondered about Kaia's silence, though. Perhaps she also wished to keep her thoughts from the others.

"Is everything all right?" Naim asked her quietly.

"Why shouldn't it be?"

What an answer.

"I've found a way for us to be together. I thought you'd be happy."

Kaia gazed forward and picked up her pace.

It wouldn't be long now. They'd go into the pole together, and she'd see. Everyone would see. He'd figured it out, and soon no one would have to live under City's capricious heel anymore. No more worrying about being torn away from others' lives and minds.

Why couldn't he help Kaia see that?

Well, he could. He was about to. As long as she went with him, everything would be okay.

The cathedral appeared on the horizon.

He spotted Ward—hard to miss him—and Aria, too, sitting on the stone steps. Ward was tinkering with some contraption and Aria was talking to someone. Why weren't they getting ready?

"Hey!" Naim called out. "The streets have changed! Come on!"

Ward and Aria, and now he could see Ondeck and Yessel, too, all looked out across the street in sudden amazement.

Naim led his group to the base of the steps. "What's going on?"

"Naim!" Aria flinched, then made eye contact.

"Whoa!" Ward jolted. "Where'd you come from?"

Everyone turned and looked at Naim's little company. "I've been shouting for you guys…"

Kaia pulled up her backpack. "Let's get going."

Ward rubbed the back of his head. "Geez. Guess I owe you guys an apology about the street changes. I had no idea…"

"Wait," Kaia said. "Do you mean that you only *just* saw the streets change?"

"Yeah." Ondeck stepped forward, wearing shorts, a t-shirt, and tennis shoes. "Everything wobbled, and Claret Crossing kind of melted into this."

Karr cast a suspicious gaze over them. "Taum's lab detected the configuration at least five minutes ago."

"Maybe it spreads out from an origin point," Ondeck suggested. "Like a wave."

"Maybe…" Kaia furrowed her brow and turned to Naim.

He brought his hand to her hair. "It'll be fine. I don't think we'll ever fully understand the shifts, but we know where the two states collapse together."

She pulled away from him and retreated down the steps.

Naim sighed. "Who's in your investigation party, Ward?"

Ward took a step forward. "Myself, Kaia, Karr—"

Naim turned a confused gaze to Karr. "I thought you were coming with me and Kaia." He'd taken her for one who'd choose escape from City, not tribal infiltration.

Karr shook her head. "I wish to learn about the Amaranthines."

"And I," Taum pulled his miniature chariot up the edge of the stairs, "wish to go with you."

Naim filled with repulsive unease. He'd certainly not expected that either. He'd imagined Taum would want to oversee the use of his bracelets.

"Sure," Naim muttered.

"Good," Taum said. "Everyone, come get your bracelets. So long as you wear these, the tribals' purple mist cannot harm you."

The entourage crowded around Taum, who pulled bracelets from a compartment at the base of his mobile platform. Naim drifted toward him and procured one of his own. Just as his mind caught up with the present and he thought to ask for one for Kaia, she stepped up and took one from Taum herself. She walked away before Naim could say anything.

"Taum?" Naim asked.

"Yes?"

"Why…?"

"Why am I going with you to the pole?"

"Yes."

"Have you ever asked me what I think is at City's pole?"

"No."

"Because you think that I am uninterested. You think that your conception of God or moral perfection or whatever it is, is all that could be of any importance at such an intersection, and that I, a person of null philosophical sophistication, would find nothing of value there. Am I right?"

Naim kept his mouth sealed, and met the scientist's scowl.

"Perhaps," Taum said, "you should have engaged in less judgment and asked more questions."

Naim found himself pulled back as dozens more members of the Collective swarmed around Taum, grasping for bracelets. He pushed through the crowd and spotted Ward at the top of the stairs. "How many?" Naim asked.

Ward turned to him. "Twenty-four. Most of the Collective's adults."

"I thought—" Naim gulped. "I thought this was reconnaissance."

Ward grinned, and in it Naim saw something he didn't like. Snide superiority. And yes—Ward was glancing at Yessel just out of the corner of his eyes. "We need a lot of reconnaissance."

"Ward..."

"You don't have an expedition without me."

"No... I don't."

Naim backed into Aria, who wore a forlorn expression. "I'd like a word with Ward, if you don't mind."

Naim nodded glumly and headed back down the stairs. With a pang of fear, he realized he'd lost track of Kaia. His relief came moments later, as he spotted her at the base of the steps. Her arms were crossed, and her head tilted toward the ground. Her beautiful hair covered her face like a veil.

Naim approached and put a hand on her shoulder. "Hey."

"Naim." She put her hand on top of his. "Let's go back to Evermore. Call this off. Can we just go to the grove with the orange flowers?"

Happy memories flooded back to Naim, but that deluge was overpowered by the sudden onrush of fear. "We don't know how long that would last. We've both been here weeks now. When the next exodus starts... I can't lose you, Kaia. I won't. I need to fix this."

"I'd rather spend my time with you than fix things. Can't we just enjoy how things are now? Let's enjoy us! I miss the Naim who used to lie by my side in the park. In the grove with the orange flowers. Please, Naim. Do you think Ward's really going to do 'reconnaissance?'"

"No, but—"

Kaia let go of his hand and turned away from him. "I said I'd go with you, so I will."

"You'll see. We'll be able to go wherever we want together."

She looked into his eyes, but her expression remained empty and distant. Her lips quivered ever so slightly, and she pulled away, tugged her backpack up, and slipped it on over her shoulders.

Naim did the same. He retreated into the mass of the Collective, and within five minutes, the entourage was underway. This was it. He was sure of it. Once he and Kaia reached the pole, she'd see it, too. City's dual states would collapse together, and they'd both see this place for what it really was. The illusion of both these false realities would finally be torn away.

A thought struck him—his home or hers? If they were forced to choose then and there where to go, they'd have to choose one or the other in order to stay together. Naim had no close relations to worry about on his world, but there was work to think about. Kaia's world had universities, but they sounded underfunded and in shambles thanks to the political movements of the last fifty years of her country's history. Not like his at all. His world had the stability and safety. But Kaia would want to stay with her family. He knew it absolutely.

He decided, after many minutes watching the weary gray facades pass by, that when they got there, he would go wherever she wanted. All these weeks she had endured him talking about maps and superpositions and wandering about the boring, pit-studded grid streets, only to have a fully detailed map fall from the sky (or rather, from Mia's mind). It was the least he could do.

He'd do better. He had to, for her.

A sharp breeze tore through the air, biting as it went. Naim and his entourage reflexively flinched. The jovial banter grew softer, sterner.

At Negative Seventy-Fifth Street, the group stopped and unpacked their backpacks. Naim, alongside everyone else, pulled thick pants, shirts, jackets, hats and boots on over their lighter clothes. He topped off the outfit with a thick, dark green wool hat.

He glanced around at his group and smiled. Everyone wore the same outfit (as they'd all raided the same camping supply store). The numerous fashion clones milled about, waiting for stragglers to finish dressing. Kaia stood at Naim's side, pulling gloves over her fingers, her lips a thin, flat line.

"Kaia—" He reached out to put his arm around her. She neither flinched nor returned the gesture. Naim could find no more words to comfort her. He wondered at the void forming within him.

He'd been repeating it to himself over and over: the pole is the answer, the pole is the answer, the pole is the answer. Repeating the mantra cleared the void. The pole, he knew, would solve all his problems.

He retracted his arm and shouted to the group. They pulled up their backpacks, now significantly lighter, and proceeded south.

It began to snow, at first wet and slushy flurries. Before long, all of City's surfaces, streets and buildings, were covered in an ever-thickening layer of fluffy, white snow. The members of the entourage pushed through it with ease. Taum's contraption flared red, and a path of snow melted in the machine's wake.

Flakes drifted down from nowhere, not a cloud in the sky. Just City's perpetual swimming tones of blue.

"There!" Ondeck pointed. A walled institution came into view, stonework architecture poking up overtop the brick fortifications. Another young man, about the same age as Ondeck, stood in front of the large gate at its entrance.

Ondeck ran past Naim, to the young man at the gate.

They seemed to shout at one another for a few moments, but as Naim grew closer, their conversation grew calmer.

"Yeah, I'm going with them," Ondeck said to the young man. He turned his attention to Naim. "This is Glorious Ramrod."

Naim smirked. "Nice to meet you."

"So, you're really not purple, huh?"

"No." Ward stepped forward. "But we are going to do a little reconnaissance in their district."

Glorious Ramrod furrowed his brow. "Huh." He turned to Ondeck. "You're really serious about this, huh?"

Ondeck nodded vigorously up and down with wide eyes.

"Well." Glorious Ramrod gave the most nonchalant of shrugs. "I guess I'm going with you. Just gimme a minute."

He retreated into his compound.

Kaia mouthed the words 'Glorious Ramrod' to Naim with a bemused expression on her face, and he chuckled.

Ondeck took a step toward them. "*Don't* make fun of his name."

Naim and Kaia exchanged glances.

"Just… it's just how he is."

Glorious Ramrod hurtled back out through the gates and slid to a halt atop the snow, now with a bag strapped across his shoulders. "Where's this, um, armband thing you wrote about?" He shut the gates behind him.

Taum rolled forward on his chariot, the snow around him liquefying. Glorious Ramrod stared up at him like a deer in headlights. Taum sternly handed down a bracelet.

Glorious Ramrod stretched out his arm, meekly at first, then registering Ondeck at his side, straightened his back and snatched the bracelet away. He turned it over in his hands. "Doesn't look like much."

"It will completely protect you from being converted," Taum said. "I invented it myself."

Glorious Ramrod nudged Ondeck with his elbow as he pulled on the bracelet. "Converted, eh? I see what your plan is now."

"Cut it out," Ondeck pushed back at him.

Taum cleared his throat. "*Under* your sleeves, young man."

Glorious Ramrod drew up his face into a mock sneer, apparently mimicking Taum. "Yes, sir."

"You wouldn't want the tribals ripping it off, would you?"

"No." Glorious Ramrod rolled his eyes. "I guess not."

Kaia pulled Naim away by the arm. She beckoned for Taum to follow. He caught their eyes and did so.

"We should hurry," she said. "If the streets change back, they'll be fine. We won't."

"I agree," Naim said.

He led the three of them to Aria, who was wearing the most forlorn expression he had ever seen upon her face.

Kaia put a hand on her shoulder. "You'll be able to keep Ward in line?"

"I think so." Aria righted her posture and turned to face the trio fully. "Go. Hurry. Don't worry about Ward. I'll keep everyone safe."

Kaia squeezed Aria's shoulder. "See you when we get back."

"See you then."

The trio backed away from the crowded Collective, all caught up in discussion with Glorious Ramrod and Ondeck about life in City's frigid tundra.

"Can you jog?" Naim asked.

Kaia nodded.

They proceeded south.

Streets with numbers in the negative nineties descended below negative one hundred. The sky grew darker. It still twisted and turned with swirling blue, just all darker tones thereof. The snow fell more densely and blew harder. Taum's contraption hummed at their side, the engine growing ever louder and the heating mechanism ever brighter.

Naim and Kaia's jog slowed to a walk as they pushed through denser and denser mounds of snow.

By Negative One Hundred and Tenth Street, City's ambient illumination had visibly dimmed. The buildings had ceased to look like habitable structures and more like stage props that might tip over or shatter at the touch of a hand. Not that any of them tried.

They proceeded in icy silence, the sky and surroundings growing dimmer and dimmer. At the intersection of Negative One Hundred and Eighteenth Street, Taum turned on the headlights of his chariot and rummaged around in one of his compartments. He produced two flashlights and handed them over to Naim and Kaia.

They continued forward, through a blinding blizzard, in the dark, at a walking pace. At least the distance between the intersections was contracting. The facades of buildings themselves even seemed to be compressing horizontally. Absurdly thin windows adorned the houses, alongside absurdly thin doors and stairs. By Negative One-Hundred and Twenty-First Street, it was clear that the vertical dimension was compressing too, though not as quickly as the horizontal. At Negative One-Hundred and Twenty-Third Street, the group stopped and stared over a row of buildings that were as tall as Taum on his chariot and as wide as Naim.

Naim and Kaia passed their flashlights over the structures, the brick and wood contorted beyond reason.

"Only one more block," Taum said. "Mia's map put the pole just after Negative One-Hundred Twenty-Fourth."

Kaia looked up at Naim with cold dread in her eyes. She winced, as though she were unable to ask, but Naim knew what she intended. She wanted to unsee this place. She wanted him to take her away to any other part of City but here.

"Just a little further then," Naim said.

He led them further down the avenue. The buildings grew smaller and more contorted, and the blizzard grew more intense. The wind howled menacingly in his ear. They crossed an intersection, but between the darkness and the snow and the contortion, they couldn't even find the sign, and then—

Black.

They all stopped.

Their headlights and flashlights shone not onto flakes of snow flying about, not more street, just emptiness.

Naim and Kaia's flashlights shot to the ground. About a meter or so beyond their feet, the ground curved downward, wrapping inward and around itself. Directly beyond them lay… nothing, a nothing so absolute that it was just dead and black. Their flashlight beams went on forever inside it, reflecting naught.

Naim's heart raced alongside his mind. What to do? What to do? His mind told him to go forward, that it might be dark and precipitous, but that it was the way out. But was this really the way he wanted? Would he get to choose, or was this way out like the other bad ways? Like the Amaranthine's way?

Kaia grasped his hand and squeezed.

His heart yearned for her. He yearned to be with her. He yearned to show her all the happy and wonderful things in the world. Things not in City. A real life. Real love, for all the rest of their days. He'd never met anyone so vivid, so smart, so funny, so profound, and he was sure he never would again.

"Forward then?" Taum asked. "From the curve, I doubt it is an actual precipice. And look."

He shot a flashlight beam from his own hand toward the sidewalk and scanned it toward where the ground curved. The buildings continued shrinking and thinning, until they reached the curve, at which point the building at the precipice stretched outward and down into the curvature of the ground.

Naim blinked a few times.

"Naim…" Kaia whispered.

"I'm going," Taum said.

He rolled his chariot forward.

Naim followed.

Kaia's hand trailed just behind his.

They walked, carefully stepping, frigid wind biting their faces. They stepped again and again, and again. Naim waited for it. He waited for his feet to step over the curve. He could feel Kaia doing the same, half-shuffling, half-walking. He heard the motor of Taum's chariot at his side, just behind the screaming wind.

He stepped and stepped.

And stepped again.

And again.

He shot his flashlight out to his sides.

Buildings on either side. Contorted, but there.

"Taum?"

"Yes?" His chariot halted.

"What happened to that curve?"

"I don't know."

"Stay facing that way," Naim said.

He turned himself around and shone his flashlight beam back the way they'd come. The inward curve now lay some five to ten meters behind them.

"What the hell…?" Naim muttered.

"Is it behind us?" Kaia asked.

"Yes," Naim said.

"Let's proceed forward," Taum said. "I have a theory."

Naim grabbed up Kaia's hand, and they did as he suggested.

"And what's that?" Kaia looked up at Taum. "What's your theory?"

"The pole is not a point in space, and City is not a perfect sphere."

Naim couldn't believe his ears. "What is it, then?"

"City is a nearly-spherical torus with intense spatial warp along its interior plane."

Naim mouthed the words and then jolted as they formed a shape in his mind. He shot his flashlight beam around the landscape. "You mean we're at the—"

His beam landed upon a signpost, highly contorted, but legible—the intersection of Negative Twenty-Third Avenue and One-Hundred and Twenty-Second Street. Positive.

"We're at the *north* pole?" Kaia yelled.

"There *are* no poles!" Taum announced, and let out a laugh.

Naim shot his light beam up to the scientist. "What the hell is so funny? Don't you realize what this means? There are no answers. There's no way out. No latch. There's nothing but… a closed loop. A möbius strip. It's all just… My god…"

"Pfft…" Taum pulled his chariot forward. "God. There is no god. There's just City. We work to understand it, and eventually we will find the way out. If I find the answer, I'll share it with you, of course."

Naim marched forward after him. "There is no way out! Don't you get it? This is all there is! This! City! Your science doesn't apply here!"

Taum swiveled his chariot around. "Science applies everywhere! Everywhere! Science is the exploration of what truly is, not some pathetic, egotistical, backward mumbo-jumbo invented to separate stupid people from their fear."

"That fear makes us human. You want to stuff it away and hide behind facts instead of facing it head on. That very schism of emotion and reason is responsible for every horror humans have ever known! Every abuse of power, every bomb, every gun, every weapon—"

Taum leveled a snarling gaze. "Oh, yes. Philosophers and priests have never become dictators or brainwashed people to serve them—"

"Stop it both of you!" Kaia shrieked.

Her chest rose and fell as she exhaled misty clouds. She held both her fists clenched. Naim turned to her and looked into her eyes.

He'd done this. Oh, dear god, he'd done this. And it couldn't be undone. The experience could never be reversed. Utter horror seeped into him, drizzling all the way down to his extremities, and finally creeping into his heart and his soul. They were stuck… in City… with…

The trio trudged southward. In the dim light and omnipresent snow, it could have been any cardinal direction for all Naim knew. And what sense did cardinal directions have on the surface of a nearly-spherical spatially-warped torus, Naim wondered—to himself.

Credulous

((before))

"Tell him what you told me," Bell says.

Window shivers and fidgets uncomfortably.

From the moment I met him, I did not like him. It's really hard to keep that back, you know. For the sake of my little Republic, I have to treat everyone fairly. But Window is both insensitive and not very bright. A terrible combination. I remind myself that he must be taught.

"Well?" I ask.

"You're all a bunch of faggots." He twists his face into an awful snarl.

I blink a few times, not comprehending the last word. He might as well have told me we were a bunch of flizblarths. I turn to Bell for support.

Bell sighs. "Evergreen kissed him, and Window called him that word he just said, then punched him in the face. Evergreen ran off and told me and Roof, and you know the rest."

Comprehension dawns me. I draw my lips up into a smile. "Oh, I get it. You're a bigot! How quaint."

Window lets out an animalistic growl. Bell grabs his arm, and Window struggles against him.

We stand in the cafeteria, our jail. There are about a dozen of us here, but Bell, Window and myself are at the center of the room between two rows of tables. The others are by the door. We all wear our outdoor clothes, except for Window, who we've stripped of everything but his underwear and a tank top.

I turn to Bell. "I've heard stories about this kind of thing in the distant past, but where I come from, we don't have any words like that."

Bell releases Window's arm. "I recognize it. Unfortunately."

"You people are disgusting," Window says.

I shake my head and furrow my brow. "Did it occur to you just tell Evergreen that you didn't want to be kissed?"

"I shouldn't have to!" he barks back. "It's disgusting. When a man lies with a man—"

He is interrupted by a roomful of groans. Bell is shaking his head in disgust. Once again, I feel lost.

"Everyone listen up," I say. "Each of you clearly has much more experience with this kind of behavior than I do. This is where I learn from you." I turn directly to Bell. "Explain please."

Bell shrugs. "He's quoting outdated religious texts with a rather unfortunate literal interpretation."

I shake my head at Window, my mouth poised for speech, but words fail me. I find myself merely staring at him incredulously.

"Fuck you." Window makes a hocking noise in throat and spits in my face.

My face grows cold even though his disgusting warm bile is sliding down the side of my nose. I nod to Pathside, who stands at the door. He picks up a folded woolen blanket at his feet, brings it to me, and hands it over. I throw it at Window's chest. Bell takes off his hat and tosses that to him, too.

I lock my eyes with Window's. "We'll slide your dinner in through there." I point to the small window at the top of the far wall near the door. The room has six others, spaced evenly around the square room.

I lead my fellow Republicans out of the cafeteria and Bell locks the door behind us. Once I'm sure that Window can't see me anymore, I wipe his spittle off my face with a quick flick of my hand.

"I want one person at each of those small windows," I tell Bell. "Not one per wall like usual."

We walk upstairs and out into the snow. Most of the others drift off to other tasks. Some stay to guard the cafeteria.

"You think that he'll actually try to run for it?" Bell asks.

I bite my lip. *Yes, I think he's that stupid*, I want to say. But I cannot say that. I must outwardly suggest that he can be made to function within our society. If I can't show them that I believe it, then my biases will infect them. And then I'll have witch hunts and tyranny… No. Our

Republic will not become a dictatorship.

"We should be extra careful with him," I say. "I'll talk to him tomorrow morning. He'll be pretty ripe by then."

Bell nods. Something seems to occur to him. "Oh! I just remembered." He shuffles around in his pockets. "This came just before Evergreen showed up. It's from Ondeck!"

I blink. "Ondeck? He's not dead?"

"No. He says there are warmer parts of City without the deadly purple goo." Bell produces a piece of paper and hands it over.

Dear Bell and Glorious Ramrod,

I am alive and well. I have discovered large, safe, and warm (!) tracts of City. There is so much here: stores full of food, a cathedral, apartment buildings, factories, a park, and so much more. And the people are very friendly. Most importantly, they are not covered in poisonous purple goo.

What they tell me is that the purple freaks are called Amaranthines or tribals. If they can stay warm, the purple is a mist, not a gel. And that mist is worse than death—it'll take over your mind and make you crazy. Hence the name "tribal."

I'm coming back soon with a big group of them. They've got armbands that can protect them from the purple mist. They want to sneak into the Amaranthine District and gather intelligence, and I want to go with them.

There's just one thing—we have to wait for the streets to change. I know that's not going to make much sense, but I saw it happen myself, right outside the walls of the Republic. Something's happening to City, something strange. I want to find out what it is. After talking with the people here, I think the Amaranthines might be involved somehow. That's why I want to go with them on their reconnaissance.

Hope to see you soon.

- Ondeck

"This day just keeps getting weirder and weirder," I tell Bell. "First we end up having to jail a… a… what did you call him?"

"A homophobe."

"First we have to jail a homophobe, and now Ondeck sends me this. Do you understand any of this?"

Bell shrugs. "It's all fairly straightforward."

"It's insane!"

Bell winces. "More insane than being trapped in City in the first place?"

I pause and ponder that over. "You make a good point. How did you get this, anyway?"

Bell smirks and stifles a laugh. "You won't believe me."

I grab his arm. "Tell me."

Bell lets out a sigh. "A miniature ornithopter landed at my feet and dropped it in the snow. Then it took off back over the wall and disappeared."

"Ornithopter? A mechanical bird?"

Bell nods.

I shake my head. "I'm going to wait by the front gates. Come get me when it's time for dinner."

"Sure," Bell says, a little bit hesitantly.

I stop and face him. "What is it?"

"You'll just be by the front gates? You're not… going anywhere, are you?"

I put my hand on his shoulder. "I'm not abandoning the Republic. I'll stay here, but I do want to keep a lookout for Ondeck, just in case. And it's important that I take the first shift." *Don't ask others to do what you are unwilling to do yourself.* "If you need me, you know where to find me."

Bell nods with a light smile and takes off in the other direction. I continue down the quad's central path toward the main gates. The snow is falling, as usual. Funny how the amount of snow on the ground and the temperature seem to remain constant. We got one of the thermometers out of the science building when I first got here. Negative two degrees Celsius. And yet, we'll wake up and the new fallen snow will have washed out all the footprints and slips and slides and remnants of snowball fights and snow angels of the previous day, while never rising more than a couple of centimeters off the ground.

I reach the gates and pull them open.

Realization of the strangeness of my surroundings strikes me. I look down the street, and it is a straight line. I can see all the way to the horizon. I shuffle, turning around myself. Both directions... the street is a straight line in both directions. There's a junkyard next to us now, which is strange. I've never seen that before. Down the other side there's a block of warehouses. I wonder if there's good food around there, but I'd hate to get lost in this mess, this orderly, straight-roaded mess.

I think back to what Ondeck's note said: *There's just one thing—we have to wait for the streets to change.* Is this what he meant? If so, is he on his way? Hopefully. If I have to stand out here for days on end, I sure am going to be pissed at him. Well, not really pissed. I'd mostly be happy he got back safe and sound.

I kick the snow, then build myself a snowman by the front gate to pass the time. I glance every so often between the horizons, but there's nothing there except City's insane sky.

I sigh, wishing I had a book. We only got half the campus. No library. Dad keeps a small library in our house. It's just across the hall from my room—shelves and shelves of books and a big sofa chair in front of a lamp. I had my nose stuck in books a lot as a kid, and dad was always suggesting new ones for me to read.

Man, I miss him.

I got the concept of standup from him. I think it was the very first time I asked him about what he does at work all day. I must have been eight or nine at the time. He didn't want to try to explain computer programming to me, so he told me about how the first thing that happens in the morning is that all the software developers stand up around a big board that has all the team's tasks on it, and they talk about what they're going to do that day.

He explained how it's part of good leadership. Instead of him going around to a dozen different people and making them explain to him what they're doing, he can get the group to keep themselves on task by making them talk to one another. If everyone knows what everyone else is doing, then the group will force consensus.

And the leader can focus on the bigger picture.

Dad was always talking about the bigger picture. I never really understood what he meant until I got here. It's as though… there are all these other guys here, and they all have their own individual desires and strengths, but they have to be encouraged to work together instead of against one another, communally instead of selfishly, or it all falls apart to chaos.

That's the big picture dad was talking about.

I hope I get to see him again and tell him what I've learned. There have been a few times when I've wished he was here. Like just now with Window. I'll bet dad wouldn't have gotten angry and let himself scowl. Might have even found something helpful to say before leaving him to his punishment.

"Let the anger go," he'd said. "Always let it go."

I glance toward one horizon, then the other—

I see shapes. A crowd rolls into view. They wear the strangest outfits, all except for one, who wears clothes more like mine, and he is running toward me.

"Ondeck!" I shout his name and take a few steps forward.

He hurtles into me. "Ramrod! You got my message?"

"Yeah." We hug, then I push him back and punch him in the shoulder. "What the hell were you thinking?!"

He looks at the snow guiltily. "Dunno. Just wanted to break the tedium, I guess. I, um, found friends though."

I break a smile. "Looks like."

"What they're doing is big, Ramrod."

I pump my eyebrows and release a vulgar chortle. It has its desired effect—he breaks out into laughter.

"Shut up. You know what I mean."

"Do I, now? Well, go do your *big* things with them if you want. Hey, did you find a boyfriend? Is that him there?"

Ondeck makes a show of sighing. "That's Naim, and beside him is Kaia. His *girlfriend*."

"What is it with you and falling for straight boys?"

"I haven't fallen for anyone!"

"Likely story. So, you want to go with them to this tribal village, huh?"

"Yeah," Ondeck says. "I do."

The group is upon us now, about two dozen at a guess. All older, too. Everyone's in their twenties or thirties or forties except us. I wonder why teenage men always end up in this part of City.

Naim and Kaia lead the group, and approach me in particular.

Ondeck turns to them. "This is Glorious Ramrod."

I love their reactions. Naim bites his lip sideways, while his girlfriend tries to hide her face from me. Totally awesome.

That's the other thing dad told me about leadership. You can absolutely be a goofball, in fact it helps, if that's who you are. You can even get to be a bit crude sometimes, especially with your guy friends, but always know the limits—know which behaviors are going to end up hurting people if you extend the joke beyond the line.

"Nice to meet you," Naim says.

"So, you're really not purple, huh?" I kick at the snow and smirk.

"No." A very tall man with broad shoulders and a deep voice steps forward out of the crowd. "But we are going to do a little reconnaissance in their district."

"Huh." I turn to Ondeck. "You're really serious about this, huh?"

Ondeck is nodding up and down wide-eyed with excitement. And he's probably a bit resentful that I didn't take his letter at face value. Never take anything at face value. That's another good lesson from dad.

"Well." I shrug. "I guess I'm going with you. Just gimme a minute."

I run back inside the Republic. I don't actually need anything in particular—I'll grab a backpack for effect—but mostly I want Bell to know what's going on. Ondeck's either going to have the time of his life, or he's in way over his head. Either way, I'm going to be there to watch his back. No one in the Republic is taking that risk but me.

I'm the leader. I can't ask anyone else to do this.

I grab up my backpack, have a hurried conversation with a very confused Bell, who seems more concerned with cafeteria security than anything else, and I run back to the front gate full tilt.

I slide to a halt in front of the gates and close it behind me. "Where's this, um, armband thing your letter talked about?"

There's a guy riding something that looks like a segway—I only half-noticed him before, but seeing him roll toward me is creepy as shit—and he reaches down, holding this dippy little gray bracelet thing. I raise an eyebrow and take it from him. "Doesn't look like much."

"It will completely protect you from being converted," the guy on the segway says. "I invented it myself."

I nudge Ondeck with my elbow as I wrap the thing around my wrist. "Converted, eh? I see what your plan is now."

"Cut it out." Ondeck is gloriously annoyed.

The creepy guy clears his throat. "*Under* your sleeves, young man."

I salute him. "Yes, sir."

But really, it's a show. I'm scared of this guy. He gives me absolutely the wrong vibe. I'm not sure I want to go anywhere with him.

"You wouldn't want the tribals ripping it off, would you?" He eyes me in a way I hate.

"No," I say. "I guess not."

Ugh. He might be enough for me to try to convince Ondeck to call the whole thing off.

Yeah, I decide I should at least try.

I pull Ondeck a bit away from the main party for a bit.

"What do you think of them?" I ask, in my serious voice.

"What? They're all on the level, I think. It'll be dangerous, sure, but everyone's bought in on Taum's bracelets—Naim, Kaia, Ward, Aria, even Yessel—he's back at the cathedral. *Everyone* trusts him."

"That Taum—" I start to say, but then I look over Ondeck's shoulder to realize that Taum, Naim, and Kaia are off on their own now. I nod in their direction. "What's up with them?"

"Oh!" Ondeck shakes his head. "Right. I forgot to mention. Naim, Kaia, and Taum have a different goal. They want to find City's south pole."

I blink a few times. "Any other different goals?"

"No. Everyone else is going into the Amaranthine District."

I scan over the rest of the group. "What about her? The tall one with the glasses. What's her name?"

"That's Karr."

"What do you think of her?"

"She doesn't talk much. The others seem to avoid her."

I give him a look. He should know what it means by now.

"Naim and Kaia found me and treated me well, and they explicitly vouched for Ward and Aria. They're running something called The Collective. It's like our Republic, actually!"

Now I'm giving him my you're-full-of-shit face. I contort my lips and kind of roll my eyes back. Ondeck once called it my O face. He has seen me mid-coitus, after all.

"Stop that." He slugs me in the shoulder.

"Are you really comfortable with them?" I ask.

He folds his arm in front of his chest. "Yes."

"Okay, then. But don't let them split us up, got it?"

"No problem."

I lead him back to the others, where Ward is dividing people up into groups. He puts me and Ondeck with himself, Aria and… Karr. Lovely. My new favorite person.

She walks up next to me and sneers down at me like I'm some kind of lower life form.

"Can I help you?" I offer.

She scoffs and turns her attention elsewhere.

I shake my head, and return my attention to Ward. He creates four more groups of four to five people each, and then talks about our approach, and what each group's priorities are. We're to sneak around the periphery of the purple mist, try to find computers or other artifacts. Take anything that's small and portable—Taum insists that the purple can't stick to inanimate objects with any permanence, only humans—and get out in under twenty minutes.

The four other groups take off, and Ward begins leading us down the road past the junkyard.

An uneasy feeling fills my gut. Mostly I think it's coming from my proximity to this Karr woman. She gives me a terrible vibe. I'm not sure I've ever met someone so blatantly full of herself. Ward is obsessed with being group dictator, so no help there. Aria has resigned herself to this, in a way. She wants to help, perhaps a bit too badly. And Ondeck, well, he's too busy having the time of his life to pay attention to any of this.

I take up a position alongside Aria.

"Aria, was it?"

"You're… Glorious Ramrod." Her smile is genuine. She is actually not offended.

"Yeah. I like it lot better than my first City name."

She smiles. "You're lucky. Most people don't get to choose."

"One of the few perks of leadership, I guess." We walk in silence for some time. I decide to get to the point. "So, um, why have you chosen now for this little excursion? Did Taum just invent the bracelets? Have they been tested?"

"Taum has sent his gatherers to the edges of the Amaranthine District with them, and they came back unharmed."

I furrow my brow. "Taum has 'gatherers?'"

She bobs her head from side to side. "The best analog is an employee. Taum controls a facility with lots of secure storage space. That's at a premium, and he can't do manual labor very easily, as you've seen, so he trades access to the space for others' help."

"Who are these others?"

"Oh, Grey, Mario, Fero, and Hyra mostly these days, but they're not here."

"Why not?"

"Three of them are children. And Grey is…" She smiles. "Well, he's grown into the role of guardian pretty well."

Ward scoffs. "I don't trust him."

"He is one of the stupidest, rudest individuals I have ever met," Karr intones.

I shoot Ondeck a look. Yeah, buddy, this sure sounds like one big, happy, fully-functional family. I note a feeling welling up me, resentment at Ondeck, that he felt the need to seek out something other than the comfortable little Republic I've built up for him.

But I've known for a while that he found it stifling. Back in his real home, he'd been just about ready to leave for college when he'd been snatched up and dropped here. He feels as though City wrecked his glorious future.

And I know it must also be hard being gay with all the rest of us only doing it for fun, all holding out for the hope that we'll get to meet girls again. He wasn't the only one frustrated with the situation, but I'm sure it felt that way to him.

The group stops. Ward motions for us to duck behind a nearby building. The snow has stopped and the ground is merely wet. I realize the weather has changed without my noticing. Ward motions for us to look out from behind the wall.

Ondeck and I peer over the edge, and that's when I see it a couple blocks beyond—wisps of purple, turning, spinning, contorting over one another. They tug and pull at the pavement and the buildings, morphing them into hideous conglomerations: ugly, twisted, unnatural shapes.

"The hell…?" Ondeck says.

I turn to the other three. "It can twist up the pavement and the buildings?"

Ward nods. "And anything else that gets near it, except us while we've got the bracelets on."

I shoot Ondeck my most serious of looks. He seems to absorb it and consider his action more carefully. For just a split second I apprehend real doubt in his eyes.

"There's no one there," Ward says. "Come on."

Ward and Aria walk in front of Karr, and we walk behind her.

"I don't like this," I whisper to Ondeck. He says nothing. He looks frightened out of his mind. And yet he follows them. I sincerely hope this is enough excitement for him for one lifetime, because after we get home I'm doing my best to make sure the story of this trip becomes the Republic's official religion. Ondeck can be its high priest.

Ward and Aria enter the miasma, side by side. The wisps retreat from their bodies as though repelled by a magnet of like pole. It twists at their feet, struggling toward a place it can't quite reach.

Karr follows them in, and then Ondeck and I shuffle into the seething purple.

Ondeck looks around. "I sure don't see anything that looks like technology."

Aria turns around to him with her finger over lips.

I whisper to him. "If I give you the word, I want you to run back to the Republic as fast as you can."

"But—"

"Please listen to me. Something is very wrong with all of this, not just this place, but this group—"

Ondeck points. Ward is beckoning us toward a building down the streets. It's not so much a building now that the purple shit has contorted it into a kind of half dome. But it will conceal us.

We scuttle toward it and join the other three.

"We'll wait here until the signal," Ward says.

Aria gives him a look. "Skylir and Brin are in on something, aren't they? Something more reconnaissance."

Ward pulls a device out of his pocket. "We can't waste this opportunity."

"Did Taum give you that?" Aria grabs his bicep. "I can't believe this, Ward."

Even though he's meandered some distance away from me, I shout to Ondeck. "Now. Go!"

Ondeck pivots, takes a few steps, and—

"Stop right there," Karr says.

We all turn to her and gasp. Ondeck falls over himself and scrambles to a stance.

The purple wisps have latched onto Karr and are spiraling up her body. Her eyes have taken on a purple sheen. In her hand she holds a dark purple pistol. Even her hands and face have begun to exude purple lines.

"Where's your bracelet, Karr?" Aria asks.

Still aiming the pistol at Ondeck, she throws out her other wrist so that we can all see—she is still wearing the bracelet.

"Taum is a traitor. If I'm lost, I will at least force you to join me as Amarathines. He must have put different bracelets on different timers. For th'sport of it!"

"Run, Ondeck!" I shout.

"Run and I will shoot!" Karr roars.

"Enough of this!" Aria snatches up Ward's device and hurls it into the nearest wall where it splinters with a sickening crunch, and the pieces clatter to the ground. Aria strides toward Karr. "You surely don't want your last act as a human being to be the creation of more human suffering. Put the gun down."

Karr whips the gun around and points it at her instead.

I nod vigorously to Ondeck, who is now fully clear of Karr's field of vision. I, unfortunately, occupy a position at its periphery. He shakes his head vigorously, and I nod more vigorously. Instead of heeding me, he creeps toward Karr.

"If you leave now," Aria says, "maybe we can reverse this. Maybe you'll be alright."

"He planned this!" Karr roars. "I know him! He thinks like me. He planned it this way. I bet, and I lost, and I'll be damned if I'm going down alone."

Ondeck creeps closer and closer to the horrible woman. My heart is racing. How much longer does he have until his bracelet betrays him?

Aria moves closer to Karr, her arms outstretched.

"Aria, stop!" Ward yells. "She's not listening to you!"

Aria is within a meter of Karr. Ondeck is within five meters behind her.

"Hand it to me, Karr."

"That is not my name." Karr fires. Blood sprays and ruptures from Aria's chest. She falls, the purple still deflected from her body. Ondeck lunges from behind, tackles her, and the guns clatters to the ground and evaporates into wisps of purple.

I run to Ondeck, and Ward runs to Aria.

Karr is shrieking and clawing at Ondeck with all her might, while he struggles to free himself from her grasp. I sock her directly in the face, and she topples to the ground, sending up a cloud of the purple mist. Ondeck pulls himself away.

We run.

Ward's sobbing resounds from somewhere behind us, and we just keep running. We reach the edge of the horrible district, and we run out to safety, away from the purple wisps. Ward's howls echo in the distance.

"The other groups…?" Ondeck asks.

"Probably the same as us. Some of them will escape, some won't."

Ondeck's face suddenly twists up in horror.

"What?" I ask.

He points at me. I realize he's pointing at my face. I can't see my face, so I look at my hands. Purple lines trace their way along my skin.

Ondeck pulls his hands up to his face, lets out a few shocked sobs.

"You need to get away from me," I say. "Run home. Now."

"But I— All my—"

"Hey! I came of my own free will. You did not do this."

"Oh, I did," Ondeck moans. "My… god!"

"Get. Back. Now. That is the first and last order I will ever give for th'Republic. You'll have to learn everything else from Bell. Go. Now."

He bites his quivering lip, mouths the words 'I'm sorry,' and rushes off.

Ward passes by me, mumbling to himself and carrying Aria's limp, dripping body. Just walks right past me.

And then he is gone.

They are all gone, and I am alone.

I'm sorry, dad. I think I screwed up real good this time. Real damn good. I guess there's such th'thing as working too hard for th'others. I should have listened to myself more and cared th'little less, I guess.

I proceed into th'purple-mist.

It's funny. It looked so horrible before, and I'm not really seeing th'different-shapes or th'different-colors than before, but it's so beautiful. What was th'torturous, distorted mess of th'ugly-forms is now gorgeous. They are th'most-beautiful-things I've ever seen.

Th'thing itches under my clothes. That itch grows into th'roar of th'discomfort. My clothes feel tight and awful. I shed them. I leave them in a pile on th'ground. My new clothes feel great. Th'luster is better than th'clothing by far.

I walk further. I want nothing to do with th'stupid-former-Karr-woman. I wonder what my own true name is.

Th'corridors form before me. I spot th'people. I run to them.

"Hello," I try.

"Hello," th'man says. "Are you new?"

I nod. "I am."

"Let's see if we can find your name." He pulls up his arm and draws upon it. Th'luster makes th'shapes and follows his finger. I didn't know it could do that. I can't wait to try it myself. I wonder what else th'luster can do?

"Ah," he says. "Got it. You are Th'Luminous Kin."

"Hmm." I smile. I think it's th'good-name.

Duplicitous

((before))

"Forward then?" I ask. "From the curve, I doubt it is an actual precipice. And look."

I shoot a flashlight beam across the landscape to show them. While they are looking, I press the button on my mobilizer that will activate the bracelets' countdown timers. Goodbye, Karr. You were very helpful. Thank you for playing your part.

My group stands at the precipice before the pole. I wasn't really sure what to expect here, but I did guess at this possibility. The trip forward into what looks like snowy oblivion will be harmless, and also a waste of time. There was the minute possibility that we would find something more akin to Naim's idiotic philosophical psycho-construct imaginings, but what we've actually found was high on my list of possibilities: the poles are connected via spatial warp. There is in fact no pole at all. That point in space is literally unreachable. We will walk forward and end up at City's northernmost reaches instantaneously.

But Naim and Kaia are still looking between one other and the void, mumbling, contemplating their emotions, I'm sure. What a waste of time.

It gives me time to ponder the potential complexities of what the Amaranthines will give me. And that's what will have made all of these roundabout interlocutions worthwhile. Oh, but how roundabout they had to be!

The missing element of my research here is the fundamental quantum energy that all of City resonates against. Discover that, and I can decohere any chunk of matter here, including the matter that comprises people, which should send them home. Even better, if I can figure out how to catalyze the effect, I could make a cascade that would tear City apart and send us all home.

Except the Amaranthines. Who knows what would happen to them? But I'm not one of them, so I can't say I particularly care.

This whole grand scheme of mine started on a perfectly ordinary day (for City). After a lot of work, I had finally gotten my lab linked up safely to the Amaranthines' computer system. It didn't take them long to notice me poking around, so I started a dialogue. I'm pretty sure it was the day I met Naim and Kaia for the first time. Yes. I remember. I had just finished sending the first message when those two showed up at my door. Kaia was poking at its control panel, and I thought she was about to trespass. Most people knock first. Or perform some other gesture of peace and goodwill. Not her. Just poked at buttons until things opened. Well, Naim's recent obsessive streak seems to have cured her of unguarded curiosity, at least.

After Naim and Kaia had left, I got back to talking with the Amaranthines, and they were wondering who I was, and what I was doing in their computer systems, and I found out that their computers are on their arms. Strange, but efficient, I suppose.

I had just discovered, thanks to Naim and Kaia, that City's streets could change, so I asked to know more about Amaranthine topography. I had an ornithopter fly them some materials they wanted, and they uploaded some data in return. It didn't take long for me to realize that the Amaranthine District was immune to the street changes, just as its inhabitants are fixed here for the duration of their lives.

The trade and exchanges went on for a while, but I could tell they were holding out on me. There were too many missing and rather major details of their holdings that they remained tight-lipped on.

So I invented the bracelets and sent a couple gatherers out to test them. The bracelets worked, and the Amaranthines were livid. They ceased communication.

Until— I kept poring over the schematics for their little 'Home,' and eventually I noticed a room. It was marked as empty, but it was in a central-ish location, right behind their leader's… their, um, Resplendent's main office.

So I asked.

At first, no response. Then a week later, I got a reply: We will not tell you what is in the room.

I asked if it was a device.

Silence.

I asked if they would trade supplies for details of what was in the room.

Silence.

I asked if they wanted people converted to their side for details of what was in the room.

That got them talking.

And, of course, the day I made that little discovery was the very day that Karr appeared right at my doorstep.

I know her kind. She will stab you in the back the moment she senses opportunity. Naturally, I built up just enough trust with her to stab her in the back first. I didn't graduate at the top of my class with honors by being nice to people.

The intentional bracelet malfunction was an interesting conundrum. Ward was insistent on sending over twenty people into the District, but the Amaranthines had requested only seven for my part of the deal. I couldn't have the Amaranthine's numbers swelling by more than twenty. I'm not an idiot. But I had to make sure they got at least seven.

So, I ran some simulations with a couple of bracelets going off the moment I hit the button, and others going off later at pre-determined intervals. After hundreds of simulations, I had built up enough data to ensure that the Amaranthines would get their seven people, and I would be spared the awkward knowledge of knowing who got which bracelet. I wouldn't have to look a person in the eyes knowing I'd sentenced them to purple oblivion. It was all up to random, unfeeling numbers.

Except for Karr, of course. I made sure she got a bracelet that would deactivate instantly. And for her, I feel no sympathy whatsoever. She would have done the same to me, and for far less of a reward. What do seven individuals matter if I can send all of us back to our real homes and end City's tyranny for good?

Finally. Naim and Kaia are walking. Good. Let's get this over with.

I roll forward through the darkness. I yawn loudly, but count on the wind to hide the noise. Naim and Kaia are probably too frightened to notice anyway.

I wait for it. They should be arriving at the conclusion that they have

not fallen into oblivion as they had been suspecting they might. I will
their dim minds to catch up to my own. I wait and wait, moving slowly
forward, thinking how utterly dense they are, and then—

"Taum?" It's Naim.

"Yes?" I halt the mobilizer.

"What happened to that curve?"

"I don't know."

"Stay facing that way," he tells me.

For the love of everything scientific. Is he working through this problem with a single functioning neuron? No wonder Kaia's fed up with him.

Naim mutters something inaudible.

"Is it behind us?" Kaia calls out.

"Yes," Naim responds.

"Let's proceed forward." I hide the exasperation from my voice. "I
have a theory."

"And what's that?" Kaia asks. "What's your theory?"

"The pole is not a point in space, and City is not a perfect sphere."

"What is it, then?" Naim asks.

It is so hard to deal with people who aren't as smart as you are. I hate
having to explain the obvious. "A nearly-spherical torus with intense spatial warp along its interior plane."

Naim pauses, struggling hard with his single neuron. "You mean
we're at the—"

"We're at the *north* pole?" Kaia yells. Not quite right, but I'm glad
someone is almost keeping up.

"There *are* no poles!" I shout with a laugh.

Naim blasts me with his flashlight beam. "What the hell is so funny?
Don't you realize what this means? There are no answers. There's no way
out. No latch. There's nothing but… the closed loop. A möbius strip. It's
all just… My god…"

"Pfft…" I am so sick of his simplistic worldview. "God. There is no
god. There's just City. We work to understand it, and eventually we will
find the way out. If I find the answer, I'll share it with you, of course."

"There is no way out! Don't you get it? This is all there is! This! City!
Your science doesn't apply here!"

I bring the mobilizer around so I can lean over him and tell him this
to his face. "Science applies everywhere! Everywhere! Science is the exploration of what truly is, not some pathetic, egotistical, backward mum-

bo-jumbo invented to keep people separate from their fear."

"That fear makes us human. You want to stuff it away and hide behind facts instead of facing it head on. That very schism of emotion and reason is responsible for every horror humans have ever known! Every abuse of power, every bomb, every gun, every weapon—"

I am livid. "Oh, yes. Philosophers and priests have never become dictators or brainwashed people to serve them—"

"Stop it both of you!" Kaia shrieks.

I realize, in that moment, that I had let myself get carried away just then. The idiocy of others can really get me worked up. I should work on not letting it get to me. It is more than my poor, fragile bones can sometimes bear, but I will make it a point to improve.

It is just so hard to talk to people who aren't as smart as I am.

Thankfully, the streets pass in silence. The sky and cityscape lighten at around One Hundred Tenth Street. By One Hundredth Street the blizzard has reduced to a light snow. By Ninetieth Street the buildings have returned to their right shapes. By Eightieth the snow is diminishing. At Seventieth, we take off our winter clothes and leave them in piles on the ground.

I turn and head away down Seventieth Street. Naim and Kaia do not call out to me, and I am thankful for their silence. I am thankful also that they gave me the opportunity they did. Everything just fell right into place, didn't it?

Why, if Naim hadn't gotten obsessed with the street configuration changes, then I never would have had the chance to manipulate The Collective the way I did. I wonder what they will do next? I can't imagine I've permanently crippled them, unless perhaps both Aria and Ward have been converted, but the odds of that happening are extremely low. Being led by Yessel means that they will not retaliate. They will merely isolate me. I will likely see no more of Grey, Mario, Fero, and Hyra.

All the better. I have enough hamburgers and chicken nuggets to last me until the next influx, and some of the new arrivals will certainly discover me and my promise of storage before they discover the Collective and its promise of abysmal leadership. Yes, I shall offer beautiful, valuable storage space, enabled by beautiful, wondrous technology. This is progress. This is humankind's future.

And we may soon be free of City before it even comes to that.

I reach my laboratory.

I open the door and pass under my on and off lights, passing through light and dark. I come to my central laboratory. I turn on my computers and check my communication programs.

A transmission for the Amaranthines—Yes! It awaits me, and I accept. The data transmits. I scan for harmful programs. No executables. Good, good. It is image data. A schematic.

I open it.

…

This is not possible.

This does not make any sense at all.

Such a construction cannot exist. It is a paradox. Imagine peeling away the layers of reality to find… No. If this were true. Not only is escape from City impossible, but everything I was doing at my university, my real home, my life's work—it is all for nothing.

Perhaps City does not follow our physical laws. Perhaps this would not apply at home. But quantum properties, atoms, subatomics, molecules, physics, everything here is the same. This abomination of a—I don't even know how to describe what it is—should be physically possible at home too, and if it does what they say it does…

No.

That would mean that my whole life is a lie.

Not just my City research, but everything before, too. All my research. Everything I have done with my entire life.

The room grows white. A powerful luminance seeps in at the edges of my vision, melting everything in its path.

What is happening to me?

What is my name?

Who am I—?

City is Paradox

(( ))

It would be a lie to say that City delights in ridding itself of individuals who disrupt harmony. As stated prior, City does not have feelings or a consciousness that would be comparable to that of a human being.

And yet, part of what makes City City, is that it must maintain a form of balance. An individual cannot force discord upon City for very long without being forced out, if only to restore a measure of equilibrium.

But there remains the problem of Naim's disruption. All this bouncing back and forth, before and after, after and before, a human one moment, an Amaranthine the next, or was it the other way around? Even City can lose track of such things. City does not operate upon linear time. That is a human contrivance.

City merely is.

Naim has reached a place where City cannot touch him.

City cannot restore equilibrium from that rupture.

And that rupture is green with envy, envy for those that get to keep what life has brought them, all the happiness and joy. Naim cannot stand it. He was unwilling to accept the fact that pain and heartbreak and sorrow were joy's necessary corollaries.

City is left with an irreconcilable paradox.

Who will reconcile it? And how?

Acerbic

((after))

Adema looked down at Tyr and Vall. "Your presence is no longer necessary. You may return to Th'Home."

The children picked themselves up and scampered away, deeper into the purple mist.

Adema and the other two adult tribals motioned to Gwei, and they too proceeded toward the Amaranthine District, albeit at a much more reasonable pace.

The moment Gwei stepped into th'luster, she had the awkward, disorienting sense of perceiving the same space in two opposing and contradictory ways. None of the physical shapes or movements of the purple mist seemed in any way doubled. Rather, her mind comprehended two different interpretations of each form and motion.

On the one hand, the purple was ugly. Its movement patterns were unnatural, even alien, and filled her with dread. It contorted the stone and metal and dirt into unnatural configurations comprised of bizarre, obtuse angles creating a nightmare profusion of ever-morphing insanity.

On the other hand, the purple was beautiful. It was light and spritely and luminescent. It danced about the landscape, crafting glorious symmetry and harmony into every object, including the minds of those individuals it inhabited. Gwei wanted to hear th'luster better. It remained a distant voice in the back of her mind, as if heard from across a great chasm. She wanted to embrace it.

And that scared her deeply.

Her forehead throbbed from the pain of her dual perceptions, and yet she gulped and followed the sound of Adema's footsteps.

They walked in silence.

Gwei decided she needed something to distract her from the contradictory visual chaos, and so she formed up beside Adema.

"Th'Resplendent?"

"Yes?"

"What do you know about the green spots?"

"Their appearance coincided with an event within Th'Home."

"Did you cause this, then, inadvertently?"

Adema shook her head. "It is but another symptom."

They know something about me, Gwei thought. *Why would they think I can solve this problem for them? But how to find out what it is they think I can do, or know, without compromising my position?*

"Can you tell me what happened?"

Adema shook her head. "I must show you."

Gwei pondered that over. A conclusion struck her: Adema couldn't tell her own people. That was intriguing. Had the green light compromised a sensitive part of the Amaranthine District?

"Did you know," Adema said, "that we gave th'gone-away-scientist th'schematics for Th'Home? Th'entire-Home?"

"No."

"We thought there might be th'connection. Th'bracelets were not th'sole-reason we took his lab. But we have his computer and his notes. Unless he destroyed records of some unknown experiment, which is unlikely, he did not cause this horrible thing."

Difficult as it was, Gwei looked over Adema's facial features and her blank purple eyes. There was something about the way she spoke. "You don't like the gone away scientist, do you?"

"I found him utterly repulsive."

"So did a lot of people, from what I've heard."

City's ambient illumination dimmed. Gwei managed to glance around enough to gain a better awareness of her surroundings. A domed ceiling of purple insanity had appeared overhead. Further before them, it descended, enclosing them with walls; a corridor formed before them. Gwei recognized components within the contortions of the structure—a bicycle wheel, a book, a telephone pole, the mast of a ship, a quilt, a steering wheel, a stone arch—but each object disappeared into the miasmic mass just as soon as it became recognizable. The constant shifting added yet another order of magnitude to the pain of the dual interpretations assaulting her brain.

Gwei threw her eyes back to the ground and followed the footsteps of her entourage.

She had started to wonder if they would pick up where they left off before, rip the bracelet from her, and subsume her in th'luster. Part of her felt sick, and another part of her wanted to heed th'luster's call more than anything in the world, which only acted to intensify her nausea.

She closed her eyes, leaned into the wall and took deep, slow breaths.

"Are you all right?" Adema asked.

She's only asking because she needs me as I am now. "I'm fine. Just… give me a minute."

"As you wish."

The entourage stood and waited for her. She could tell they were all there, even with her eyes closed. Those others would never do anything that might inadvertently upset Th'Resplendent. How did she know that?

She opened her eyes a bit and pushed off the wall. "Let's go then."

They marched forward.

Minutes passed in agony as they marched through hall after excruciating hall. Gwei caught the faint outlines of other passing tribals in her peripheral vision as they went. It felt so surreal—all of their shifting tattoos and purple eyes, and walking about stark naked.

Gwei realized a small part of her disliked the stuffy, cramped feeling of her clothing. She extrapolated the feeling to behaviors she might take, were those feelings amplified, and she understood the Amaranthines. They didn't see themselves as naked. Th'luster itself was clothing. It was *better* than clothing. At least, it felt that way.

They came to a room, and Adema motioned Gwei inside while the adult tribals took off further down the hall. Adema pulled a chair out from the table at the center of the room, and Gwei blearily took a seat.

"Is this the place?" Gwei asked.

"No." Adema loomed over the table. A new pair of adult tribals entered the room and took up positions at either side of the door.

"Why am I here?"

"Because… most of th'brethren cannot see what you will you see. They cannot know what you will come to know. And you must know that when you know these things, if we get even th'slightest-hint that you will tell th'others, we will take you. We will make good on our bargain only if you vow th'absolute-silence regarding th'things you learn. Do you understand?"

Gwei nodded and clamped her eyes shut to keep the horrible contradictions out.

"Is it difficult for you be in Th'Home…?" Adema's voice carried a tinge of uncertainty.

Gwei pulled her eyes as far open as she dared and looked up at Adema. "It's just, when I look at things here, I see everything twice. It's very disorienting."

"Ah. You are th'first to be partially converted. It has never happened before."

"I see."

"Your unique position has th'potential to save us all, I think. I will return." Adema walked out the door, leaving Gwei alone at the table, across the room from the guards.

Gwei closed her eyes and took deep breaths, focusing solely on alleviating her mental agony. As the contradictions fell away and she gained a better grasp of her mental faculties, she turned her mind to her predicament.

Something struck her just then—something she'd seen as Adema had exited.

Gwei opened her eyes and looked over the guards at the door. The one man was unremarkable, but the other… When Gwei looked at him, she felt none of the double-natured reaction that she felt toward the rest of Th'Home. His skin swam with tattoos, and th'luster did seem to dance about his body, but he didn't *feel* double to her.

She focused on him and opened her eyes all the way, really *looked* at him.

Dear god. It was Bolt. Bolt was standing before her, naked, with purple eyes and tattoos, and th'luster all about him, but he wasn't really a tribal.

He pulled his lips up into a light smile. 'Don't betray my cover,' he seemed to be saying.

So Gwei closed her eyes. It made no sense—Bolt's life had been in mortal danger, and Sez was no doctor of that caliber… and yet here he was, in the form of a tribal, but not a tribal in substance. He was still himself, but he'd been camouflaged somehow, even created th'simulation of th'luster. Th'Home's first true infiltrator, it seemed. She recalled Naim's tale of the disastrous, failed incursion that had left Ward an emotional wreck and fragmented The Collective.

She rubbed her hands over her face.

What to do? What to do?

If Adema found out that she could do nothing, that this second awareness would not correct whatever problem the green had created for them, she would certainly become a tribal.

She had to stay herself long enough to gain more information. That, or go back outside and wait for the green to swallow everything up.

A low rumble sounded and her table and chair shook. She opened her eyes despite the pain and grasped the seat of her chair to steady herself. Bolt and the tribal braced themselves against the doorframe. Then the shaking stopped.

Bolt motioned to the other tribal and pointed to the corner behind Gwei. She swung around and saw it, too. A kind of lattice structure, interwoven hexagons, had fixed itself in the wall, unchanging like the rest of it; the thing radiated bright green.

The door swung open.

"Hey!" the tribal guard shouted.

A boy appeared in the doorway. "Oh, sorry, I just wanted to see—"

Gwei shot to a stance. "Ma—!"

She clamped her mouth shut, remembering what had happened to the twins.

"Gwei?" He looked up at her with sad eyes.

Before her stood Mario, naked, and covered in swirling purple tattoos.

Stalwart

((after))

I watch her die for what seems like an eternity. I try to hold her, comfort her, but she contorts and wreaths so badly, and her strength! I'm not sure how many minutes pass. It is utter torture to be sitting on the ground spellbound at the writhing of this woman who has saved my life at the expense of her own. All at once, a spasm hits her, and a snapping sound erupts from her body and she just falls limp on the floor like a rag doll.

I bawl.

I cry my eyes out and yell and then I stand up and tear apart her little alcove in a blind rage.

I fall to the floor and stare at the green… thing in front of me, the one that left a hole in the door leading to the stairwell. What the hell is it? I look around for more damage. The bed is a mass of splinters. Most of the furniture has been broken against the telescope. I'll be surprised if anyone can repair any of it.

I look at my hands, scratched and bloody, dripping onto the wood floor. I am so very tired of people dying. And I am even wearier of feeling ignorant and helpless.

Then I remember what Sez told me. It was just minutes ago maybe, but it feels hidden beyond an eternity of mental history. I struggle to pull it up through my cataclysm of emotions: "Help Gwei. Don't blame yourself."

I breathe deep breaths.

She wanted me to help Gwei. I want to help Gwei.

Gwei is going to the Amaranthine District.

Fat lot of good the bracelets did. The tribals run around naked, covered in living, purple tattoos and have blank purple eyes. Even with a bracelet, there's no sneaking into their compound. A normal human stands out like a sore thumb. To get anywhere near her, I'd need a disguise. The purple eyes could be doable with contact lenses, but I don't have any of those. And the tattoos? What about the way that the purple mist twirls around their bodies?

A phrase pierces my thoughts—'Holographic Amaranthine Infiltration System.' I'd seen it written in the scientist's lab on a computer. The figure that morphed and gained the tattoos. Yes!

I tear open the door of the room, and begin down to the stairs, then halt and turn. I look over Sez's body, lying broken on the floorboards, surrounded by the mess I've made of her room. I'm torn. She told me to go help Gwei, but I can't just leave her here—can I? I decide that I can. For now. She made her wishes clear. Her dying wish wasn't 'have as proper a funeral as City will allow.' No. Sez, from what little I knew of her, was practical if nothing else.

I race down the stairs, through the central auditorium, push through the enormous entrance doors, and I'm out into City's blazing light. I spot a couple more objects turned neon green—a part of a lamp post and half of the window of a nearby house.

That's not right.

I mean, City's not right, but that's extra not right.

Okay, so the scientist's laboratory… I don't know how I got here. I was unconscious. It occurs to me that I am running full tilt now, fully cognizant, although just minutes ago, turning my head made me so dizzy I'd nearly thrown up.

A renewed sense of obligation to Sez sends me hurtling faster down the street. I stop a moment and take a look at the debris. A crushed paper cup lies in an adjacent intersection. Recently crushed?

I turn and head that way.

I wish I could remember how they got me into that room. They couldn't have carried me. Maybe the vehicle they used could have left some sign.

I hurtle through intersection after intersection.

It occurs to me also, as I run, that I have heard a lot about how the grid streets are supposed to be some rare occurrence—a freak reorganization of City's "usual" order. And yet, I feel as though, in my day or so here, I've spent just as much time traversing this grid as I have the other configuration, if not more.

A figure appears in the distance. I don't see any purple mist, so I run faster.

The figure is female, a woman, maybe in her late thirties or early forties. She has long, blonde hair and blue eyes. And she's wearing flower pattern dress. Looks like something out of my world from over a century ago.

I slow to a halt. "Hello."

"Hello," she says, dejectedly.

"What's your name?" I ask.

She winces slightly at that. "Mia," she says quietly.

"I'm Bolt. Nice to meet you."

"Nice to meet you, too."

"I apologize, Mia, but I'm in a bit of trouble. My friend Gwei—"

"I know Gwei. Naim introduced us."

"Gwei is in trouble."

"A number of my family portraits have turned green."

I blink at her a few times, not sure how we ended up at this point in our conversation.

"Is that normal for City, Bolt? Or is it just something I'm imagining? I mean, I didn't want to risk something like Mary showing up, so I left the glowing, green pictures on my table and started out on a walk."

I have no idea who Mary is, but I make a reasonable guess at Mia's conundrum. "I don't think it's normal for City. And it's not your imagination, either."

"Oh dear. Well, I was about to say 'thank goodness,' but that really would be quite inappropriate under the circumstances, wouldn't it?"

I nod.

"If you'll excuse me, Mia. I have to find the gone-away scientist's laboratory, and I don't have a lot of time—"

"Take this road seven blocks West, then turn south (that will be a left) then eleven blocks later you'll be at his lab, but I heard that's Amaranthine territory now. Oh, and if the streets change back, you'll probably be over... Lavender Alley, just where it touches Tangelo Relief. Turn right on Tangelo, and you'll want to take it all the way to the end where it intersects Cesious Boulevard. Another right will put you at the edge of the lab."

I blink. "Thank you, Mia."

She smiles. "You are quite welcome."

I wave and run off.

I push as fast as I can down the grid streets, counting blocks as I go. At the seventh block, I turn left, just as Mia said, and begin counting again. I wonder if City will change on me, thwarting Mia's goodwill, and I'm sweating and panting now. This aerobic stuff isn't really my thing. But thinking of Sez propels me forward.

I reach the seventh of the eleven blocks, and already I can see the purple mist on the horizon. I glance down at my bracelet. It protected me once. Here's to hoping it works again.

I slow at the edge of the miasma, treading carefully inside. The purple wisps are repelled.

I hurtle into the laboratory. Under the influence of the purple it has twisted and contorted into something even more monstrous than it was before. The hallway is barely recognizable and even more dimly lit. The purple miasma glows brighter than the intermittent light bulbs in the ceiling.

I throw open the door to Taum's laboratory. It has become a similar contortion of equipment and materials. I walk to the computer, whose screen is a distorted mess. It refuses to turn on, and I frown in frustration. This one's part of the wall, though. I take a look around the objects atop tables. They appear less distorted than the room itself.

I pick up something that looks like a tablet computer, and it activates at my touch. A holographic display appears before me. Not the one I wanted. I tear into the pile of computer tablets, throwing each useless device onto the ground, until—

Holographic Amaranthine Infiltration System.

After ten frustrating minutes of prodding and poking the screen, I have prepared my disguise, and I'm reasonably sure the computer is targeting me.

I activate the program.

I look down at my hands—purple tattoos dance across my skin, and I smile. I scan the room for a mirror and spot a tower of glass cubes near the door, twisting and congealing under the power of the mist, but they'll do. I take a look at myself. My reflection is as contorted as the room, but I can see that my eyes are indeed purple, and I even have the appearance of miasma swirling about my body.

I wonder what to do with the computer, and then I notice a toggle for adhesive and another for stealth mode.

The computer shimmers to invisibility, and I latch it to my side. I have no idea how to make it visible again, but I'll worry about that later.

Now, the most awkward part. The holograms have added miasma and tattoos and covered my pupils with purple, but they haven't done anything about my clothing. I take off my shirt, shoes, socks, pants, and underwear, and throw them in a pile on the floor.

I take a deep breath. Here goes nothing. I'll know soon enough whether or not the disguise works.

Gwei got a good head start on me, so I guess that she's already in the Amaranthine District. I walk out of the scientist's laboratory and into the street as nonchalantly as I can. Even knowing that this is 'normal,' it's hard for me to feel comfortable wearing absolutely nothing. But the tribals all run around like it's the most normal thing in the world, so I think about keeping my back tall and walking with purpose, even though I'm not sure I'll even pull that off well.

I feel utterly vulnerable. Not a feeling I'm used to.

A domed ceiling appears overhead and walls before me. I enter a tunnel of sorts, all of its surfaces constantly twisting and turning, a scattered mess of random objects pulled and skewed by purple.

I turn left with the hallway, then right. Still no one.

Finally, I spot an older man and a younger woman. The man stands with his back against the nearby wall. The woman has her arms crossed and is listening to him intently.

I decide that the first test is to see if I can just pass by them without garnering any unwanted attention.

"…This new thing, th'green-thing, it's unnatural," the man says. "I know Th'Resplendent insists that it can be contained and controlled, but I don't see th'evidence of that. Have you?"

"No."

"I wonder how long this will last."

"You don't mean Th'Home, do you?"

"No, I mean th'position of Th'Resplendent Adema. No one likes her. We ascended her because there was th'crisis at th'time and there was no one better."

Their conversation fades as they recede behind me.

I exhale a bit in relief. The charade works, at least visibly. But I didn't realize how different the Amaranthine's speech patterns were. I now worry that I will be caught as soon as I open my mouth.

Those two seemed to say 'the' a lot, and they said it really fast. I decide to try that out and see how far it gets me.

The hallway opens up into a larger chamber, this one swarming with tribals, maybe two dozen. Some work with pieces of mechanical equipment, others stood at makeshift stands, which morph and twist like everything else. Those at the stands appear to be engaged in barter. Three Amaranthine children scamper along the far side of the room. They come to a halt and talk in one corner.

I gulp.

Children turned into tribals. I twitch in disgust, then realize that a scowl might garner attention, and I shove the feelings away.

I walk through the room, listening to bits of conversation.

"—I heard th'new-green-thing showed up near th'office of Th'Resplendent and she hasn't done anything about it—"

"—Where do you think we should expand to next? Further to th'north or to th'east? Don't say th'west—"

"—That food is th'days old! You don't expect me to eat that swill, do you—?"

On and on I go, trying to grasp the rhyme and reason of their language. Fairly soon, I will be forced to mimic them.

"—They need th'guards for th'—half-convert! They've got th'half-convert! Can you believe that?"

My ears perk up and I turn to the young man who'd spoken. "Excuse me, did you say th'half convert?"

"Yeah."

"Th'female?"

"Yeah…" He poked at the tattoos on his arm. "She's th'woman."

"I want to be th'guard. Where should I go?"

The youth grins. "Yeah, you look like th'guard alright. They're taking her to Th'Incandescent-Halls while Th'Resplendent preps Th'Chamber. It's all in th'message."

Lovely. I decide not to ask where the Incandescent Halls are. It seems like the kind of thing I'm supposed to know.

"Thank you." I walk away.

I maintain a neutral face, but inside I am frowning. I count eight exits out of the huge barter chamber, and any one of them could lead to the Incandescent Halls. Which one? Where to go? And who to ask? The young man had seemed to think that I should be able to get all the information I need from a message I have no way of accessing.

I find myself wandering closer to the children.

"I don't care!" one boy shouts at the other two, twins from the looks of it. "I'm gonna see Gwei!"

I can't stop myself from cracking a smile.

The boy scampers off down a nearby corridor. The twins run after him, and I follow at a reasonable distance, able to keep up at the pace of a brisk walk. They weave around many corners and intersections, and then they stop. The twins have caught up to the boy, and are now holding him by the arms. He twists his head back and forth and struggles, insisting that he be allowed to see Gwei.

I walk past them. Hopefully the boy has brought me close enough. I turn a corner and see them—Gwei is walking into a room behind a very tall woman. This Resplendent everyone's been talking about, maybe? There are a few other tribal adults with her, too. She's definitely not fully converted. Why have they let her keep her bracelet on?

Gwei and the tall woman enter the room.

"Are you here for th'guard-duty?"

One of the men shouts to me.

I walk toward him. "Yes."

"What's your name?"

I am paralyzed with fear. Amaranthines do not have normal names. I remember Gwei telling me that before. If you use their real City name, they lose their power.

I need to say something, I reach into my recent memory and pluck out something familiar. "Blindrage."

He blinks at me a few times. "You new, Blindrage?"

"Yes."

"That's th'name most odd."

"I'm not happy with it myself."

"We'll get you th'name-appeal later. What's your rank?"

Can he see that I'm sweating beads? Please let the holograms cover those up.

I pray that I haven't depleted my luck on reaching into my memory for something at random. "Th'Incandescent." I'm sure I've done it now. He'll call the others and they'll figure out my disguise and convert me.

It's over.

"Th'Incandescent Blindrage. I don't know. Kind of long, but altogether, that has th'nice-ring to it."

He motions for me to enter the room.

"Thank you," I say. "I'll consider keeping it."

I walk around him and toward Gwei's room. At the door I meet another man, pretty well built, but I'm pretty sure I could take him. As a normal person, he could probably work construction.

"Hello," I say.

He grunts at me.

Okay, maybe he couldn't work construction. A bad attitude on a team is a good way to get injuries or, god forbid, deaths.

Death.

How precariously close Gwei and I are.

I see her now, as we enter the room. She's sitting at the table with her head down. The tall woman and her are talking quietly.

It's okay, Gwei. I'm here. I've got your back. Let's give 'em hell.

Crestfallen

((after))

They warned me.
Sting.
Everyone told me it was th'bad-idea.
Sting.
And now, here I am. I can't even think th'two of th'words without—
sting—th'stupid-luster—*sting*—fucking stop!
Sting.
I throw myself into th'wall and cross my arms. I try to slide my back
down it, but th'pointy-thing pokes out of th'wall and hurts my back. I
cry out and throw myself on th'floor instead.
They told me.
Sting.
"Th'Dim Doge?" An adult stands above me.
I peel my face off th'floor. "That's me."
"Stand up. Show th'dignity."
I put my face back on th'ground. "I don't know what th'dignity is."
He scoffs. "Clearly." And walks away.
I liked my last name so much better, th'one that Grey gave me. I'm
not sure whether to be angry with Grey or not. He did tell me to stay put.
I didn't do what he said. I just didn't want him to get hurt. I didn't want
him to end up like I am now—*sting*.
Th'luster is wonderful, th'luster is wonderful, th'luster is wonderful.
Sting.
Fuck. It can tell when I'm lying.

I open my eyes and crawl, so at least I am sitting on th'floor instead of lying face down. I'm in Th'Bazaar. Th'people swarm around me. Th'most look at me with th'disgust.

They decided I was Th'Dim. Th'Dim. *Sting.*

And now I'm stuck with that the rest of my life. *Sting.*

Because I was so sure I was right. *Sting.*

"Guess who's here." Vall stands in front of me. That used to be Hyra. And of course there's Tyr next to her. That used to be Fero.

I cross my arms and turn my head away from her. "Don't care."

"Yes you do," Tyr says.

"No I don't!"

Vall rolls her eyes. She grabs th'arm of her brother. "C'mon. We've got better things to do."

Tyr smirks and resists her grasp. He looks directly at me. "Gwei is here. And she's only th'partial-brethren."

I blink. "Th'partial-brethren? What's th'partial-brethren?"

Vall throws down th'arm of her brother. "She's got th'luster on her hands and her feet, but not th'rest of her. She probably hears th'luster only th'little."

I shoot to my feet and brush th'dirt off myself. "Where is she?"

Tyr shakes his head at Vall. Vall looks th'little bit afraid, th'little bit suspicious.

"That's th'idea most stupid." Vall crosses her arms.

Tyr sneers at me. "She's with Th'Resplendent."

"I don't care!" I shout. "I'm gonna see Gwei!" I begin manipulating th'luster on my arm, looking for th'information. Tyr grabs my arm, and I push him away. Th'luster stings my mind, but I focus on finding th'location of Gwei. There must be th'message…

Vall comes at me, but I push her away, too. She falls on her butt, and now th'twins are really pissed.

I find th'information—Th'Incandescent Halls, th'fourth-rotund, th'seventh-block!

I take off running down the halls, and I can hear Tyr and Vall running after me, but I focus all my energy on going faster. Why do they care so much? If they didn't want me to go to Gwei, why did they tell me? So what if I'm punished? They never liked me, even back when we were Fero and Hyra and my old name. They were jealous of how Grey liked me better. How I could use th'skateboard better. I want those days back. I want to grind down Tangelo Relief with Grey again. But I can't. Because of th'stupid-stupid-luster. *Sting*.

Th'thing slams into me from th'behind and I fall to th'ground. It's Tyr.

I struggle to th'stance. "Get offa me!"

"Stay outta there!" Tyr grabs at my arms.

Vall is on me now too. She takes my other arm.

I struggle against them. My anger grows. I wrench my right hand away from th'grasp of Vall, pull it back into th'fist, and wallop Tyr in th'face.

Tyr stumbles back, th'blood running out his nose.

My anger turns to th'shock. I hurt him. I really hurt him.

"I'm sorry—" I say.

"Fuck you," Tyr says. Th'luster wafts up his nose, wiping away th'blood.

"You really are Th'Dim." Vall forms up alongside her brother. "I knew it even before you got th'rank."

"I—"

They walk away.

I gulp and walk around th'corner.

Th'door is unguarded.

I wonder if Th'Resplendent is inside. No way to know. Th'luster won't tell me that. It's more like th'computer. Probably Th'Resplendent can ask it where people are, but Th'Dim-Brethren can't do that.

Th'Dim Doge.

I hate my new name so much.

Sting.

I take th'deep-breath, and I open th'door.

City is Möbium

(( ))

As City nears its end, so nears its beginning.
 Does one ever really move anywhere? Does anything truly ever change?
 Perhaps the philosopher was right, and perhaps all the internal movement is not so much a permanent alteration as a reconfiguration of the universal whole. But then how to account for the fact that, once done, once altered, once changed, things can never go back to the way they were before?
 Humans, unfortunately, fixate.
 The time the human spent with his loved one. The time the human and her friends had the most glorious fun. The time the human and his coworkers built amazing things. The time the human learned important truths about her life and humanity as a whole.
 But then the humans move out of such times and can come to view the new configurations as less worthy than the configurations of those past. They might even believe, naïvely, that they should have been able to fix the configurations of the past for all time.
 There is only one eternity, one universal form, and the human's current configuration is as much a part of it as any of her past.
 City now alternates between purple and green. Purple and Green. Purple and Green.
 But to what end?
 City needs deliverance.
 Something is yet… missing.

Broken

((before))

"Say something, Naim."

Kaia's voice sounded a million miles away. Naim turned to see that she stood right beside him. He found he couldn't look her in the eyes. "There's no answer."

"We don't need an answer! We just need us, right here, right now. Isn't that enough?"

He still couldn't look her in the eyes.

I can't lose you.

He would have said the words, but found that he couldn't. He couldn't do anything. He was useless, a useless wreck of a philosopher trudging through an urban wreck next to the woman he loved and could not keep.

"Let's go back to the park, Naim."

"I'm going back to the convenience store. I'll look over the maps again—"

She yanked his arm, brought herself around to stand in front of him. Her chest heaved up and down. "Enough maps. Enough configurations, and poles, and cats, and latches. No more. Let's just please do something together that's not about City."

Naim paused. He dug deep within himself and found... nothing. Nothing but his desire to stay with Kaia. Nothing. "I have to... I can't help but..."

"Fine."

They resumed walking.

"Fine?"

"Fine. We'll go to the convenience store."

"Okay."

And so they walked. They walked for many blocks, around rubble and debris, the pitted, scarred roads of City-as-Grid. Memories of other seemingly important things would flit into Naim's conscious: How had the reconnaissance gone? What had they learned? What was The Collective's next step? But City's oppression overwhelmed such thoughts.

It seemed so simple—he wanted to stay with the woman he loved. Was City really so callous? Was it really hellbent on driving them apart? Or rather, had it been him applying force to the wedge? He had free will, hadn't he? But that would have meant submerging himself in blissful ignorance, sticking his head into the sand and insisting that City would never painfully force their separation, despite his reason telling him otherwise.

They reached the convenience store, a small, rundown bungalow with half of its fluorescent lights busted out, and row after row of empty, white metal shelves covered in dust. It had run out of food long ago, and Naim had therefore considered it an excellent spot for his scrawlings of the various buildings and roads of the two City configurations.

In the back room, probably the one-time manager's office, he'd plastered the walls with them. A single bulb hung from a beaded metal chain fixed to the ceiling.

So many circles, across all the walls. Mia's featured most prominently in the center. After weeks of pasting together his incomplete maps, Mia had simply drawn it all from out of nowhere.

Naim sat down in the center of the room and scanned his eyes over them. The secret had to be there somewhere. It had to be. He couldn't lose her.

Kaia towered over him. "So?"

Naim shook his head. "I don't know."

She exhaled, a long and doleful sound.

"Naim…"

"Yes?" His eye remained fixed on the maps.

"I'm going to step outside for a bit. Get some air."

He thought to tell her he loved her. He thought to ask her to stay. He thought to suggest they go to the park, or to the cathedral, or even down to find Ondeck's Republic, any number of things they could possibly do together. He thought of all the times they'd spent together, all the people they'd met.

But his eyes remained fixed on those maps, and his mind on the broken promise with City that he could have the one little thing that he desperately desired—a way out for them both together. He found he could not tear his eyes from the maps.

He stared at them.

He stared at them for a very long time.

His stomach rumbled, and his heart ached, and it occurred to him that he could tell her again that he loved her, and that maybe they could find some food and water and go to the park, and that would be quite nice, and they could find their grove. Maybe he could take a break from worry for just a bit.

He looked around the room.

It was empty, save for the light and the maps.

He stood.

He tried to call out her name.

…And failed.

He tried again.

He struggled.

He willed his lips to make the syllables.

No. No no no no no.

"Noooooo!" he wailed, failing to find any other words.

Tears streaming down his face, he threw open the door to the manager's office, still trying to force his lips to say the name that had been wrenched out of his mind. He roared inchoate syllables, crashed through the shelving and wire mesh stands that once held artificially-saccharined confections.

He threw open the glass door, stumbled into City's streets, and wailed anew.

He ran.

Screaming and crying and yelling all at once, he ran, trying to turn his slurred speech into the name his brain and his lips could no longer make.

All their time together, how they met, how they fell in love, how they made love, how they found the grid streets, how he found his maps, how she grew more distant, all there. All the memories right where they should be. He could see her face, her beautiful eyes. He could remember how she would smile, how she would sleep, even how she would frown when she was sad or angry.

But no name.

His feet crunched onto gravel. Trees all around.

He threw apart the vines of orange flowers and ran up to the top of the hill. He knelt, and he wailed up at the sky, the horrible, twisting blue sky that took, and took, and took. And the one thing he'd wanted—he'd wanted one simple thing—had been taken away. It had taken her.

It was easy to blame City, but he also knew that he had failed. He had failed to listen to her about Yessel and The Collective, about the grid streets, about the pole. Everything. It would have been so easy. If only he had just *let go*...

No! City did this. No! He did this.

Blame City! Blame himself!

He looked at his hands, gasping and panting. Whose hands were these? They were the claws of a monster. A terrible monster who refused to give the woman he'd loved affection instead of obsession.

He roared at the sky again.

"What is—?" A female voice. It stopped abruptly.

Naim looked down. A woman stood at the base of the hill, across the grove from him. She wore a white apron over a blue dress and white sneakers. The long socks beneath them bore polka dots. She had curly brown hair. A rather vapid expression adorned her face. She stood and stared about.

Naim stared at her, his countenance sinking further and his frustration growing by the moment.

"Where am I?" She asked. "Who are you? Why can't I remember my name?"

Naim's lips quivered.

Okay. He'd squandered his brief time with his girlfriend. City had taken her. That hurt, but it was a manageable hurt. However... *to replace her* with some stupid, ugly, idiot of a woman. No! He would not tolerate that insult.

Naim scowled, stood and marched toward her as he spoke. "This place is called City. It's an abomination of an urban landscape inhabited by tortured souls who have been torn away from their home realities to this nightmare sphere where the sky is always blue and shifting even though there's no sun, and you can't remember your name or the names of anything else for that matter, and even when people get taken away out of City—they just disappear for no good reason, same as how they arrived—you won't remember their name after they're gone either. So now if you have no more questions I'd like you to get out of my grove and go find your name and leave me with my abject misery, please."

Naim now stood mere inches from her.

The woman quivered and looked up at him with beady, frightened eyes.

"Um." She gulped. "I… um…"

Naim's rage boiled over. "Go away, go away, GO-AWAY!"

She shrieked, turned and scampered out of the grove, through the wall of flowery vines.

Naim collapsed on the ground and sobbed once more.

"No…" he muttered.

He stood. It took so much energy, but he pulled himself to a stance.

He could be angry, and he could be hurt. But he could not be cruel. If he were going to start being cruel to people, he should just walk into the tribal miasma and end his human existence. He should either fully become a monster, or he should behave like a human being.

He'd take behaving like a human being.

"Wait!" he called out.

He pushed through the flowery vines. He expected to burst into a sprint, but he looked down at his feet instead.

The woman sat huddled on the ground, sobbing.

"Hey…" Naim said. He crouched beside her. "I'm sorry. I'm really, really sorry."

"What's happened… what's happening to me?"

"It's City." He sat down cross-legged beside her. "I'm sorry I yelled at you."

"I don't understand."

"You won't at first. But you'll learn."

She sniffed. "Is it dangerous, this City?"

"Some parts, yes. Most of it's safe, though."

"Will I remember my name?"

"No." He tried to put his arm around her. "May I?"

She took a deep breath and nodded. He slid closer and hugged her. She wasn't his girlfriend, and he knew it. It wasn't like that. But it did feel good. It felt much better to comfort than to dole out pain. It felt far,

far better.

"You'll get a City name eventually—" Something struck him. She already had her City name.

"What is it?" the woman asked.

Naim winced. "I accidentally named you."

"What do you mean?" She turned to face him.

Naim took a deep breath. "I said, 'Go away, go away, go-away.'"

She furrowed her brow and shook her head a bit. "So?"

"Your name is Gwei."

Resilient

((after))

"So, um," Gwei gulped. "What's your name now?"

Mario turned his adorable little face up into an awful sneer. And his eyes... "Th'Dim Doge."

"Dimdoge?"

Mario shook his head. "No. Th'Dim is my rank."

"Rank?"

"Yeah. There are th'ranks. I'm Th'Dim."

Gwei scoffed, revolted. "They call you dim?"

"They call everyone in my rank Th'Dim."

"Actually, you're very bright, Ma— Doge."

"That's not what they said." Mario looked at the ground.

"You shouldn't be here," the guard who was not Bolt intoned, eyeing Mario.

Gwei looked to him. "Is it dangerous for him?"

"These are th'halls of the Th'Incandescent. He is Th'Dim. If Th'Resplendent finds him here..."

"I see."

She stood up, despite her vertigo, walked to Mario, knelt, and put a hand on his shoulder. "You're going to be okay. Stay strong. You're smart and kind. You'll make it through this. We all will."

Mario nodded and smiled a sad little smile, then turned and ran out the door the way he'd come.

Th'Dim Doge... What kind of horrible society would do such a thing to a child...?

She felt a very weak prickling sensation in the back of her mind, much like the sensation she'd experienced when thinking of Naim earlier. Was th'luster punishing her for her thoughts?

Ugh.

She disliked this luster the more she learned about it.

Another prickle.

That confirmed her suspicions.

She stood and walked back to the chair at the table. Bolt still stood, doing a great impersonation of an Amaranthine. How had he managed it? How had he healed? She had to get them out of this, if only to learn the story of the last few hours of his life.

The door swung inward, and Adema reappeared.

"Are you well enough to walk?" Adema asked.

"Yes," Gwei said. She stood and approached the door. Adema exited, and Gwei followed. Bolt and the other guard trailed behind them.

Gwei found the act of steadying herself even more taxing than before. She leaned into corners and closed her eyes frequently during straightaways. The endless churning of the walls and ceiling only exacerbated her suffering. Each new object that appeared was a thing that produced a new dual conception within her mind, and each new dual conception carried with it a twinge of nausea.

The corridors grew narrower and more sparsely populated.

When Gwei thought she could go no further, they came to a door set against the dead end of its hallway.

"Where are we?" Gwei asked.

"This room is called Th'Chamber," Adema said. She turned to the guards. "You will wait here. Do not move. Enter only upon my command."

She opened the door and ushered Gwei inside.

Gwei walked into the room, her eyes fixating on the enormous structure at its center. A towering, hourglass shaped construct emerged from the floor and ceiling. It was made of the same material, or rather, was like them in that its component parts were constantly shifting and morphing under the power of th'luster. But within this construct, the closer one's eyes moved to its center, the faster and more violent the transformations became. The size of the objects also changed, growing smaller closer to the center of the hourglass shape. Very near its center, the objects changed so rapidly that they could not be distinguished, and th'luster swirled about the center in a purple vortex of endless change. Its very center shone a white light so bright that it hurt to look at it directly.

Adema closed the door.

"What is this?" Gwei asked.

"We don't know," Adema replied. "That is what you must tell no one. Two ancient groups in City, Th'Technos and Th'Sophos, built th'weapons to hurt each other. But they were all taken away. Those who came after them did not understand th'weapons, and accidentally combined them into this. That was th'knowledge of Th'Former-Resplendent, anyway."

Gwei looked up at Adema. Her face was hard. She wouldn't give all this away for nothing. "What do you think I can do?"

"Th'luster is th'faint-whisper for you?"

"Yes."

Adema pointed. "Th'luster is changed."

Gwei followed Adema's gaze and saw it. A part of the hourglass near the ceiling had fixed into green neon glow.

"Th'change here is th'change to th'all of th'luster. It is th'change to th'all of us. We cannot fix this problem, even our brightest, as we cannot comprehend th'thing that has changed. Those who do not have th'luster at all cannot comprehend this room. Now, you will tell me of what you have learned of Th'City, and how we can remedy this… abomination."

Gwei looked up at Adema and her stern, imposing gaze.

This would be it, then. Either she would offer up a solution to the green chunk of void afflicting their 'chamber' or Adema would tear off her armband.

"Well?" Adema asked.

"Let me think. When did this happen?"

Adema drew with her finger upon her forearm. "Nineteen hours, twenty-seven minutes and thirty-two seconds ago."

Gwei mouthed the numbers. "… Naim."

Adema curled up her lips ever so slightly.

Gwei perked up. "You know him?"

"No."

Adema was lying. But if she were, how could that have possibly been? Naim hadn't ever mentioned going into the Amaranthine District. He had said he'd gone to the pole instead of joining the reconnaissance mission. And Adema couldn't have come to him, because tribals weren't able to leave th'luster for long.

Adema put her hands on her hips. "You do not know, do you?"

Gwei shook her head. "The time you mentioned is roughly the time Naim went away."

Adema narrowed her eyes. "Went away? But we can remember his name."

"Exactly." Gwei shook her head. "He didn't go away the normal way."

Adema exhaled. "That does explain some things."

"Like what?"

"I am asking the questions."

"Do you want my help, or not?"

Adema tapped her foot and bobbed her head back and forth, seeming to think it over. "Guards!"

Oh no.

Bolt and the other guard entered the room.

"Remove her bracelet," Adema said.

Bolt and the other guard walked toward her. Gwei stood stiff as a board. Just as the one guard grabbed at her arm, Bolt grabbed his arm and threw it away.

"What are you doing?" Adema roared.

Bolt turned and looked at Gwei, with all the kindness she had ever known of him apparent on his face. "It's something Naim knew. That's the answer. I don't know what it is, but he knew something, and he told you. Just remember what it was."

"Who—What are you?" The other guard roared and tackled Bolt.

Adema marched toward Gwei, who scurried around the far side of the hourglass through dizziness and nausea.

Think, think, think.

Something Naim knew. What did Naim know? He'd told her so many things.

After scampering around the hourglass each direction three times, Adema gave up chasing a more nimble Gwei and began drawing on her forearm while Bolt and the other guard struggled on the far side of the chamber.

Naim had told her about his girlfriend, about the falling out they'd had. He'd introduced Yessel and Ward, and Grey and Mario and Fero and Hyra and Sez and Zen. He'd taken her to the funeral for Aria, who'd died in the failed reconnaissance. He'd told her about the Republic of Fuckknowswhere far to the south in the snowy part of City, about Ondeck and the goofy but charismatic young man named Glorious Ramrod, who'd been converted to a tribal.

Three more tribal guards burst into the room and moved to surround Gwei.

What Gwei had noticed earlier—Adema had known Naim. Had he known her? That shouldn't have been possible. How could that have been possible—? Unless Adema had been recently converted. Yes. Yes! He had known her before her conversion. But it wasn't Sez, who she'd seen recently. And neither Mia nor Zen either. They weren't tall enough. Then who?

The new guards closed in, arms outstretched. Gwei's back hit the wall. Adema grinned, arms crossed, standing next to Bolt and the struggling guard.

Gwei's eyes locked onto her, and she smiled back, wide and proud.

"Karr!" Gwei shouted.

Adema shrieked and tore at her skin as purple miasma tore into her, wrenching skin and blood and flesh apart. The approaching guards and the guard struggling against Bolt collapsed, their hands wrapped around their heads. They opened their mouths as if shrieking but emitted no sound.

"That's your name." Gwei strode closer to her.

The woman's skin, what was left of it, had grown red, drenched in blood.

She looked up at Gwei with bloodshot eyes, no longer purple. "What will you do now? You have solved nothing. The green is still there. There will be a new Resplendent."

Bolt approached her side and joined her in glaring down at the former Amaranthine leader.

"All this purple…" Gwei said. She looked down at her own hands, still swirling with miasma. Her left hand moved to her right wrist, and she pushed the bracelet down toward her fingers.

Bolt grabbed her shoulder. "What are you doing?"

"It's okay," Gwei said. "I think… I think I can fix it."

"By becoming a tribal?"

"Not exactly."

Gwei pushed the bracelet off completely. Bolt squeezed her shoulder. A rush of purple euphoria filled her. Th'voice of th'luster grew from th'dull whisper in her mind to th'resounding-roar. She turned and strode toward th'hourglass-thing, holding her hands in front of her.

"Purple and green are both wrong!" Gwei shouted. She fought back against the lustrous voice with all her energy. She was not *a* 'Definite Incarnate.' Nothing in City was definite. Nothing. Not even the center of this stupid chamber.

She looked up at Bolt. "The balance is off. Purple and green…"

"Orange?" Bolt suggested.

Gwei smiled. "Orange."

Orange, she thought to the luster. *Orange, orange, orange.*

The wisps around her hands took on an orange hue and glowed ever so brightly. The hourglass portion of the chamber twisted inward and contorted around itself. Orange veins spread and rippled through the purple, outward from the white center. The white center itself dimmed.

"Gwei!" Bolt yelled.

The orange light radiating from her body dimmed his features. She turned to look up at him. "Thank you, Bolt."

The hourglass collapsed, falling apart into column after column of sparkling orange, like unfurling vines full of flower blossoms. The voice of the luster in her mind grew into a roaring scream.

And then it was silent.

All became black.

Earthbound

((now))

"Hi, Gwei."

A hand before her, shrouded in green wisps. Gwei looked up. "Naim!"

She was on the ground, on all fours. Soft, clumpy soil lay beneath her fingers. She raised her head, reached out her hand, swathed in orange, and took his. He pulled her to a stance. She looked into his eyes, and he smiled back. He looked happy, and she realized it was the first time she'd ever seen him that way. He'd been sad the entire time she'd known him. Here, his clouds were gone.

"I've missed you," Gwei said.

Naim nodded. "I've missed you, too. I've missed everyone."

"Where— what is this?" She looked around. It was like the grove where she'd met Naim, where she'd first arrived in City. But the flowers hanging from the vines were white instead of orange. They looked like they could almost be true orange blossoms. Perhaps they were—?

"I don't know," Naim said. "I think that's the beauty of it, though."

"What do you mean?"

"I don't need to know. My answer is admitting that I don't know the answer. That's philosophy's fatal flaw, I guess. We want to answer too much, like the philosopher who tried to prove God mathematically, or the scientist who opened up the box of the universe and found a cat that was both dead and alive at the same time."

Gwei pondered that over. "We answered all the questions though."

"Did we?"

"Well, we found a way out of City. We've kept ourselves intact—"

"If we haven't, would we know? The Amaranthines all thought they were perfectly normal."

"I suppose. And you are covered in green mist."

Naim chuckled. "And you in orange."

"Fair enough." Gwei punched him playfully on the shoulder. "But… I fixed things, right? No more Amaranthine District and the quakes and green things will stop appearing in City, right?"

Naim shrugged. "Probably. I guess. I'm not really sure."

"And the people we met?"

"Let's wish them all the best."

Gwei couldn't argue with that.

"Do you want to go see what's beyond the vines? I can't move them alone, but I think with the two of us…"

"Sure," Gwei said.

They walked hand in hand toward the vines with white flowers. This felt good. This wasn't like before. Gwei felt their connection had grown stronger, and she got the impression that Naim felt it, too.

Just as they approached the vines, Gwei stopped. "Wait. Before we go…"

"Yeah?"

"Something we didn't solve. I never figured out City's two configurations, one with twisting streets and one with grid streets. I mean, sure, there are two configurations, but what was causing them to flip?"

Naim shook his head. "I never figured that out, either."

"You said… You said that we're like the scientist's cat. City was flipping between two equally real states. Well, doesn't that imply that some scientist was lifting open the 'lid' of City's box, and her observation was changing the streets to one configuration or the other?"

"I suppose that could be. But we'd have no way of knowing if that were true. We'd never be able to prove it."

"I guess not." Gwei frowned.

"Something the matter?"

"Well… the changing streets caused us so much trouble, you especially. Do you think if the observer knew how much sadness she was causing, she would have stopped? Or maybe she didn't know that by watching, she was pushing us in one direction or the other. What would our lives have been like if the streets had never changed?"

Naim shook his head. "They're nice questions. Maybe someday we'll answer them. But new questions will always take their place. Let's leave it for others to work out. There are people with all the time in the world. Ours is limited, and there's so much outside this grove to experience."

"Hmm," Gwei said. "A mystery for another day, then."

"Right. Let's go."

Gwei smiled. "Sounds exciting."

"The time of our lives."

Hand in hand, they walked forward. Together, they pushed apart the vines of orange blossoms and proceeded out of the grove—onward, forward, and away.

Appreciative

(( ))

I have a great many people to thank for helping me bring this novel into existence.

I believe I got my first inkling of what *Schrödinger's City* would be when my friend Evan Witt brought my attention around to the fact that I had tended to write a lot of protagonists who were gay, male programmers in their teens or twenties. And while it was exciting to see a writer try to put that viewpoint into the world, after three books, I probably needed to expand the kinds of viewpoints my writing accommodates.

At the same time, I found myself arriving at a conclusion that contradicts the common wisdom regarding how independent writers should approach the craft. Namely, that it's fine for a writer to adhere to the 'rules of writing' while he's still trying to gain his bearings, but once a concept has been understood and internalized, further mastery can only result from breaking the rules intentionally, as the new goal becomes the discovery of the various effects that breaking the rules generates, thus allowing utilization of that effect to productive ends.

For example, common writerly wisdom has it that narrative point of view should be consistent throughout a novel, reserving the narrative entirely to the thoughts and feelings of a single character. I paired Evan's advice with my new stance on rules, and City's twenty-seven unique points of view were born in spirit, if not quite yet in form. That would take a bit more mental churning on my part.

I am indebted to China Miéville, whose writing has filled my imagination with fantastic and powerfully evocative cityscapes. And also Ursula K. Le Guin, whose world of Earthsea helped me understand the importance and power of names.

My partner Alex has always had my back, in all endeavors: programming, writing, publishing, everything. None of this would have been possible without him.

I would also like to thank Scott Roberts, who lent his considerable medical expertise to my endeavor of rendering the effects of the damage inflicted to Bolt's head.

And finally, my supportive and insightful readers get the biggest thanks of all. Alissa Berger, Michael Blackbourn, Justin Gilman, Nan Hickman, Mark Gyscek-Strauss, Victor Legros, Kelly McPike, Matt Sayer, and Dan Thompson read this novel in advance of its publication, and their feedback has been invaluable.

Thank you all.